金笛

杨正方 杨莲秀 罗纪宽 演唱

张立玉 张扬扬 英译

[美]H.W. Lan 审校

刘德荣 张鸿鑫 陶永华 搜集整理

"十三五"国家重点图书
中国南方民间文学典籍英译丛书

丛书主编 张立玉　丛书副主编 起国庆

MAGIC FLUTE

出品单位：中南民族大学南方少数民族文库翻译研究基地
云南省少数民族古籍整理出版规划办公室

武汉大学出版社

·汉英对照·

图书在版编目(CIP)数据

金笛:汉英对照/刘德荣,张鸿鑫,陶永华搜集整理;张立玉,张扬扬英译.—武汉:武汉大学出版社,2019.11(2022.1重印)
中国南方民间文学典籍英译丛书/张立玉主编
"十三五"国家重点图书
ISBN 978-7-307-21063-9

Ⅰ.金… Ⅱ.①刘… ②张… ③陶… ④张… ⑤张… Ⅲ.苗族—叙事诗—中国—汉、英 Ⅳ.I222.7

中国版本图书馆 CIP 数据核字(2019)第 152045 号

责任编辑:郭　静　　责任校对:汪欣怡　　版式设计:韩闻锦

出版发行:武汉大学出版社　(430072　武昌　珞珈山)
(电子邮箱:cbs22@whu.edu.cn　网址:www.wdp.whu.edu.cn)
印刷:湖北恒泰印务有限公司
开本:720×1000　1/16　　印张:24.5　　字数:297 千字
版次:2019 年 11 月第 1 版　　2022 年 1 月第 3 次印刷
ISBN 978-7-307-21063-9　　定价:78.00 元

版权所有,不得翻印;凡购我社的图书,如有质量问题,请与当地图书销售部门联系调换。

丛书编委会

学术顾问

王宏印　李正栓

丛书主编

张立玉

丛书副主编

起国庆

丛书编委会成员（按姓氏笔画排列）

邓之宇　王向松　艾　芳　石定乐　龙江莉　刘　纯
汤　茜　李克忠　杨　柳　杨筱奕　张立玉　张扬扬
张　瑛　和六花　依旺的　保俊萍　起国庆　陶开祥
鲁　钒　蔡　蔚　藏军娜

序

  近年来，民族典籍英译捷报频传，硕果累累。韩家全教授等人的壮族系列经典翻译陆续出版，王宏印教授等人的系列民族典籍英译研究著作已经问世，李正栓教授等人的藏族格言诗英译著作不断在国内外出版，王维波教授等人的东北民族典籍英译著作纷纷付梓，李昌银教授等人的"云南少数民族经典作品英译文库"于2018年年底出版，其他民族典籍英译作品也接踵而至。

  近日，中南民族大学张立玉教授传来佳音：他们要出版"十三五"国家重点图书——"中国南方民间文学典籍英译丛书"。虽叫民间文学，其实基本上都是民族典籍。这一系列包括十本书，它们是：《黑暗传》《哭嫁歌》《哈尼阿培聪坡坡》《彝族民间故事》《南方民间创世神话选集》《查姆》《召树屯》《娥并与桑洛》《金笛》《梅葛》。其中，好几本是云南少数民族的。只有一本是汉族典籍，即《黑暗传》。很有意思的是，这些典籍展示了不同民族的创世史诗或诸如此类的东西。

  《黑暗传》以民间歌谣唱本形象地描述了盘古开天辟地结束混沌黑暗，人类起源及社会发展的历程，融合了混沌、盘古、女娲、伏羲、炎帝神农氏、黄帝轩辕氏等众多英雄人物在洪荒时代艰难创世的一系列神话传说。它被称为汉族首部创世史诗。《哈尼阿培聪坡坡》是一部完整地记载哈尼族历史沿革的长篇史诗，堪称哈尼族的《史记》，长5000余行，以现实主义手法记叙了哈尼族祖先在各个历史时期的迁徙情况，并对其迁徙各地的原因、路线、途程，各个迁居地的社会生活、生产、风习、宗教，以及与毗邻民族的关系等，均作了详细而生动的辑录，因而该作品不仅具有文学价值，而且具有重大的历史学、社会学及宗教学价值。《南方民间创世神话选集》包括一些创世神话，主要是关于世界起源和人类起源的神话。本书所列包括生活在广泛地域的民族，如门巴族、珞巴族、怒族、基诺族、普米族、拉祜族、傈僳族、毛南族、德昂族、景颇族、阿昌族、布朗族、佤族、独龙族、水族、仡佬族、布依族、仫佬族、高山族和侗族等。这些神话不仅讲述了世界的起源，也讲述了人类的始祖，以及人类对世界的改造。《梅葛》是彝族的一部长篇史诗，流传在云南省楚雄州的姚安、大姚等彝族地区。"梅葛"本为一种彝族歌调的名称，由于人们采用这种调子来唱彝族的创世史，因而创世史诗被称为《梅葛》。《查姆》是一部彝族史诗，是彝族人民唱天地、日月、人类、种子、风雨、树木等起源的长篇史诗，被彝族人民当作本民族的历史来看待。

其余几本书展示了一些少数民族的风俗习惯、恋爱故事、斗争故事等。《哭嫁歌》是土家族文化典籍。"哭嫁"是土家族姑娘在出嫁时进行的一种用歌声来诉说自己在封建买办婚姻制度下不幸命运的活动，是指土家族姑娘的抒情歌谣，富有诗韵和乐感，融哀、怨、喜和乐为一体，以婉转的曲调向世人展示土家人独特的"哭"文化。《彝族民间故事》是一部以流传于云南楚雄彝族自治州彝族人民中间的民间故事为主体，同时覆盖全省包括小凉山等彝族地区的民间故事集。这些故事丰富多彩，从中能看到民族民间故事的各种形态和生动、奇妙而颇具彝族民族特色的文化特征。《召树屯》是傣族民间长篇叙事诗，叙述了傣族佛教世俗典籍《贝叶经·召树屯》中一个古老的传说故事。这部叙事诗一直为傣族人民所传唱，历久不衰。《娥并与桑洛》是一部优美生动的叙事诗，一个凄美的爱情悲剧。《金笛》是一部苗族长篇叙事诗，富于变幻性和传奇性，尽情铺叙扎董丕冉与蒙诗彩奏的悲欢离合，热情赞颂他们在与魔虎的激烈斗争中所表现出来的坚贞不屈、英勇顽强的精神，许多情节含有浓郁的民族特色。

这些故事都很引人入胜，都很符合国家文化发展需求，向世人讲述中国故事，传播中华文化，并且讲述的是民族故事，充分体现了党和国家对各民族的关怀。

民族典籍英译是传播中国文化、文学和文明的重要途径，是中华文化"走出去"的重要组成部分，是国家战略，是提高文化"软实力"的重要方式，在文化交流和文明建设中起着不可或缺的作用，对提升中国国际话语权和构建中国对外话语体系以及对建设世界文学都有积极意义。

中国民族典籍使世界文化更加丰富多彩、绚丽多姿。我国各民族典籍中折射出的文化多样性极大地丰富了世界多元、特色鲜明的文化。人们对多样性形成全新的认识角度和思维方式，有助于开阔视野，丰富思考问题的角度，挖掘这些经典中的教育价值和文化价值，对世界其他民族都有指导和借鉴意义，并且有助于建设我国的文化自信。

民族典籍翻译与研究事业关乎国家的稳定统一，关乎民族关系的和谐发展，关乎世界多元文化的实现。在中国，民族典籍资源极为丰富，有待进一步挖掘、翻译，仍有许多少数民族典籍亟待拯救，民族典籍翻译与研究工作任重而道远，民族典籍翻译事业大有可为。

李正栓[①]

2019 年 7 月 19 日

[①] 李正栓，中国英汉语比较研究会典籍英译专业委员会常务副会长兼秘书长；中国中医药研究促进会传统文化翻译与国际传播专业委员会常务主任委员。

前　言

苗族历史悠久，其先祖可追溯到原始社会时代活跃于中原地区的蚩尤部落。商周时期，苗族先民在长江中下游建立"三苗国"，从事农业稻作。苗族在历史上曾多次迁徙，大致路线是由黄河流域至湘（湖南）、至黔（贵州）、鄂（湖北）至滇（云南）。

苗族有自己的民族文字，最早见于甲骨文中。唐宋以前，曾有"三苗""南蛮""荆蛮""五陵蛮"等称呼。这些称呼往往将苗和其他族称混同在一起。宋朝以后，苗才从若干混称的"蛮"中脱离出来，作为单一的民族名称。直到1949年以后，统称为苗族。目前中国境内苗族人口超过942万，在中国55个少数民族中排第五位。

《金笛》是一部苗族叙事长诗。它是苗人在苗族悠久的历史长河里集体创作并世代口耳相传的民族文化的一块瑰宝。

《金笛》整首诗歌由十一章组成，可分为三个部分——扎董丕冉与蒙诗彩奏相恋——魔虎横刀夺爱——扎董丕冉灭虎救心上人。故事情节曲折，富于魔幻色彩和传奇性。全诗生动叙述了扎董丕冉与蒙诗彩奏的悲欢离合，热情赞颂他们在与魔虎的激烈斗争中所表现出来的坚贞不屈、英勇顽强的精神，许多情节带有浓郁的民族特色。

《金笛》历经口耳相传，不断得到丰富发展，不仅记录了扎董丕冉和蒙诗彩奏的爱情故事，也反映了苗族先民的风土人情，是研究苗族古文化的宝库。

我们深知，作为一部少数民族典籍《金笛》的英译实为不易。在翻译中，我们竭力用英语展现《金笛》真实的文化样貌，尽量减少翻译过程中的文化损耗。比如《金笛》中多处出现的"阿支""阿奈""扎董丕冉""蒙诗彩奏"作为苗家特色文化现象，我们采取异化原则，运用音译方法，译为"A Zhi" "A Nai" "Zha Dong Pi Ran" "Meng Shi Cai Zou"保留了苗族文化中对年轻男女和父母的特有称呼。译文中也运用归化的原则，向英语世界展示直观文化现象，如"干巴"的英译，译者在咨询当地苗族文化专家后，了解到"干巴"是一种便于携带、保存的肉类腌制品。因而译为"jerky"，向英语世界说明苗族"干巴"的特性。

本书为"中国南方民间文学典籍英译丛书"的一个分册。全书以汉英对照本形式出版，汉译本则采用云南省少数民族古籍整理办公室主编（收录入2012年7月云南出版集团公司云南教育出版社出版的《云南少数民族叙事长诗全集》下卷）的汉语原文本。

译者几经打磨修改，竭力忠实展现苗家文化原貌，努力在专有名词、文体风格上达成一致，但是由于水平有限，对原文理解和表达不妥之处在所难免。读者若有发现，敬请批评指正，以便修订时改正。

张立玉　张扬扬
2019年3月于南湖书斋

目录 Contents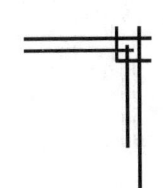

目　录

第一章　夜梦 …………………………………………… 2
第二章　赠笛 …………………………………………… 24
第三章　相恋 …………………………………………… 48
第四章　拦路 …………………………………………… 82
第五章　中计 …………………………………………… 130
第六章　试刀 …………………………………………… 166
第七章　追虎 …………………………………………… 186
第八章　沉睡 …………………………………………… 200
第九章　血溅魔窟 ……………………………………… 242
第十章　苦守坟台 ……………………………………… 302
第十一章　悲去喜来 …………………………………… 330

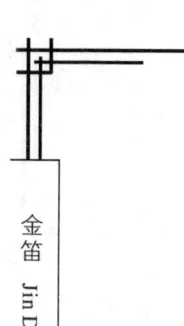

金笛 Jin Di

Contents

Chapter One   Dreams ·· 3
Chapter Two   A Gift ··· 25
Chapter Three Love ·· 49
Chapter Four   Tests ··· 83
Chapter Five   The Trap ··· 131
Chapter Six   Preparations ··· 167
Chapter Seven The Putsuit ·· 187
Chapter Eight Deep Sleep ··· 201
Chapter Nine   The Bloody Fight ····································· 243
Chapter Ten   The Tomb Guard ······································· 303
Chapter Eleven New Beginning ·· 331

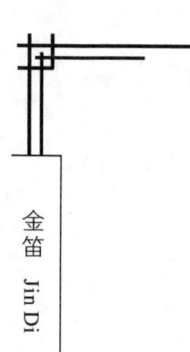

第一章　夜梦

一

夺戈底地方，
是蒙诗的故乡。
从古到今多少年，
有支口才歌在传唱。
口才歌唱的是什么？
一对恋人的悲欢离合；
口才歌唱得是哪样？
一支金笛奇妙无双。
这金笛呀，
能吹出心中的欢乐；
这金笛呀，
能奏出满腹的忧伤。
这对恋人呀，
就靠这金笛传情意；
这对恋人呀，
就凭金笛诉衷肠。

第一章 夜梦 Chapter One Dreams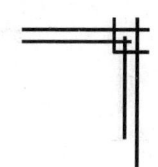

Chapter One Dreams

1

Duo Ge Di

is home to Meng Shi.

Throughout history and till today,

one of the best songs has been sung from generation to generation.

What is the story that people sing?

It is about the joys and sorrows of two lovers;

what else is the story about?

It is about a most magical Jin Di.

This Jin Di①

could express the delights of the heart;

this Jin Di

could show the sorrows of the mind.

Those two lovers

relied on the Jin Di to exhibit their affections;

those two lovers

resorted to the Jin Di to tell their innermost thoughts.

---

① Jin Di is a Kind of Chinese flute.

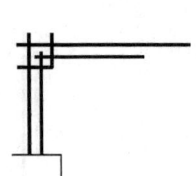

二

夺戈底的山很高很高，
抬头望不见峰顶；
夺戈底的树很密很密，
透不过一线阳光；
夺戈底的河流宽无边啊，
水手也不敢把波涛闯。

在那宽宽的大河旁，
在那高高的山顶上，
在那密密的树林里，
住着蒙诗的夫妻俩。

他们未生小咪朵，
也没怀过小咪彩。
夫妻各满五十岁，
孤零相依度时光。
阿支勤劳又诚恳，
阿奈贤惠又善良。
日子虽然苦，
心中却欢畅。

第一章 夜梦 Chapter One Dreams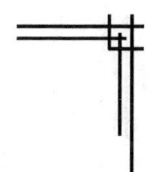

2

The mountains in Duo Ge Di were so high
that the mountaintops were out of sight;
the trees in Duo Ge Di were so thick
that the sun could not shine through;
the rivers in Duo Ge Di were so wide
that expert sailors did not dare to steer through.

By the side of one of those wide rivers,
on top of one of those high mountains,
and in the midst of one of those dense forests
lived a couple of the Miao nationality.

They didn't have a Mi Duo,
or a Mi Cai①.
The couple were both fifty years old,
leading a solitary life and relying on each other.
A Zhi was industrious and honest,
and A Nai② was considerate and kind.
Though life was hard,
they were content and happy in their hearts.

---

① Mi Duo and Mi Cai mean young male and female children in the Miao dialect.
② A Zhi and A Nai are ways to address older people in the Miao dialect, like Mr. and Mrs. in English.

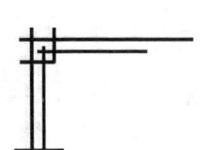

金笛 Jin Di

一天清晨,
阿支在楼下打长刀,
一只蜜蜂飞到他身旁。
忽前忽后围着转,
一边飞舞一边唱:
"你打长刀打大点,
打出大刀有用场。
拿在手上有分量,
好砍山地好开荒。"

阿支听了叹口气:
"长刀打大了,
年老抬不动。
我无儿又无女,
大事小事没人帮。
谁替我使刀砍山呀,
谁帮我种地开荒?"
蜜蜂说:
"大刀打好有人使,
劝你莫着急;
开荒种地有人帮,
劝你别忧伤!"

蜜蜂的话很蹊跷,
话中有话费思量。
阿支眨眼正想问,
蜜蜂早已不知飞何方。

第一章 夜梦 Chapter One Dreams

One early morning,
when A Zhi was forging a long machete downstairs,
a bee came to him.
Circling around him,
the bee was dancing and singing:
"You should forge the long machete bigger,
and it will be useful in the future.
The weightier the machete is felt in the hand,
the easier it is for cultivating and tilling the farmland in the mountains."

On hearing this, A Zhi sighed:
"A big long machete
is not for an older person.
I don't have a son or a daughter,
so nobody can give me a hand for things serious or minor.
Who will use the machete to cut the firewood for me?
Who will help me cultivate the farmland in the mountains?"
The Bee said:
"Just make the big machete, and someone will use it,
so don't worry;
someone will help you cultivate and till the land,
so don't be sad!"

The bee's words sounded puzzling,
with meaning between the lines and hard to fathom.
Blinking his eyes, A Zhi was just about to ask a question,
but the bee had already flown away.

金笛 Jin Di

阿支拉风箱,
风箱呼呼响;
阿支舞铁锤,
铁锤响叮当。
打了三天又三夜,
大刀打得九十九寸长。
一称足有九十斤,
从头到尾明晃晃。
阿支老了使不动,
把它挂在篱笆上。
这把大刀到底谁来使?
阿支天天在思量。

一天傍晚,
阿奈在楼上织麻布,
一只凤凰飞到她身旁。
忽左忽右围着转,
一边飞舞一边唱:
"你织麻布织长点,
织出麻布有用场。
左裁右剪随你意,
好做裙子和衣裳。"

阿奈听了叹口气:
"麻布织长了,
年老用不完,

第一章 夜梦 Chapter One Dreams

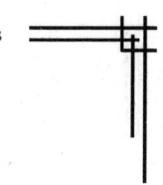

A Zhi pumped the bellows,
and the flames roared;
A Zhi wielded the hammer,
and the hammer clacked away.
Working for three days and three nights
he produced a machete that was ninety-nine cun① long.
It weighed a good ninety jin②,
gleaming from one end to the other.
A Zhi was too old to use it,
so he hung it up on the fence.
Who indeed would use this big machete?
A Zhi wondered every day.

One evening,
when A Nai was weaving the linen upstairs,
a phoenix came and landed by her.
Circling around her left and right,
it danced and sang:
"You want wave the liene longer,
and it will be useful someday.
You can tailor it at will,
be it making shirts or skirts."

On hearing this, A Nai sighed:
"If I make it longer,
I can't use it up at my old age,

---

① A Chinese *cun* is about 1.3 inches.
② A Chinese *jin* is one half of a kilogram.

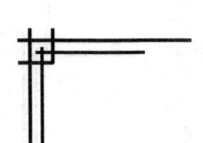

金笛 Jin Di

我无儿无女,
大事小事没人帮,
织出麻布谁来帮我染?
做出衣裙留给哪个穿?"

凤凰说:
"织出麻布有人染,
劝你莫着急;
衣裙缝好有人穿,
劝你别忧伤!"

凤凰的话很奇怪,
话语之中有名堂。
阿奈瘪嘴正想问,
凤凰早已不知飞何方。

阿奈理麻线,
麻线长又长;
阿奈使飞梭,
梭穿如燕忙。
织了三月零三天,
麻布织得九十九尺长,
这多的麻布两老咋个用得完?
卷成一筒放在枕头边。
这多麻布到底谁来穿?
阿奈心中有个疑团!

第一章 夜梦 Chapter One Dreams

for I don't have a son or a daughter,
have no help with my work, serious or minor,
so who will help me dye the linen when it is woven?
Who will wear the shirts and skirts when they are made?"

The phoenix said:
"Someone will dye the linen when it's made,
so don't worry about that;
someone will wear the shirts and skirts once they are made,
and don't be sad about it!"

The phoenix's words sounded odd,
intriguing and suggestive.
 A Nai motioned her mouth and was just about to inquire further,
but the phoenix had already flown away.

A Nai disentangled the twines,
the twines that were long;
A Nai used the shuttle,
the shuttle that moved like a busy swallow.
Weaving for three months and three days,
she made the linen ninety-nine *chi*① long.
How could the older couple use up this much cloth?
She rolled it up and put it by the pillow.
 Who would be the one to wear the clothes made of all this linen?
 A Nai had not a clue!

---

 ① A Chinese *chi* is about 1.09 feet.

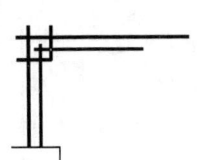

三

星星分外明，
月亮挂山顶。
阿奈躺在床上做了个梦——
梦见到河边洗褶裙。

那只凤凰又飞来，
口衔葡萄亮晶晶；
葡萄放在阿奈手，
叽叽叫几声：
"你将葡萄吃下去，
就会越活越年轻。
好花自由好雨淋，
好人自有好福分……"

阿奈手捧葡萄暗思忖：
"想来凤凰是好心。"
她将葡萄吃下去，
果然满嘴甜津津。

就在同天同一晚，
阿支也遇好梦境——
他到深山去打猎，
蜜蜂嗡嗡眼前飞：

第一章 夜梦 Chapter One Dreams

3

The stars shone more brightly than usual,
and the moon hung over the top of the mountain.
A Nai had a dream—
she dreamed that she went to wash the pleated skirt by the river.

The same phoenix came to her again,
with a glistening grape in its beak;
placing the grape in A Nai's hand,
it twittered:
"Eat it,
and you will become younger as you live longer.
Just as the fairest flowers will be showered by the timely rain,
virtuous persons will have their rewards…"

With the grape in her hand, A Nai thought to herself:
"I think the phoenix good-hearted."
She ate the grape,
and it indeed tasted very sweet.

On that same night,
A Zhi also had a good dream—
He went hunting deep in the mountains,
and the bee buzzed right in front of him;

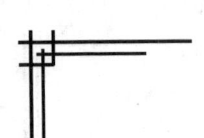

金笛 Jin Di

"山再高也有路穿林,
命再苦也会交好运,
祝你喜事临门!"

阿支好纳闷:
"枯树上开不出花朵,
我年过半百能交什么好运?
莫拿假话来骗人!"

蜜蜂说:
"给好马配鞍要配新的,
跟好人说话要说真的,
我说的话不会假,
不久你家就会有贵子生。"

四

天空说晴就放晴,
地上有水庄稼就返青;
自从吃了红葡萄,
阿奈果然变年轻。
脸上皱纹天天少,
不久怀中有了孕,
十个月后坐月子,
一个咪朵坠地生!

第一章 夜梦 Chapter One Dreams

"High as a mountain is, there are still paths through its trees,

just like hard as the fate it, good fortune can smile upon you,

so best wishes to you for the happy event to come to your doorsteps!"

A Zhi wondered:
"Since flowers won't grow on a dead tree,
what good fortune could visit upon me with fifty years old?
You have got to be kidding!"

The bee said:
"Just as the saddle for a good horse must be new,
the words spoken to a good person must be true.
I am serious,
and you will soon have a lovely son."

4

When the timing is right, the sky can clear up quickly,
and when the water returns, the crops can turn green in no time;
since eating the red grape,
A Nai did become younger.
With less and less wrinkles on her face day by day,
she soon was pregnant,
and, in ten lunar months,
a Mi Duo was born!

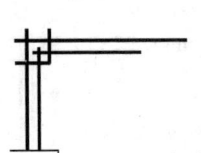

金笛 Jin Di

咪朵眼睛亮闪闪,
配着一对弯弯眉。
别人生下地来嘛,
第一声是哇哇哭,
这咪朵生下地来呀,
咯咯笑出第一声。

阿支最称心,
望着小宝宝,
就是不吃饭,
肚子也饱了。

阿奈最如意,
抱起小宝宝,
就是不吃蜜,
嘴里也甜了。

咪朵的笑声,
传遍几十里。
凤凰听到了,
翩翩飞来祝贺;
蜜蜂听到了,
嗡嗡赶来道喜。

吊脚楼上好热闹,
阿支阿奈真欢喜。
阿支要给咪朵取名字,
想了五天没想出;
阿奈要给咪朵取名字,
想了七夜没想起。

第一章 夜梦 Chapter One Dreams

The Mi Duo's eyes were bright
with curvy eyebrows matching them.
Other Mi Duos on being born
cried to utter their first sound,
but this Mi Duo on being born
giggled to utter his first sound.

A Zhi was so content that
looking at the baby,
without eating his meals,
he was not hungry.

A Nai was so satisfied that
holding the baby,
without eating honey,
she could taste its sweetness.

The Mi Duo's laughter
spread far and wide.
When the phoenix heard about this,
it came to give its congratulations;
when the bee heard about this,
it buzzed over to give its blessings.

Their stilted house was bustling with activities,
and A Zhi and A Nai were overjoyed.
A Zhi wanted to give Mi Duo a name,
but for five days he could not think of one;
A Nai wanted to give Mi Duo a name,
but for seven nights she could not think of one.

凤凰蜜蜂一齐出主意，
你一言来我一语。
最后取名扎董丕冉，
这名字响亮又好听，
夫妻两个都满意。

阿支对蜜蜂说：
"你说把刀打大点，
原来其中有道理。
如今这刀有人使，
我要感谢你！"

阿奈对凤凰说：
"你说把布织长点，
现在解了这个谜。
如今这布有人穿，
我要报答你！"

吊脚楼边的桃树，
开花十五次，
山坡地里的小米，
播种十五回，
扎董丕冉渐渐长大了，
满了十五岁；
扎董丕冉慢慢长高了，
比青松还俊美。

第一章 夜梦 Chapter One Dreams

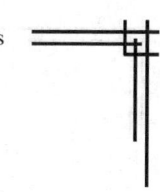

The phoenix and the bee tried to help,
each offering their ideas.
They finally settled on the name Zha Dong Pi Ran,
a name that had a resonant and nice sound
and that made the couple both happy.

A Zhi said to the bee:
"You told me to make the machete bigger,
and now I understand.
Someone will indeed use the machete,
and I must thank you for it!"

A Nai said to the Phoenix:
"You told me to weave the cloth longer,
and now I get the key to the riddle.
Someone will indeed wear the clothes made of this cloth,
and I must repay you for your kindness!"

The peach trees by their stilted house
had blossomed fifteen times,
and the millet in the land on the hillside
had been sown fifteen times.
Zha Dong Pi Ran grew up
and turned fifteen;
Zha Dong Pi Ran was tall,
more handsome than the green pine trees.

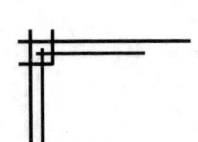

金笛 Jin Di

树上桃子千万个,
他是最甜的那一个;
夜空星星千万颗,
他是最亮的那一颗。

苗山上的咪朵,
个个长得很结实,
但是没有一个哟,
像他那样健壮;
苗寨里的咪朵,
人人生得很好看,
可是没有一个哟,
像他那么俊美。
即使有他那样的身材,
也没有他标致;
即使有他那样的容貌,
也没有他端庄;
即使有他那样的性格,
也没有他诚恳;
即使有他那样的品德,
也没有他高尚。

扎董丕冉呀,
像蜜蜂一样勤劳;
百里苗山呀,
就数他灵巧。
他像阿支一样能干,

第一章 夜梦 Chapter One Dreams

Of tens and thousands of peaches on the trees,
he would be that sweetest one;
of tens and thousands of stars in the night sky,
he would be that brightest one.

All the Mi Duos in the Miao mountain
were very strong,
but none of them
was as strong as he was;
all the Mi Duos in the Miao village
were handsome,
but none of them
was as beautiful as he was.
Even if they had the same stature,
they did not have his features;
even if they had the same looks,
they didn't have his poise;
even if they had the same personality,
they were not as genuine as he was;
even if they had the same character,
they were not as noble as he was.

Zha Dong Pi Ran
was as industrious as a bee;
within hundreds of miles in the Miao mountain
he was the most resourceful.
He was as able as A Zhi,

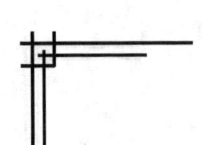

金笛 Jin Di

会犁会耙会砍柴；
他像阿奈一样利索，
会洗会煮会撒荞。
他像阿支一样风趣，
芦笙吹得最好听；
他像阿奈一样开朗，
调子唱得最动人。
他是小咪朵呀，
又是小咪彩，
他是阿支的希望哟，
他是阿奈的依靠。

第一章 夜梦 Chapter One Dreams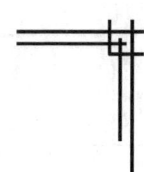

ploughing, raking, and cutting the firewood;

he was as organized as A Nai,

washing up, cooking, and sowing the buckwheat seeds.

He was as humorous as A Zhi,

and played the Lu Sheng① most beautifully;

he was as cheerful as A Nai,

and sang most movingly.

He was a Mi Duo

but also a Mi Cai,

like the morning sun for A Zhi

and a ship anchor for A Nai.

---

① Lu Sheng is a kind of reed-pipe wind instrument used by the Miao ethnic group.

第二章　赠笛

五

清早太阳升起来,
扎董丕冉上山去砍柴,
身背大刀走到泉水边。

捧口泉水喝下肚,
坐在石上歇口气。
一阵微风送来荞花香,
一只蝴蝶飞到眼前。

蝴蝶生得很美丽,
两只翅膀现五彩。
飞来又绕去,
活像两根花飘带,
扎董丕冉看得发了呆。
忽然蝴蝶一闪身,
眨眼飞出三丈外。
飞到花丛间,

第二章 赠笛 Chapter Two A Gift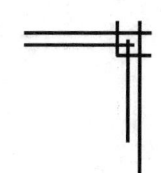

Chapter Two   A Gift

5

An early morning as the sun was rising,
Zha Dong Pi Ran went up the mountains to cut firewood,
and, with the big machete on his back, he came to a spring.

He scooped up some spring water and took a big mouthful
and then sat on the stone to take a break.
A gentle breeze wafted the scent of the buckwheat flowers to him
and, with it, a butterfly came in front of his very eyes.

The butterfly was very beautiful
with two colourful wings.
Flying around,
just like two ribbons,
it astounded Zha Dong Pi Ran.
Suddenly, the butterfly took a turn,
flying out thirty feet in the blink of an eye.
Into the flower bushes,

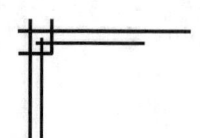

金笛 Jin Di

飞入金竹林,
飞进一片树林里,
再也没有飞出来。
扎董丕冉东边寻,
扎董丕冉西边找,
四处寻找都不见。

忽然一道金光闪,
一只凤凰站在眼前。
凤凰披着金羽毛,
抖动翅膀舞起来;
凤凰跳舞真迷人,
扎董丕冉乐得心花开。

扎董丕冉呀,
心中暗思量:
"莫非那只蝴蝶有情意,
故意引我见凤凰?"
扎董丕冉呀,
自言自语讲:
"可爱的金凤凰呀,
看你长得多漂亮。
红头黄尾金羽毛,
真不愧是个百鸟王!
如果你愿跟我做伴,
我要找个金笼来喂养……"

第二章 赠笛 Chapter Two A Gift

then the golden bamboo grove
and then a patch of forest,
it never returned.
Zha Dong Pi Ran searched here;
Zha Dong Pi Ran searched there;
Zha Dong Pi Ran searched everywhere, but to no avail.

Suddenly, a flash of the golden light
and then a phoenix appeared in front of him.
The phoenix, donning gold feathers,
fluttered its wings and began to dance;
the phoenix's dance was so charming that
Zha Dong Pi Ran was intoxicated by it.

Zha Dong Pi Ran
murmured to himself:
"Could it be that the butterfly
arranged this meeting of me and the phoenix?"
Zha Dong Pi Ran
said to himself:
"Lovely golden phoenix
how pretty you are.
With a red head, a yellow tail, and golden feathers,
no wonder you are number one among the birds!
If you would like to accompany me,
I will build a golden abode for you…"

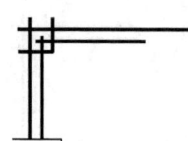

金笛 Jin Di

扎董丕冉正在想心事，
一只老虎猛然下山冈。
它张牙舞爪一声吼，
扑向那只金凤凰。
这是一只魔虎呀，
凤凰一见就惊慌。
想跑，难抬起双脚，
想飞，难张开翅膀。
即使抬起双脚，
也跑不了几丈；
即使张开翅膀，
也飞不过山梁。
凤凰拼出力气，
一飞一落，
东躲西藏。
老虎施展魔法，
一跳一跃，
紧追不放。
凤凰筋疲力尽，
跌跌撞撞；
魔虎怒吼狂嚎，
天摇地晃。

眼看疯狂的魔虎，
就要抓着金凤凰，
扎董丕冉呀，
愤怒生力量。

第二章 赠笛　Chapter Two　A Gift

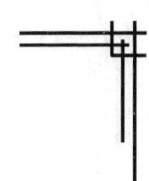

As Zha Dong Pi Ran was musing
a tiger suddenly rushed down the hill.
Swiping its paws, showing its fangs, and roaring,
the tiger charged at the golden phoenix.
It was a demon tiger,
so the phoenix panicked.
Trying to flee, it could hardly move its feet;
trying to fly, it could hardly spread its wings.
It stumbled around
for just a few feet;
its winds could not open enough
for it to fly over the mountain ridge.
With all its might, the phoenix
went up and down in the air
and dodged left and right on the ground.
The tiger cast a spell,
was sprinting and pouncing,
and would not let it go.
The phoenix was now exhausted
and began to stagger around;
the tiger gave out such a ferocious roar
that it rocked the sky and shook the earth.

Just when the crazed tiger
almost caught the phoenix,
Zha Dong Pi Ran
felt a rush of anger and found extraordinary strength.

他举着大刀追过去。
要跟魔虎斗一场。
他左砍右杀,
势不可挡;
魔虎前闪后避,
只能退让。
直斗得满山树发抖,
直杀得遍地土飞扬。
扎董丕冉越杀越猛,
大魔虎却防不及防。
阿支打的大长刀,
这时有了大用场。
魔虎再凶恶,
还是怕刀光。
最后它大吼一声,
夹着尾巴逃进了林莽。

六

凤凰终于得救了,
站在石上扇翅膀。
对着扎董丕冉点点头,
伸长脚足开喉唱:
"就是小蚂蚁,
也知糖最甜。
就是小飞蛾,
也知灯最亮。

第二章 赠笛 Chapter Two A Gift

Wielding his big machete, he started to run
and entered a fight with the demon tiger.
Hacking left and right,
he was invincible;
dodging forward and backward,
the demon tiger had no choice but to back own more and more.
They fought till the trees all over the mountains trembled,
and they battled till the dust shrouded everything.
The more Zha Dong Pi Ran fought, the stronger he fought,
while the tiger was passively warding off, only unsuccessfully.
The big long machete that A Zhi made
was put to great use now.
Fierce as the demon tiger was,
it was still afraid of the flashing lights of the machete.
Howling a final cry,
it fled into the woods with the tail between its legs.

6

The phoenix was finally saved,
now standing on a rock and flapping its wings.
It nodded at Zha Dong Pi Ran,
stretched its feet, and started to sing:
"Even a little ant
knows that sugar is sweet.
Even a small moth
knows that light is bright.

金笛 Jin Di

我虽是山中一只鸟，
也知道冷暖和炎凉。
是善是恶呀，
我也能分得清清楚楚。
扎董丕冉哟，
你有一副好心肠。
杀退大魔虎，
让我免遭殃。
你的勇敢和机智，
我永远不能忘！
我要真心感谢你，
请你在这儿等一下。"

凤凰唱完歌，
把身子晃一晃。
钻进树林里，
树林深处闪金光。
金光一闪就消失，
凤凰不知飞何方。

扎董丕冉心里想：
"凤凰怎样谢我呢？
为何叫我等一下？
给我一坨真金子，
还是一件新衣裳？
给我一张粟木弓，
还是一个花箭囊？
我是正直人，

第二章 赠笛 Chapter Two A Gift

Though I am a bird in the mountains,
I still know cold and warmth, heat and cool.
Good and devil
I can see clearly.
Zha Dong Pi Ran,
you have a kind heart.
Defeating the demon tiger,
you saved my life.
Your courage and quick-thinking
I will never forget.
I want to thank you sincerely,
so please wait here for a moment."

When the phoenix finished singing,
it swayed its body a couple of times.
As it disappeared into the woods,
a golden light came from deep in the wood.
When the golden light disappeared,
the phoenix was nowhere to be found.

Zha Dong Pi Ran wondered,
"How will the phoenix thank me?
Why did it ask me to wait?
Will it give me a bar of pure gold,
or a new shirt?
A bow made of the Su-wood,
or a handsome arrow sac?
I am an upright man,

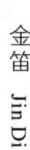

金笛 Jin Di

除恶是天良。
遇虎就杀虎,
逢狼就打狼。
要是接礼物,
那就不应当。"

东猜西想正入神,
凤凰飞回他身旁。
凤凰嘴里叼金笛,
金笛闪闪现金光。

凤凰唱:
"扎董丕冉哟,
这支金笛送给你,
请你收下有用场。
愁闷时候吹一吹,
你的心情就舒畅;
高兴时候吹一吹,
你就更加喜洋洋。
它是你最好的伙伴呀,
你要时刻带它在身上。"

要是别的礼物呀,
扎董丕冉定然会谢绝;
眼前这件礼物不寻常,
扎董丕冉没有再推让。
凤凰唱完就起飞,
腾云驾雾到远方。

34

第二章 赠笛 Chapter Two A Gift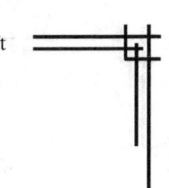

and weeding out the wicked is what I do.
I rid off tigers
and chase away wolves to save lives.
If I accept gifts for doing so,
that's not right."

He was still deep in thought
when the phoenix flew back to his side.
It had a Jin Din (the Golden Flute) in its mouth.
the flute glittering with golden light.

The phoenix sang:
"Zha Dong Pi Ran,
let me give this Jin Di to you,
and please accept it as it will be useful one day.
Play it when you are upset,
and you will be happy;
play it when you're happy,
and you will be happier.
It will be your best partner,
so keep it with you at all times."

If it were any other gift,
Zha Dong Pi Ran would have surely refused it;
but this was an unusual present,
so he accepted it.
When the phoenix finished singing,
it flew away on the misty clouds.

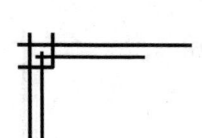

金笛 Jin Di

扎董丕冉拿起金笛吹起来,
学着凤凰的调子越吹越欢快:
"布哩布哩布哩噜,
布哩布哩布哩……"
吹了一遍又一遍,
笛声阵阵传天外。
画眉听了不敢再唱歌,
蝴蝶听了不敢恋花来,
金蝉听见着了迷,
八哥听到呆住了。
笛声就像珍珠滚银盘,
清脆悦耳响叮当;
笛声就像悬崖滴水落千尺,
咚咚哒哒动听又欢畅。

扎董丕冉吹金笛,
越吹越高兴,
觉得身子像云彩,
缥缈又轻盈。
扎董丕冉吹金笛,
越吹越激动,
四肢如同风摆柳,
如痴如梦。

第二章 赠笛 Chapter Two A Gift

Zha Dong Pi Ran picked up the Jin Di and started to play,

mimicking the phoenix's melody and becoming happier and happier.

"Bu li bu li bu li lu,

bu li bu li bu li…"

He played it over and over,

sending the sound of the Jin Di beyond the horizon.

On hearing it, thrushes dared not sing anymore;

butterflies were afraid of going to the sweet nectar again;

golden cicadas became entranced;

and crested mynas were astonished.

The Jin Di sounded like the pearls rolling in a silver plate,

crisp, pleasant and resonating;

the Jin Di sounded like the water droplets falling from a thousand-foot cliff,

plinking, alluring, and delightful.

The more Zha dong Pi Ran played the Jin Di,

the happier he became,

and the more he felt like a cloud

ethereal and light.

The more Zha Dong Pi Ran played the Jin Di,

the more overjoyed he became,

and the more he moved his limbs like the willows swaying in the wind,

mesmerized and fanciful.

金笛 Jin Di

七

这支金笛很美观,
世上笛子就数它好看。
笛面又亮又滑,
笛眼又密又圆。
筒子不大不小,
笛身不长不短。
上下镶金嵌银,
头尾画着图案:

这面是——
双龙跃身闹海底;
那面是——
双凤展翅傍云天。
这头是——
鱼眼排队排
那头是——
鸳鸯面对面。
中间吊着小花穗,
五颜六色多鲜艳。
这支金笛最神秘,
世上笛子没有它稀奇
只要把它放在嘴边上,
就可吹出千歌和万曲;

第二章 赠笛 Chapter Two A Gift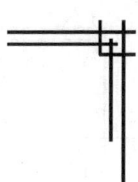

7

This Jin Di was so good looking

that it was the most beautiful in the world.

Its surface was bright and smooth,

and its holes were close to each other and round.

The tube was neither too large nor too small,

and it was neither too long nor too short.

With its top and bottom both inlaid with gold and silver,

It had pictures carved on it at both ends:

On one side

were two bouncing dragons rough-housing at the bottom of the sea;

on the other

were two flying phoenixes with their wings touching the floating clouds.

At one end

were the fish-eyed holes arranged in perfect order;

at the other

were mandarin ducks facing each other.

In between were little flowers,

colorful and bright.

This Jin Di was so mysterious

that nothing in the world was as peculiar.

As long as it was placed by the mouth,

it could play tens and thousands of songs;

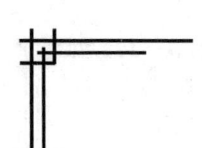

金笛　Jin Di

只要把它放在两唇间，
还可吹出虫声和鸟语。
想吹哪调吹哪调，
想唱哪曲唱哪曲。
吹出欢快的调子，
可使小河无声息；
吹出高昂的调子；
可使飞鹰落下地；
吹出抑郁的调子，
可使百兽难呼吸；
吹出幽怨的调子，
可使高山把头低。
吹出悲伤的调子，
可使万人都哭泣。

这支金笛最珍贵，
世上笛子没有它值钱。
它是凤凰珍藏的宝贝，
它跟凤凰的命运紧相连。
千两黄金呀，
买不下它一根穗子；
万两白银呀，
换不来它一个图案。
虚伪狡诈的歹徒，
永远不能跟它沾边；
只有诚实勇敢的人哟，
才能跟它做伴。
凤凰将它送给扎董丕冉，
这是对他的信任呀，
这是对他的爱恋！

第二章 赠笛 Chapter Two A Gift

as long as it was placed between the lips,
it could play the buzz of insects and chirping of birds.
It could play any tune
and sing any song.
Its happy tune
could silence the small river;
its noble tune
could attract eagles to the ground;
its melancholy tune
could dishearten all animals;
its tragic tune
could force mountains to bow their heads.
Its sad tune
could make tens and thousands of people weep.

This Jin Di was the most precious
and nothing in the world was more priceless.
It was the treasure of the phoenix,
closely linked to its fate.
A thousand taels of gold
couldn't purchase a piece of its fringe;
ten thousand taels of silver couldn't buy a pattern in its picture.
Hypocrites, swindlers, and crooks
could never have anything to do with it;
only the honest and the brave
could keep it company.
That the phoenix gave it to Zha Dong Pi Ran
showed its confidence in him
and its affection for him!

41

金笛 Jin Di

八

扎董丕冉在家吹金笛,
忘记上山砍柴;
扎董丕冉在外吹金笛,
忘记回到家来。
他对着阿支吹金笛,
阿支也忘了赶街;
他对着阿奈吹金笛,
阿奈也忘了洗菜。

阿支笑着说:
"这支金笛真好看,
看见它的样子呀,
我的皱纹就平了!"

阿奈笑着说:
"这支金笛真稀罕,
听到它的声音呀,
我的白发变黑了!"
这支金笛呀,
扎董丕冉最喜欢。
不管出门和进门,
随时别它在腰间。
它是扎董丕冉的朋友,
它是扎董丕冉的伙伴。

第二章 赠笛 Chapter Two A Gift

8

When Zha Dong Pi Ran played the Jin Di at home
he forgot to go to the mountains to cut the firewood;
when Zha Dong Pi Ran played the Jin Di outside of the house,
he forgot to return home.
When he played the Jin Di to A Zhi,
A Zhi forgot to go shopping;
when he played Jin Di to A Nai,
A Nai forgot to wash the vegetables.

A Zhi said, smiling:
"This Jin Di is so beautiful,
when I look at it,
my wrinkles are disappearing!"

A Nai said, smiling:
"This Jin Di is so rare,
listening to its sound
my grey hair is turning black!"
This Jin Di
Zha Dong Pi Ran cherished the most.
Whether he was at home or outside,
the Jin Di was carried at his waist.
It was Zha Dong Pi Ran's friend
and it was Zha Dong Pi Ran's companion.

金笛 Jin Di

他放牛时候吹金笛,
爱打架的黄牛不打架;
他挑水时候吹金笛,
爱点水的蜻蜓不点水;
他打猎时候吹金笛,
爱爬树的猴子不爬树;
他踩花山时候吹金笛,
姑娘小伙围着他打转。

这支金笛呀,
最懂得扎董丕冉的心愿。
春天来了,
扎董丕冉爱看鲜花,
他把金笛吹起来,
满山百花越开越艳。
夏天来了,
扎董丕冉爱吃山果,
他把金笛吹起来,
遍岭百果越结越香甜。
秋天来了,
扎董丕冉要收小米,
他把金笛吹起来,
坡上小米长得更饱满。
冬天来了,
扎董丕冉想晒太阳,
他把金笛吹起来,
天上阳光变得更温暖。

第二章 赠笛 Chapter Two A Gift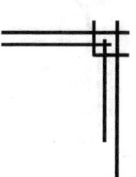

When he played the Jin Di while herding the cattle,
the cantankerous yellow cattle were content;
when he played the Jin Di while carrying water,
playful dragonflies stopped dipping in it;
when he played the Jin Di while hunting,
climbing monkeys quit going up the trees;
when he played the Jin Di while strolling in the mountains,
young women and men surrounded him.

This Jin Di
understood Zha Dong Pi Ran the best.
When spring came,
Zha Dong Pi Ran enjoyed looking at the fresh flowers,
so as he played the Jin Di,
the flowers covering the hills became brighter and brighter.
When summer came,
Zha Dong Pi Ran was fond of wild fruits,
so as he played the Jin Di,
the fruits blanketing the ridges became sweeter and sweeter.
When autumn came,
Zha Dong Pi Ran was to harvest the millet,
so as he played the Jin Di,
the kernels of the millet carpeting the slope became fuller and fuller.
When winter came,
Zha Dong Pi Ran liked to bask in the sun,
so as he played the Jin Di,
the sun in the sky became warmer and warmer.

金笛　Jin Di

一年四季呀，
金笛与扎董丕冉形影相伴，
它能使他得到欢乐，
它能帮他消除痛苦。
有了这支金笛呀，
他就觉得不孤独；
有了这支金笛呀，
他就感到更幸福！

第二章 赠笛 Chapter Two A Gift

Throughout the four seasons each year,
the Jin Di and Zha Dong Pi Ran were inseparable,
it bringing him happiness
and eliminating his sufferings.
With this Jin Di,
he didn't feel lonely;
with this Jin Di,
he felt happy!

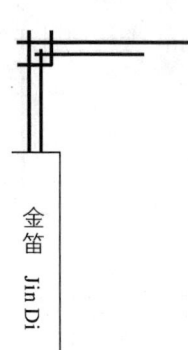

第三章　相恋

九

当阳的荞菜长得快，
叫你越看越新鲜。
扎董丕冉满了十八岁，
长得比牛犊还矫健。
四肢就像大碓杆，
粗壮又结实；
身躯就像嫩冬瓜，
丰满又浑圆。
他的人品嘛，
没人和他比；
他的容貌呀，
盖过苗家山。

可是树不开花不结果，
天不下雨地就旱。
扎董丕冉不开口，
姑娘跟他就难交谈。

第三章 相恋 Chapter Three Love

Chapter Three   Love

9

The buckwheat-scallion grew fast under the sun,
looking more and more fresh everyday.
Zha Dong Pi Ran reached the age of eighteen,
stronger than a calf.
His four limbs were like big poles,
thick and sturdy;
his body was like the fresh winter melon,
full and stout.
His character
had no equal;
and his looks
surpassed the picturesque mountains of the Miao village.

But trees would not bear fruit without blooms,
and drought would strike without the rain.
Until Zha Dong Pi Ran broke his silence,
young women could hardly talk with him.

金笛 Jin Di

不是姑娘不爱他,
爱他的姑娘数不完。
眼前的姑娘虽然好,
扎董丕冉就是不喜欢。

清早起来时,
扎董丕冉坐在竹楼上,
抬眼朝着树林看。
姑娘轻声唱起歌,
故意逗他下来玩。
可是他假装搓绳子,
看也不看她一眼。

吃过晚饭时,
扎董丕冉去挑水,
走到寨头清泉边。
姑娘等在半路上,
有意帮他换换肩。
可是他假装没看见,
匆匆走过她面前。

踩花山时,
扎董丕冉吹金笛,
跑着要去爬花杆。
姑娘打开花撑子,
要想罩住他的脸。
可是他钻进人群里,
过了半天不露面。

第三章 相恋 Chapter Three Love

It was not that young women were not attracted to him;
those who were attracted to him were countless in number.
Even though those were fine young women,
Zha Dong Pi Rang was yet to find the one.

Early one morning while sitting upstairs in the bamboo house,
Zha Dong Pi Ran Looked up at the woods.
A young woman was singing softly,
wanting him to join her.
He pretended he was weaving the rope
and did not look at her.

After dinner
Zha Dong Pi Ran went to fetch water
and stopped by the spring at the end of the village.
A young woman waited for him on the way,
hoping to help him switch the water to the other shoulder.
He pretended to be unaware,
hurrying through right in front of her.

During the Mountain Treading Festival,
Zha Dong Pi Ran played the Jin Di
and ran up to climb the ribbon-decorated pole.
A young woman opened an umbrella,
trying to cover his face.
He rushed into the crowd
and kept out of sight for a long while.

金笛 Jin Di

跳芦笙时，
姑娘向他抛花带，
故意逗他心喜欢。
可是任凭花带缠满身，
他却不理也不看。
只顾吹着芦笙调，
在地上滚滚又翻翻。

就是这样呀，
年满十八没情人，
还是一个单身汉。
不是他无情又无意，
只因他要挑又要拣。
蝶恋鲜花鸟恋林呀，
鹰爱蓝天鱼爱潭。
扎董丕冉爱的是哪个？
太阳在打听，
月亮在偷看……

这年春天桃花开，
蜜蜂忙着来采蜜。
苗家山上很热闹，
家家忙着种小米。
偏偏就在这时候，
家中忽然出岔子。
为了儿子的婚事，
阿支心烦闷，
阿奈也焦急。

第三章 相恋　Chapter Three　Love

Dancing to the Lu Sheng music he was playing,
young women tossed ribbons at him
to please him.
Even with ribbons all over him,
he did not pay attention to or look at them.
Focusing on nothing but playing the Lu Sheng,
he was rolling and summersaulting on the ground.

This was why
at age eighteen
he was still a bachelor.
It was not because he was heartless,
but that he was particular about the one.
Butterflies loved fresh flowers and birds loved the forest;
eagles loved the blue sky and fish love the pool.
Who was the love of Zha Dong Pi Ran?
The sun was asking
and the moon was watching…

One spring, the peach trees were blossoming
and bees were busy gathering nectar.
The mountains of the Miao Village were full of hustle and bustle,
and every family was busy with planting the millet.
Just at this time
something went wrong at home.
Anxious about their son's marriage,
A Zhi was unhappy
and A Nai was worried.

金笛 Jin Di

双双愁出一身病，
躺在床上爬不起。
你看阿支呀，
不吃不喝只呻吟；
你瞧阿奈呀，
不说不笑光叹气。
眼看节令快晃过。
还没打算去犁地。
今年小米种不下，
明年怎样过日子？
想起这件事情呀，
别说扎董丕冉犯了愁，
就是那头牯牛也怄气！

凡是耕田种地人，
节令就是命根子。
要是节令错过了，
来年就是啃树皮。
普天之下都晓得，
这是一个大道理。
一定不能再等了，
得要赶快拿主意！
扎董丕冉清早就起身，
扛上那张黄木犁。
包起冷饭做晌午，
吆牛上山种小米。
孤孤零零一个人，
又撒种子又犁地；

第三章 相恋 Chapter Three Love

Both fell ill
and became bed-ridden.
A Zhi
did not eat or drink but only groaned;
A Nai
did not talk or laugh but only sighed.
The spring was almost slipping away,
yet there was still no plan for when to plough the field.
If the millet wasn't planted this year,
what would they live on next year?
The thought of this
not only worried Zha Dong Pi Ran,
but even the ox was mad!

For all farmers,
missing the season is losing their livelihood.
Missing the season means
chewing on the tree bark the coming year.
Everyone knows this
very important fact.
It could not wait any longer,
and something had to be done soon!
Zha Dong Pi Ran got up early one morning,
putting the plough on his shoulder.
Having packed some cold lunch,
he hollered at the ox up the hill to plant the millet.
All by himself,
he sowed seeds and ploughed the fields;

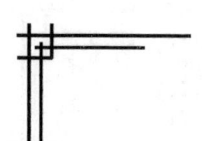

金笛 Jin Di

犁完一沟撒一沟,
撒完一沟又来犁。
来来往往忙半天,
才种完一块小坡地。
累得浑身大汗如雨淌,
腰酸眼花腿无力。

十

四山八岭传笑声,
扎董丕冉乱了心。
他抬眼向着远处看,
越看越烦恼。

别家做活都有伴,
人多手快热腾腾。
男的呦牛打犁沟,
女的撒种在后跟,
男耕女播多火热呀,
有说有笑有歌声。
调子出口传得远,
种子落地就生根。
累了双双到地头,
大树底下好躲荫。

56

第三章 相恋 Chapter Three Love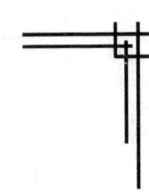

ploughing one row and then seeding it,

seeding a row and then ploughing another.

he was busy for a long while,

but he merely finished a small piece of the land on the hillside.

Exhausted, he was dripping with sweat that fell like the rainwater,

his back being sore, his eyes seeing stars, and his legs feeling heavy.

10

Laughters spread through the great mountains,

causing Zha Dong Pi Ran to lose his focus.

He looked at the distance

only to become more and more anxious.

Others worked in pairs,

more people, faster pace, and livelier environment.

The men steered the plough behind the oxen to plough the field,

while the women sowed seeds right after,

how lovely the ploughing men and sowing women,

full of talk, banter and songs.

The songs once sung were carried far away,

while the seeds once sown took root in the soil.

When tired, the couples went to the end of the field

sheltered from the sun and under the great trees.

金笛 Jin Di

打开饭包吃晌午,
吃在嘴里甜在心。
男的递给女的吃,
女的接过抿嘴笑;
女的递给男的吃,
男的接过挤眼睛。
恩恩爱爱甜如蜜呀,
亲亲热热情意深。

扎董丕冉越看越懊恼,
犁地撒种没精神。
别人成双又成对,
只有自己孤零零;
别人有说又有笑,
只有自己闷沉沉。
他跑到树下吹金笛,
金笛声声诉苦情:

布哩布哩布哩噜,
太阳偏西过晌午。
我又犁泥沟又撒种,
满身汗水湿衣襟。
忙酸了四肢,
累散了骨筋,
可怜我扎董丕冉呀,
为何这般受苦楚?

第三章 相恋 Chapter Three Love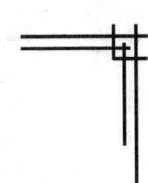

Opening their lunch boxes,

they tasted the lunch in their mouths and felt the sweetness in their hearts.

The men handed food to the women

who accepted with a smile;

the women passed food to the men

who accepted with a wink.

The love was so sweet,

and the affection, so deep.

The more Zha Dong Pi Ran looked at them, the more upset he became,

his mind wandering away from ploughing and sowing.

Others were in pairs,

but only he was alone;

others were talking and laughing,

but only he was depressed.

He ran to under a tree to play the Jin Di

to use it to tell his grievances:

"Bu li bu li bu li lu,

the sun is to the west, and the day has passed noon.

I both ploughed the land and sowed the seeds,

with my shirt drenched with sweat.

My four limbs are sore

and my bones ache.

Wretched me, Zha Dong Pi Ran,

why am I suffering from all this?

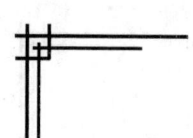

金笛 Jin Di

可怜我扎董丕冉呀,
何时才会有人来呀,
何时才会有人来帮助?"

笛声阵阵多惆怅,
幽怨婉转绕山岗。
一直传到九霄云,
惊得太阳也无光。
只见天上起火闪,
照得四周明晃晃。
就在这时候
怪事出一桩。
空中忽然传来木叶声,
一声一声多响亮。

"布哩布哩布哩噜,
扎董丕冉别心急。
只要你不嫌我手脚笨,
我一定会来帮助你!
人到难时有人怜呀,
鸟到山边有林栖。

木叶声从哪里来?
来自天上云彩里。
扎董丕冉听到木叶声,
呆呆站着出了神。
这声音很像凤凰叫,

第三章 相恋 Chapter Three Love

Wretched me, Zha Dong Pi Ran,
when will some one come,
come to help me?"

How woeful was the sound of the Jin Di,
a sense of bitterness circling around the mountains.
It flew into the sky,
startling the sun and dimmed its shine.
Just then a fiery flash was seen in the sky,
lighting up the entire area.
It was at this moment,
something astounding happened.
Out of the sky suddenly came the sound of the Mu-leave,
over and over, loud and clear:

"Bu li bu li bu li lu,
Zha Dong Pi Ran, don't be anxious.
As long as you don't think I am too clumsy,
I will come to help you!
In hard times, one will be pitied by others,
 just as, reaching the edge of the mountains, birds will find woods to inhabit."

Where did the sound of the Mu-leaf come from?
It came from the clouds in the sky.
Listening to that sound of the Mu-leaf,
Zha Dong Pi Ran stood in a daze.
It sounded like the loud cry of the phoenix,

金笛 Jin Di

清脆响亮最好看。
扎董丕冉越听越畅快，
像喝口泉水甜透心。
他抬头朝着天上看，
只是听见声音不见人。
这木叶是谁吹的呢？
吹得真迷人！
扎董丕冉吹金笛，
调调吹出心里话；
这人吹的木叶呀，
曲曲吹的是真情。
扎董丕冉已明白：
他已经找到好知音；
扎董丕冉已知道：
他到难处有人怜。
他的知音是哪个？
就是这个吹叶人！
可怜他的是哪个？
也是这个吹叶人！
这人究竟是谁呢？
扎董丕冉在判定：
寨子里的姑娘呀，
木叶也还吹得成，
可是她们嘴不灵，
没有这个好本领。
她们吹起木叶来，

第三章 相恋 Chapter Three Love

crisp, clear, and striking.

The more Zha Dong Pi Ran listened to it, the more joyous he became,

like tasting the heart-sweetening spring water.

He looked up into the sky

but could only hear the voice without seeing anyone.

Who was playing the Mu-leaf?

It was played so mesmerizingly!

Zha Dong Pi Ran played the Jin Di again

to express his thoughts;

the one who played the Mu-leaf

showed true emotions.

Zha Dong Pi Ran had realized that

he has found a confidant;

Zha Dong Pi Ran had learned that

when he found himself in trouble someone felt sorry for him.

Who was the confidant?

It was the one who played the Mu-leaf!

Who felt sorry for him?

It was also the one who played the Mu-leaf!

Who was it?

Zha Dong Pi Ran was trying to decide:

The young women in the Miao village

could indeed play the Mu-leaf,

but they were limited

and not this skillful.

When they played the Mu-leaf,

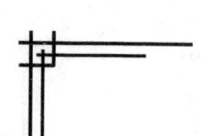

金笛 Jin Di

好瞧不好听；
她们吹出调子来，
入耳不入心。
如今这个吹叶人，
来历怕是有原因。
绝不是寨里的小姑娘，
定是远方来的好客人！

扎董丕冉正猜想，
忽然眼前闪金光。
一个姑娘微微笑，
已经站在他身旁。
花衣彩裙随风舞，
项圈手镯响叮当。
头顶有颗夜明珠，
就像星星在眨眼；
鞋尖有对红玛瑙，
晶莹璀璨在发光。
浑身上下亮闪闪，
活像一只金凤凰。

扎董丕冉前边瞧，
扎董丕冉后边看，
扎董丕冉左边看，
扎董丕冉右边望。
最后站在对面不动了，
就像一颗木桩桩。

第三章 相恋 Chapter Three Love

they looked better than they sounded;
the tune they played
went into the ear but didn't touch the heart.
This Mu-leaf player today
might have a reason to come here.
It couldn't be some young woman of the Miao village
and must be a guest from afar.

While Zha Dong Pi Ran was pondering,
a gold light flashed before his eyes.
A young woman with a smile on her face
was already standing by him.
Her colorful shirt and skirt waved in the wind,
as were her bracelets and necklaces
jingling in the wind.
A luminous pearl was on her head,
twinkling like a blinking star;
at the tips of her shoes was a pair of red agate stones
that were sparkling and gleaming.
Her whole body was flashing brilliance,
just like a golden phoenix.

Zha Dong Pi Ran looked at the front of her,
and he looked at the back of her,
and he looked at the left side of her,
and he looked at the right side her.
He finally stopped in front of her, facing her
like a post.

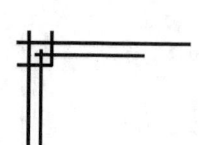

金笛 Jin Di

他见过姑娘千万个,
可是面前这个呀,
谁也比不上!
她的眉毛像月牙,
又细又弯真好看;
她的眼睛像湖水,
又明又亮清汪汪;
她的脸庞像桃花,
又红又润粉泱泱;
她的头发像青丝,
又长又软拖到地面上。
蝴蝶围着她跳舞,
蜜蜂绕着她歌唱。
扎董丕冉笑眯了眼睛呀,
姑娘羞红了面庞。

扎董丕冉望着姑娘不眨眼,
金笛落地他也顾不上了。
不知过了几多时,
他才如梦初醒眼发亮。
赶忙爬上一颗老桃树,
摘下一朵红桃花,
轻轻插在姑娘的鬓角上。
扎董丕冉低声问,
心中却是有点慌:
"你是天上的仙女,
还是林中的凤凰?
你怎么生得这样美?
高山因你增颜色,

第三章 相恋 Chapter Three Love

He had met many, many young women,
but the one in front of him
beat them all!
Her eyebrows were like the crescent moon,
slender, curved, and pretty;
her eyes were like a lake of water,
bring, clear, and glassy;
her face was like a peach blossom,
rosy, smooth, and flawlessly madeup;
her raven tress as like the black threads,
long and soft trailing on the ground.
Butterflies danced around her
and bees sang around her.
Zha Dong Pi Ran was grinning from ear to ear,
and the young woman was blushing.

Zha Dong Pi Ran stared at her without a blink,
even ignoring the Jin Di when it fell to the ground.
This went on for no one knew how long
before he emerged from his reverie with bright eyes.
He hurriedly climbed up an old peach tree,
plucked a peach blossom,
and gently placed it in her hair and by her ear.
Zha Dong Pi Ran whispered
nervously:
"Are you a fairy from the sky
or the phoenix of the forest?
How can you be endowed with such beauty?
Mountains become more radiant because of you,

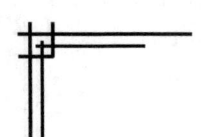

河水因你泛银光!"

姑娘脸上飞红云,
启动双唇轻开腔:
"我是一只金凤凰,
住在遥远的地方……"
她顿觉自己已失口,
赶忙改了腔:
"不,不……
我不是凤凰,
我是蒙诗彩奏,
我的家在山顶上。
看见你一个人种小米,
我特地来帮忙。"
蒙诗彩奏笑盈盈,
欠欠身子显得很端庄。
弯下腰去拾起那金笛,
亲手别在他的腰带上。

十一

蒙诗彩奏抬起脚,
迈走进小米地,
扎董丕冉想阻止,
可是没有来得及。
她右手扶犁耙,
左手拉牛鼻索,
口里不住吆着牛,
一铧铧犁过去。

第三章　相恋　Chapter Three Love

and rivers sparkle more silverily because of you."

With rosy cheeks like the pink clouds,
the young woman replied softly,
"I am a golden phoenix,
who lives in a faraway place..."
Immediately she realized she had let her origin slip
and corrected herself:
"No, no...
I am not a phoenix
but Meng Shi Cai Zou,
living at the top of the mountain.
Seeing that you were planting the millet all by yourself,
I came to give you a hand."
Meng Shi Cai Zou smiled,
and bowed slightly with respect and poise.
She bent over, picked up the Jin Di,
and reattached it to his belt by herself.

11

Meng Shi Cai Zou started walking
towards the field of the millet.
Zha Dong Pi Ran wanted to stop her
but it was too late.
With her right hand holding the handle of the plough,
her left hand pulling the nose ring of the ox,
she hollered at the ox now and again
and ploughed the field one row after another.

金笛 Jin Di

姑娘也会犁地呀!
扎董丕冉觉得很稀奇。
看着她那苗条的身影,
心中又有些不过意:
"还是让我来犁吧,
莫弄脏了你的彩裙和花衣!"

"游鱼离不开池塘,
蒙诗彩奏离不开土地,
怕脏怕累就不是苗家女。"
扎董丕冉赶紧拿起一个大粪箕,
撮了一些小米种,
沿沟撒种赶上去。

扎董丕冉撒着种,
就像喝醉酒一样。
一步一摇跟她走,
两眼不住朝她望。
一粒一粒小米种啊,
全都撒在沟帮上。

蒙诗彩奏心里暗发笑,
脸也觉得有点发烫,
开口轻轻唱起歌,
教他不该分心肠:

第三章　相恋　Chapter Three　Love

A young woman could plough the field!
Zha Dong Pi Ran was amazed.
Seeing her slim figure,
he felt somewhat guilty:
"Let me do it,
so that you don't dirty your skirt and floral shirt."

"Just like fish cannot leave the pound,
Meng Shi Cai Zou cannot leave the land,
so those who are afraid of hardships are not daughters of the Miao Village."
Zha Dong Pi Ran quickly picked up the shallow basket,
grasped the millet seeds,
and started to plant them by the furrows.

Zha Dong Pi Ran sowed the seed
as if he were drunk.
Following her each step,
he could not help staring at her.
The seeds of the millet
were spread all over the wall of the furrows.

Meng Shi Cai Zou, amused by this,
felt her cheeks slightly burning
and started to sing quietly,
telling him not to be distracted:

金笛 Jin Di

"种子撒在石头上，
不会生根不会长；
种子撒在沟帮上，
会被鸟雀全吃光；
种子埋得太深了，
就会沤烂在泥塘；
种子盖得太浅了，
将来苗棵长不壮。
我的阿哥哟，
乱撒种子的人，
他的收成无指望！"

这歌像股清泉水，
潺潺流进他心房，
他边撒种子边唱歌，
也用歌来答姑娘：

"是你天仙般的美貌呀，
使我神乱心发慌。
我的阿妹呀，
我一定专心撒好种，
等到秋天收割时，
定让小米装满仓！"

歌没唱完小米已撒完，
整整撒了三块大坡地。

第三章 相恋 Chapter Three Love

"Seeds thrown on the stone
will not take roots and grow;
seeds thrown on the walls of the furrows
will be eaten up by birds;
seed buried too deep
will rot in the mud;
and seeds buried too shallow
will not grow strong.
My dear,
those who sow aimlessly
have no hope for a good harvest!"

The song was like a stream of spring water
flowing into his heart,
and he started to sing as he sowed the seeds
to reply to the young woman also with a song:

"It is your heavenly beauty
that made me distracted and nervous.
My dear,
I will focus on sowing the seeds,
so that the harvest in the fall
will fill the granary up with the millet!"

The planting was done before the singing was finished,
three large patches of the field on the hillside.

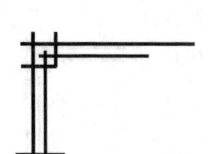

金笛 Jin Di

两人你看我来我看你,
还有多少话儿埋心底。
可是这时日落天将晚,
只好依依不舍相别离。
扎董丕冉看着她,
慢慢走进树林里。

十二

夏天地里杂草长,
长得跟小米一样齐。
扎董丕冉铲杂草,
铲一阵呀,吹一回笛:

"布哩布哩布哩噜,
太阳当顶正晌午。
红火辣日头,
铲草最辛苦……"

只听一阵木叶响,
声声传到他耳里:
"布哩布哩布哩噜,
铲草阿哥莫心急。
天热太阳辣,
我来帮帮你……"
木叶声刚停,
蒙诗彩奏又来到地里。
两人一边铲草一边唱,

第三章 相恋 Chapter Three Love

They looked at each other,
still having many words buried at the bottom of their hearts.
But the sun was set and it was getting late,
so reluctantly they had to say goodbye.
Zha Dong Pi Ran looked at her,
as she slowly disappeared into the woods.

12

In the summer the weeds in the field
were as tall as the millet plants.
Weeding the field, Zha Dong Pi Ran
worked for a while and then played the Jin Di:

"Bu li bu li bu li lu,
at noon, the sun is directly overhead.
Under the red hot sun,
weeding is quite a slog…"

Just then the sound of the Mu-leaf
reached his ears:
"Bu li bu li bu li lu,
my weeding dear, do not worry.
Since the day is hot and the sun, scorching,
let me help you…"
As soon as the sound of the Mu-leaf stopped,
Meng Shi Cai Zou appeared in the field again.
They two were then weeding and singing,

金笛 Jin Di

太阳不再辣,
热风也像有凉意。

你一铲,
我一铲,
一直铲到日偏西;
你一调,
我一调,
一直唱到月升起。

铲完三块大坡地,
两人恋恋不舍又分离。
扎董丕冉看着她,
见她姗姗隐进夜幕里。

秋天小米一片黄,
穗子粗又长。
扎董丕冉割小米,
孤单一人心惆怅。
他想起心上人,
又把金笛来吹响:
"布哩布哩布哩噜,
小米丰收人幸福。
可是人少地多收不完,
怕要收到日落月亮出。
叫声蒙诗彩奏呀,
请你快快来帮助!"

第三章 相恋 Chapter Three Love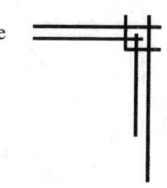

no longer feeling the scotching sun,
and even the hot wind feeling cooler.

One weeded,
and the other did, too,
weeding until the sun set in the west;
one sang a tune,
and the other did, too,
singing until the moon rose.

After all three pieces of the land on the hillside had been weeded,
reluctantly, the two had to say goodbye again.
Zha Dong Pi Ran watched her
as she slowly disappeared into the darkness of the night.

In the autumn the millet had ripened,
with strong and long spikes.
Zha Dong Pi Ran was harvesting the millet
alone by himself and gloomy.
Remembering his sweetheart,
he played the Jin Di again:
"Bu li bu li bu li lu,
the millet yields a good harvest, and people are happy.
Yet being shorten-handed I cannot finish,
and I'm afraid I will still have to harvest well into the moon is up.
My dear Meng Shi Cai Zou,
please come quickly and lend me a hand!"

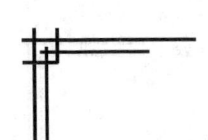

金笛 Jin Di

远处又是一阵木叶响：
"布哩布哩布哩，
小米丰收人欢喜。
人少地多不要紧，
妹妹来帮你！"

随着悠扬的木叶声，
蒙诗彩奏又来到地里。
两人心相印，
一起收小米。
他割得快，
她掼得勤。
又割又掼不歇气，
很快收完三块大坡地。
小米堆得像金山，
两人相对笑嘻嘻。

十三

春天犁地种小米，
夏天铲草薅小米，
秋天来到割小米，
他俩都是在一起。
金笛诉衷肠，
木叶传情意。
小米黄澄澄，
心中甜蜜蜜。

第三章 相恋 Chapter Three Love

At a distance came the sound of the Mu-leaf again:
"Bu li bu li bu li,
rejoice at this good harvest of the millet.
It's okay to have much work with fewer people,
because I am coming to lend you a helping hand!"

With the sweet sound of the Mu-leaf,
Meng Shi Cai Zou reappeared in the millet field again.
With their minds and hearts set on the same goal,
the two harvested the millet side by side.
He cut the crop fast,
and she bundled it quickly.
Cutting and bundling without a break,
they soon finished the three pieces of the farmland on the hillside.
The millet piled up like the golden hills,
and they smiled at each other.

13

Planting the millet in the spring,
weeding the field in the summer,
harvesting the crop in the autumn,
they were together during all those times.
The Jin Di expressed true feelings,
and the Mu-leaf conveyed genuine care.
The millet now looked golden,
and their hearts felt sweet and joyful.

金笛 Jin Di

种小米的时候,
他俩播下种子,
也播下爱情;
薅小米的时候,
小米长得旺盛,
爱情也生了根;
小米收割了,
何时才能收割爱情?
扎董丕冉有点纳闷。
小米收完了,
蒙诗彩奏又要别离,
扎董丕冉更加伤心:
"我的阿妹呀,
今天分别了,
何时才相见?
是三年五载,
是几个秋夏几个冬春?"
蒙诗彩奏微微笑:
"我的阿哥呀,
不要三年五载,
也不要几个秋夏冬春,
正月初三踩花山,
我们来相逢,
我俩来对歌,
那时我俩把亲定,
阿哥你莫错过好时辰。"

第三章 相恋 Chapter Three Love

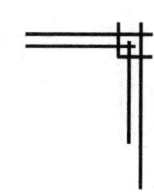

When they sowed the millet,
they also sowed
the seed of their love;
when they weeded the field,
the millet thrived
and their love took roots;
now that the millet had been harvested,
when would the love be ready for harvesting?
Zha Dong Pi Ran wondered.
After the harvest,
Meng Shi Cai Zou was to depart again,
and Zha Dong Pi Ran was saddened:
"My sweetheart,
when we part today,
when will we see each other again?
How many years will there be
or how many seasons?"
Meng Shi Cai Zou smiled:
"My dear,
it won't take years
or seasons,
but at the Mountain Treading Festival on the third day of the first month,
let's meet again then,
sing responsorially,
and get engaged,
an auspicious time you do not want to miss."

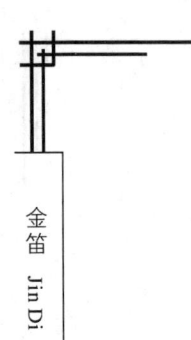

第四章　拦路

十四

八月过了到九月,
九月过了到十月,
十月过了到冬月,
冬月过了到腊月,
时间就像撵兔子,
紧跑快追不停歇。

正月初三来到了,
欢欢喜喜度佳节。
正月初三踩花山,
高山顶上立花杆①。
红绸挂在花杆上,
飘飘扬扬真耀眼。
群群姑娘和小伙,
说说笑笑上花山。
扎董丕冉穿新衣,

---

① a traditional festival activities of the Hmong, (The Mountain Treading Festival) People choose tall pines to make a pole, decorate it with flowers and climb to the top of the pole in different ways.

第四章 拦路 Chapter Four Tests

Chapter Four   Tests

14

The eighth month passed, and then came the ninth,
the ninth month passed, and then came the tenth,
the tenth month passed, and then came the eleventh,
the eleventh month passed, and then came the twelfth.
time flew by just like rabbit chasing,
always running, never stopping.

The third day of the first month arrived,
festival and delightful.
During the Mountain Treading on the third of the first month,
a pole decorated with ribbons was set up on the top of the mountain.
The red ribbon hanging from the pole
brilliantly fluttering in the air and dazzling the eye.
Groups of young women and men
were chatting and laughing as they went up the mountain.
Zha Dong Pi Ran, dressed in new clothes,

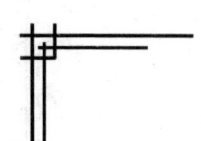

金笛　Jin Di

拿起金笛跨出门。
顺着弯弯小路走,
越走越精神。
因为他到花山上,
就要会情人。
一边赶路一边吹金笛,
金笛吹遍山和岭。

蒙诗彩奏等在大树脚,
隐隐听到金笛声。
凭着笛声来判断,
知道扎董丕冉已来临。
她站在地上摇摇身,
摆动一下长褶裙,
使个法术隐真形,
变成另外一个人。
变成糯珠彩奏呀,
她要试探他的心。

扎董丕冉来到泉水旁,
一颗心儿在跳荡。
马上就要见到情人面,
止不住阵阵脸发烫。

他在泉边停住脚,
俯下身子望一望。
身影映在水里头,

第四章 拦路 Chapter Four Tests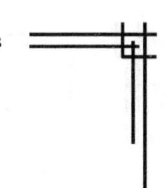

with his Jin Di, went out the door.
Walking along the winding path,
he became more and more inspirited.
He was going up the mountain
to reunite with his love.
As he walked, he played the Jin Di,
the sound of which resonated everywhere in the mountain.

Meng Shi Cai Zou was waiting under a big tree
when she heard the indistinct sound of the Jin Di.
Judging by the sound of it,
she knew Zha Dong Pi Ran had arrived.
She stood up, shook her body,
swayed her long pleated skirt,
and magically transfigured
into another person.
She was now a Nuo Zhu Cai Zou,
just to test his loyalty.

Zha Dong Pi Ran came by the spring,
his heart racing with excitement.
He would soon see his love,
and he couldn't help blushing and his cheeks burning.

He paused by the side of the spring fountain
and bent over to have a look at himself.
His reflection in the water

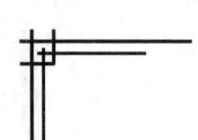

金笛　Jin Di

随着水波在荡漾。
一边望来一边理头发,
又伸出手来扯衣裳。
泉水清清多明净,
自己的身影更漂亮。
看着影子微微笑,
自言自语诉衷肠:

"蒙诗彩奏呀,
正月初三来相会,
我俩定下好时光。
收拾打扮来会你,
见面就在花山上。
请你耐心等着我,
照照影子我就上山梁。"
忽然水面影子闪,
水里现出一个小姑娘。
姑娘生得很漂亮,
紧紧挨在他身旁。

她扭着身子咪咪笑,
脉脉含情把话讲:
"扎董丕冉,
我是糯珠彩奏,
只因你生得像金鹿,
我早就偷偷把你爱上。

第四章 拦路 Chapter Four Tests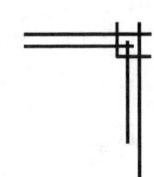

buoyed with the ripples.
He looked at himself, adjusting his hair
and then straightening his shirt.
The spring water was clear and clean
but his reflection was even more attractive.
Looking at his figure, he smiled
and said to himself:

"Meng Shi Cai Zou,
we meet again on this third day of the first lunar month,
the auspicious time you and I have chosen.
I am all dressed up to come to see you
on top of the Flower Mountain.
Please be patient and wait for me,
for I'm coming up the ridge of the mountain right after this final inspection."
Suddenly, another reflection appeared in the water,
one of a young woman.
She was very beautiful
and was right next to him.

Twisting her body and giggling,
she spoke to him tenderly:
"Zha Dong Pi Ran,
I am Nuo Zhu Cai Zou,
who loves your golden deer-like physique
and has been your secret admirer for a long time.

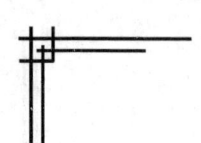

金笛 Jin Di

你有一支神奇的金笛,
能吹出欢乐和忧伤。
我特地在这里等着你,
把贴心的话语跟你讲。
望你不要嫌弃我,
定要将我贴心上。
今天踩花山,
我俩正好配成双。"

扎董丕冉看着她,
一下被她迷住了,
她的腰身像柳枝,
匀称又苗条。
她的脸盘像葵花,
眼睛像葡萄。
她比蒙诗彩奏还好看,
一颗心止不住咚咚跳。
又仔细瞄她一眼,
频频向着她微笑。
接着吹起金笛来,
笛声在她耳边绕:

"布哩布哩布哩噜,
我把心事给你来倾吐。
你的好心又使我佩服。
但我不能爱上你呀,
我的心早已有归宿。
我已爱上蒙诗彩奏,

第四章 拦路 Chapter Four Tests

You have a mysterious Jin Di
that could express joy and sorrow.
I came here just to wait for you
to share my deepest thoughts with you.
Please do not be annoyed with me
and please keep me in your heart.
On this Flower Mountain Treading day,
you and I will make a perfect couple."

Zha Dong Pi Ran looked at her
and became enthralled by her.
Her waist was like a willow branch,
gorgeous and slender.
Her face was round like a sunflower,
and her eyes were like grapes.
She was even more beautiful than Meng Shi Cai Zou,
and his heart was racing.
Glancing at her again,
he smiled at her.
He then started to play the Jin Di,
the sound of which rang in her ears:

"Bu li bu li bu li lu,
let me tell you my story.
I appreciate your kindness,
but I can't love you,
because my heart has found its own home.
I am in love with Meng Shi Cai Zou,

金笛 Jin Di

她会给我人生的幸福。
要是我再爱你呀,
那我就连禽兽也不如!
一双鹿子歇个窝,
一对锦鸡栖一树;
我跟蒙诗彩奏已相爱,
永远只能将她牢记住。
她在花山上面等着我,
从早等到正晌午。
为了趁早去会她,
我正忙赶路。"
糯珠彩奏不死心,
紧紧跟住他。
扎董丕冉上高山;
她也追到高山上;
扎董丕冉走进石旮旯,
她也撵到石旮旯。

追了一山又一山,
撵了一程又一程。
糯珠彩奏追不着,
可是心中很高兴。
她想扎董丕冉没变心,
正是她的意中人!
可是她又打主意,
钻进一片大树林。
摇身变成花太彩奏,

第四章 拦路 Chapter Four Tests

who will give me happiness.
If I gave my heart to you,
I would be worse than a beast!
A deer couple rest in one nest,
and a golden pheasant pair inhabit on one tree;
I and Meng Shi Cai Zou have already fallen in love,
so I can but always keep her in my mind.
She is waiting for me up in the mountains
from morning till noon.
To see her as soon as possible
I must keep walking along."
Nuo Zhu Cai Zou doesn't want to give up.
Nuo Zhu Cai Zou would not let go,
following hard on his heels.
Zha Dong Pi Ran climbed up the mountain,
so did she;
Zha Dong Pi Ran walked in a rocky nook,
so did she.

She chased after him one hill after another,
one league after another.
Although Nuo Zhu Cai Zou couldn't really keep up with him,
she was very happy.
She knew now that Zha Dong Pi Ran didn't change his mind
and was just as she thought of him!
But still she thought of another idea
and then disappeared into the forest.
She shook her body and changed into a Hua Tai Cai Zou,

金笛 Jin Di

花枝招展真迷人。
要论她的容貌呀,
比糯珠彩奏美十分。
穿戴齐整又华丽,
石头见了也动心。
她坐在河边弹口弦,
弹出曲曲好歌音。
故意等着扎董丕冉来,
二次试探他的心。

一会扎董丕冉走过来,
她闪动一双大眼睛。
立刻伸出一只手,
紧紧拖住他的大衣襟。
又将口弦举起来,
嘴里唱得更迷人:
"我是花太彩奏,
家住金碧辉煌的宫殿里。
虽说山高路又远,
早已听见你的好名声。
你是苗家最出众的男子,
早就使我动了心。
收下我的口弦吧,
请你莫嫌礼物轻。
它是我的好伙伴,
它是我的命根根。
你若把它收下了,

第四章 拦路 Chapter Four Tests

gorgeous and alluring.
Her appearance was
even prettier than that of Nuo Zhu Cai Zou.
She was so well-dressed and looked so splendid
that even the stone would be moved.
Sitting on the riverbank and playing the Kou Xian①,
she performed every song beautifully.
Waiting for Zha Dong Pi Ran,
she wanted to test him a second time.

Presently, Zha Dong Pi Ran came,
and she blinked her baby-like eyes at him.
Immediately reaching out one hand
she held tightly onto the lapel of his jacket.
Then with the other hand she held up the Kou Xian,
singing charmingly:
"I am Hua Tai Cai Zou
from a splendid palace.
Despite the mountainous and long distance,
I have heard about your good reputation.
You are the best among the Miao young men
and have touched my heart for a long time.
Please accept my Kou Xian,
and do not reject it as a gift too trifle.
It is my good friend
and the essence of my life.
If you accept it,

---

① Kou Xian is a kind of Chinese mouth harp.

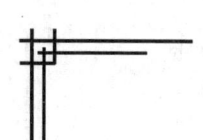

金笛 Jin Di

我俩就算定了情。
我俩在一起,
就像一对小蜜蜂。
你会犁地种小米,
我会织布裁衣裙。
我俩勤勤恳恳过日子,
同甘共苦心贴心。
我俩在一起,
就像一对小白灵。
你吹金笛很好听,
我弹口弦也动人。
你一吹,
我就应。
我俩永远在一起,
欢欢乐乐过一生。"

扎董丕冉一见她,
不禁赞叹她的好人品。
她的脸蛋呀,
像刚剥的竹笋一样白嫩;
她的眼睛呀,
像荷花上的水珠一样透明。
绣花的锦缎上衣,
配着美丽的长裙,
手镯是拿金子铸造,
项圈是用珍珠串成。
如果跟她相爱,
定是美满婚姻……

第四章 拦路 Chapter Four Tests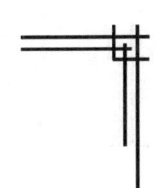

you and I will be engaged.

You and I together

will be like a couple of bees.

You can plough and plant the millet,

and I can weave and tailor clothes.

We work hard and lead our happy lives,

sharing sorrows and happinesses.

We will be together

just like a pair of white larks.

You can play the Jin Di wonderfully,

and I can play the Kou Xian movingly.

Once you play,

I will respond.

We can be together forever

and live happily forever.

Looking at her, Zha Dong Pi Ran

couldn't help admiring her.

Her cheeks

were white and tender like the bamboo shoots freshly peeled;

her eyes

were clear and bright like the dewdrops on the loutus buds.

Her embroidered blouse was of silk brocade

matched with a long beautiful skirt.

Her bracelet was made of gold,

and her necklace was made of pearls.

If he fell in love with her,

he would for sure have a happy marriage…

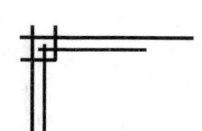

金笛 Jin Di

扎董丕冉越想越甜蜜,
昏昏沉沉像是入梦境。
可是耳边好像有人在说话,
那是蒙诗彩奏的声音:
"正月初三踩花山
我们来相逢……"
扎董丕冉心一惊,
立刻就猛醒!

他又拿起金笛吹,
金笛声声传真情:
"布哩布哩布哩噜,
你是皇家贵公主。
我是一个穷小子呀,
跟你配不住。
你再生得美,
我不能把心转向你;
你再长得好,
我不能把情移给你;
你再说得甜,
我不能把爱向你倾吐。
你的口弦我不能接,
你的心意我只能惋惜,
我已爱上蒙诗彩奏,
她是我心中的一颗明珠。
衣裳可以穿两件,

第四章 拦路 Chapter Four Tests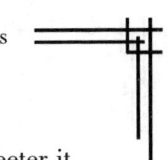

The more Zha Dong Pi Ran thought about this, the sweeter it became,

as if he were entering into a dream.

But someone seemed to be whispering into his ear,

like the voice of Meng Shi Cai Zou.

"At the Flower Mountain Treading on the third of the first month

let's meet again…"

Suddenly, Zha Dong Pi Ran

woke up startled.

He picked up the Jin Di and played,

sincerely and seriously:

"Bu li bu li bu li lu,

you are a royal princess.

I am a poor man

and was no match for you.

You can be born a beauty,

but I can't give my heart to you;

you can be in perfect shape,

but I can't give my affections to you;

you can speak the sweetest words,

but I cannot express my love to you.

I cannot accept your Kou Xian

and I am sorry but I cannot return your feelings.

I am in love with Meng Shi Cai Zou,

the bright and shining pearl in my heart.

One can wear two outfits

97

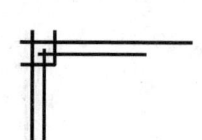

金笛 Jin Di

烂了可以再缝补;
情人只能有一个,
纯洁的感情容不得亵渎。
她在花山上面等着我,
从早等到正晌午。
为了趁早去会她,
我得立刻就赶路。"

花太彩奏脸发红,
故意嘟着嘴巴唱一曲:
"蒙诗彩奏不爱你,
她是财主家的小幺女。
你是一个穷小子,
她怎把你放眼里?
我见她打着花伞上花山,
跟着一个小伙子唱调子,
唱完调子就说话,
亲亲密密坐在一起。
她已爱上别个人,
早就忘了你!
劝你不要再想她,
再想也无益。
虽说我是皇家大公主,
却是真心爱着你!"

扎董丕再哈哈笑,
吹起金笛回答道:
"布哩布哩布哩噜,

第四章 拦路 Chapter Four Tests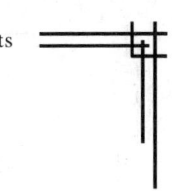

and can mend them when they are worn out;
but true love one can have only one,
the undefiably pure love.
She is waiting for me up in the mountains
from morning till noon.
To see her as soon as possible,
I must keep walking along."

With the redness of blush on her face,
she sang a song:
"Meng Shi Cai Zou doesn't love you,
herself a daughter of a wealthy man.
With you being a poor nobody,
how could she take you seriously?
I saw her holding an umbrella and going up the Flower Mountain
with a young man singing chatting,
and sitting intimately next to each other.
She has fallen in love with another one
and had forgot about you a long time ago.
I urge you to stop thinking about her,
because doing so can do you no good.
Though I am a royal princess,
I am your true love!"

Zha Dong Pi Ran burst out laughing,
replying by playing the Jin Di:
"Bu li bu li bu li lu,

99

金笛 Jin Di

请你不要再啰嗦。
顽石堵不住山泉的水,
臭藤缠不死爱情的花。
我跟蒙诗彩奏早交心,
死死活活都要成一家。
她贴肝贴肺爱着我,
我直心直肠想着她。
要是她去爱别人,
除非石头会开花!
请你不要纠缠我,
让我早点去会她!"

花太彩奏一点不轻松,
仍然把他拦在大路边。
又弹口弦又是唱,
在他身边团团转。
他被缠得无路走,
只好假意答应她:
"请你别再把路拦,
我愿跟你结伙伴。
我们二人一路走,
双双同去踩花山。"

花太彩奏心里想:
"莫非是他已变心?
等我同他一路走,
看他可会跟我来谈情?
他若不跟我谈情,
也就没变心。"

第四章 拦路 Chapter Four Tests

please stop talking.
Rocks can't block the spring water from flowing,
and the rotten vine can't strangle the blossom of love.
Meng Shi Cai Zou and I have long known each other's heart,
and are destined to be together in life and in death.
She is deeply in love with me
and I whole-heartedly miss her.
She would love another
only when stone could blossom!
Please stop hassling me,
so that I could see her soon.

Hua Tai Cai Zou would not give up,
trying to detain him by the side of the road.
Playing the Kou Xian and singing songs,
she was circling around him on and on.
He could not get on his way,
so he pretended to accept her demand,
"Please don't block my way,
and I agree to be your companion.
Let us walk up together
to celebrate together the Flower Mountain Treading festival."

Hua Tai Cai Zou wondered:
"Has he changed his mind?
On our way there,
I will see if he courts me.
If he doesn't,
he has not changed his heart."

金笛 Jin Di

花太彩奏让开路，
扎董丕冉朝前奔。
花太彩奏忙追赶，
跨沟翻梁又过岭。
扎董丕冉跑得快，
一会就不见踪影。

他越跑得快，
她就越高兴。
"他没跟我同路行，
没唱曲，
没谈情，
看他确实没变心。
不过还得考验他，
三次才会有定准。"

花太彩奏又使法，
忙将身子扭几扭。
只听一阵风吹过，
她就变成竺妞彩奏。

竺妞彩奏驾云雾，
悄悄绕到他前头。
一直跑到花杆下，
静静在等候。
她打着一把花撑子，
坐在那里等得久。
扎董丕冉一到来，

第四章 拦路 Chapter Four Tests

Hua Tai Cai Zou stepped aside,
and Zha Dong Pi Ran bolted out.
Hua Tai Cai Zou ran after him quickly,
over the valleys, the ridges, and the hills.
But Zha Dong Pi Ran ran so fast
that he was soon out of sight.

The faster he ran,
the happier she became.
"He doesn't accompany me,
or sing a tune,
or talk love,
so it seems he indeed didn't change his mind.
But there needs to be another test of him,
because only after three times can it be known."

Hua Tai Cai Zou played a trick again,
twisting her body several times.
With a gust of wind,
she turned into Zhu Niu Cai Zou.

Zhu Niu Cai Zou, riding the clouds,
quietly got ahead of Zha Dong Pi Ran.
She ran all the way to the decorated pole,
under which she waited for him silently.
Holding a floral umbrella,
she waited for quite a while.
When Zha Dong Pi Ran arrived,

金笛 Jin Di

就拿撑子罩住他的头。
扎董丕冉被罩住,
觉得很害羞。
以为蒙诗彩奏在眼前,
不禁喜上眉梢头。
他抬眼瞅见姑娘很美丽,
不禁吃一惊,
再把姑娘细端详,
认出她不是蒙诗彩奏,
不禁浑身发起抖。
他不愿再打听,
也不敢再停留。
一把掀开花撑子,
立刻就逃走。

扎董丕冉跑得快,
一下跑到斗牛场;
竺妞彩奏追得紧,
跟着追到斗牛场。

扎董丕冉跑得急,
忽然钻进人群里;
竺妞彩奏撵得狠,
跟着撵到人群里。

扎董丕冉没有地方躲,
重新跑回花杆下。
这时爬杆比赛才开始,
花杆底下的人多如麻。

第四章 拦路 Chapter Four Tests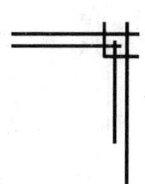

she covered his head with the umbrella.
Zha Dong Pi Ran, with his head covered,
felt shy.
Thinking that Meng Shi Cai Zou was right in front of him,
he was delighted.
But raising his head to look at the beautiful young woman,
he was startled,
and at a closer look,
he realized that she was not Meng Shi Cai Zou
and couldn't help feeling shivers sent down his spine.
He didn't want to ask,
nor dared he to tarry.
Throwing off the umbrella,
he sprinted off instantly.

Zha Dong Pi Ran ran fast
and soon came to the bullring;
Zhu Niu Cai Zou chased after him closely,
following him to the bullring.

Zha Dong Pi Ran ran huriedly
and dived into the crowd of people;
Zhu Niu Cai Zou was at his heels,
pursuing him into the crowd.

Running out of place to hide,
Zha Dong Pi Ran returned to under the pole.
The pole climbing game had just begun,
so there was a countless number of people under the pole.

金笛 Jin Di

小伙子们显身手,
一个跟着一个爬。
没有一个人,
能够爬到花杆顶,
爬了一半就滑下。
个个累得汗水淌,
人人急得眼发花。

扎董丕冉跳过去,
抱住花杆往上爬。
倏倏倏!
刷刷刷!
一下爬到花杆顶,
引得全场笑哈哈。
小伙齐欢呼,
向他抛彩带;
姑娘齐拍掌,
向他甩鲜花。
扎董丕冉来这里,
不是爬杆比输赢。
只是为脱身,
才几下爬到花杆顶。
说不巧来也很巧,
他夺得爬杆第一名。
使得全场都轰动,
发出阵阵喝彩声。
竺妞彩奏站在花杆下,

第四章 拦路 Chapter Four Tests

The young men were showing off their talents,
climbing up the pole one by one.
But none of them
could get to the top of the pole,
but all slid down after reaching only half way of it.
Everyone was exhausted dripping with sweat,
and all were frustrated with their eyes seeing stars.

Zha Dong Pi Ran now had reached the pole
and, holding onto it, he started to climb up.
Swish, swish, swish!
Swoosh, swoosh, swoosh!
He reached to the top without taking a break,
the entire crowd bursting out cheering.
The young men were shouting,
throwing ribbons at him;
the young women were applauding,
tossing fresh flowers at him.
Zha Dong Pi Ran came here
not to win the game of pole-climbing.
It was to free himself from being pursued
that he was now on the top of the pole.
Whether it was a coincidence,
he was the winner of the game.
The whole crowd was buzzing with excitement,
applauding and cheering again and again.
Zhu Niu Cai Zou was standing under the pole,

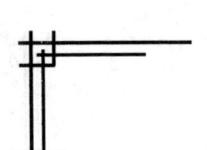

金笛 Jin Di

不住向他表深情:
"我是竺妞彩奏,
我要跟你成亲。
多好听的话呀,
我也不会说,
我只有一颗真心,
我只有一片痴情;
多甜蜜的话呀,
也不要你讲,
只要你点头,
只要你答应!"

扎董丕冉见她那容貌,
又比花太彩奏美十分。
只见她——
身上裹着红霞紫雾;
又见她——
头上戴着明月良星。
好一派仙女风度呀。
怎能不使人迷恋,
怎能不叫人倾心。

是拒绝她的求婚呢,
还是答应跟她成亲?
扎董丕冉的心中,
就像海浪在翻腾,
他悄悄定一定神,
赶忙闭上眼睛:

第四章 拦路 Chapter Four Tests

continually expressing her feelings for him:
"I am Zhu Niu Cai Zou,
and I want marry you.
The beautiful words
I have none,
but I have the true love
and affection for you;
the sweet words
I have none,
but I only need you to nod
and to agree!"

Zha Dong Pi Ran looked at her,
the beauty that was so much more than that of Hua Tai Cai Zou.
Look at her—
as if wrapped in the red cloud and purple mist;
look at her again—
as if crowned with the bright moon and lucky star.
She had the air of a fairy.
How could anyone not love her
or not be attracted to her.

To turn down her proposal
or to accept it?
Zha Dong Pi Ran's heart
was churning like the sea waves,
so to pull himself together,
he closed his eyes:

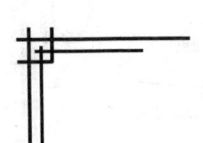

金笛 Jin Di

"不,不能答应!
一定不能答应!
什么仙女下凡,
我决不能迷恋,
决不能动心!"

他随手取出金笛来,
就在花杆顶上吹出声:
"布哩布哩布哩布哩,
心中有苦难说出。
我与蒙诗彩奏早约定,
花山上面来相会,
好把真情诉。
好不容易等到踩花山,
我心中感到最幸福。

赶忙换上新衣裳,
翻山越岭过深谷。
本想趁早来会她,
可是三个姑娘呀,
死搅活缠来拦路。
一个叫糯珠彩奏,
一个叫花太彩奏,
一个叫竺妞彩奏,
一个更比一个漂亮,
一个更比一个杰出。
她们个个都爱我,
抢着跟我诉肺腑。

第四章 拦路 Chapter Four Tests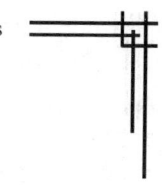

"No, I can't accept it!
Absolutely not!
It doesn't matter if she is some fairy descending the world,
and I can't be infatuated with her
or change my mind!"

Taking out the Jin Di,
he started playing on the top of the pole:
"Bu li bu li bu li bu li,
it is hard for me to explain the pain I am suffering.
I had a date with Meng Shi Cai Zou
up here on top of the Flower Mountain,
so that we could have a heart to heart.
I waited long and hard for the Flower Mountain Treading festival
and was happier than I ever was.

Hurriedly changing into the new clothes,
I then traveled across the mountains and valleys.
I thought I could come early to see her,
but three young women have hassled me on the way.
One is named Nuo Zhu Cai Zou;
another, Hua Tai Cai Zou;
a third, Zhu Niu Cai Zou.
One was more beautiful than another,
more outstanding than another.
All were in love with me
and couldn't wait to open their hearts to me.

111

金笛 Jin Di

"最清亮的泉水呀,
是从山箐沟里淌来;
最甜蜜的话语呀,
就从她们心中流出。
个个说的都入耳,
叫我心里热乎乎。
不过我也不迷糊,
我心中有数。
因为我爱的是蒙诗彩奏,
想的是蒙诗彩奏。
我只有找到她,
才会心满意足。
找不到蒙诗彩奏呀,
才是我最大的痛苦!

"蒙诗彩奏呀,
你今在何处?
莫非你病了,
还是事情有变故?
请你快来搭救我,
快将我的痛苦解除!
要是你再不来呀,
眼下我也没生路。
蒙诗彩奏呀,
如今你究竟在何处?"

竺妞彩奏说:
"你想蒙诗彩奏呀,

第四章 拦路 Chapter Four Tests

"The pellucid spring water
comes from the woods in the mountains;
the sweetest words
flew out of those young women's hearts.
Their words were easy on my ears
and warmed my heart.
But I am not confused
and I know what I want.
For the one I love is Meng Shi Cai Zou,
and the one I miss is Meng Shi Cai Zou.
Only when I have found her
will my heart be content.
Not being able to find Meng Shi Cai Zou
will be most painful to me.

"Meng Shi Cai Zou,
where are you now?
Did you fall ill,
or has something gone wrong?
Please come quickly to rescue me,
helping to relieve my pain!
If you still don't show up,
I have no way to live either.
Meng Shi Cai Zou,
where in the world are you now?"

Zhu Niu Cai Zou said:
"Oh, you miss Meng Shi Cai Zou

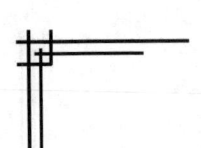

金笛 Jin Di

想得快要发疯啦。
可是你俩分手后,
她已埋进深山洼。
只因害了一场病,
灵丹妙药难救她。
如今她的坟头上,
野蔓荒藤到处爬。
劝你还是死了心,
不要再牵挂。
我真心实意爱着你,
我俩快成家!"

扎董丕冉听她说,
心痛如刀扎。
气得两眼冒金星,
哽咽哽咽难说话。
他又拿起金笛吹,
泪珠滚滚湿衣裯:
"布哩布哩布哩布哩,
世上男子千万个,
就数我命苦。
只望来到花山会情人,
哪知情人早已进黄土!
蒙诗彩奏呀,
你别抛下我,
我也要跟你走一路。
我俩共埋一座坟,
去到阴间在一处。

第四章 拦路 Chapter Four Tests

so much you're going crazy.
But since you parted your ways,
she has been buried in a ditch in the mountains.
She fell so ill
that there was no medicine that could save her.
On her grave today
are already wild vines crawling all over.
Listen to me and give her up,
and stop concerning yourself with her.
I love you with great earnestness and sincerity,
so let's get married as soon as possible!"

Hearing her words, Zha Dong Pi Ran
felt as if a knife was poking through his heart.
So upset was he that he saw stars,
and so wretched was he that he could hardly speak.
Picking up the Jin Di again, he played,
with tears falling and soaking his shirt.
"Bu li bu li bu li bu li,
among tens and thousands of men,
I am the most unfortunate.
I wanted to see my love in the mountain,
not knowing she was long buried!
Meng Shi Cai Zou,
don't leave me by myself,
for I want to go with you.
Let's be buried together
and live together in the underworld.

115

要我再爱别人呀,
除非地陷井枯!"

十五

竺妞彩奏听完这支歌,
心中快乐。
扎董丕冉情意真,
三次引诱心不动,
不愧是个好哥哥。
她越想越高兴。
两颊笑出小酒窝。
走到僻处摇摇身,
一道金光在闪烁。
现出蒙诗彩奏真身子,
亭亭玉立像天鹅。
打开那把花撑子,
坐在那里抿嘴角。
拿起一片木叶吹,
美妙歌声出心窝:
"布哩布哩布哩,
扎董丕冉莫心急。
我早就来到花山上,
坐在这里等着你。
竺妞彩奏说我得病已死去,
你泪流满面吹金笛。
金笛声声好凄惨,

第四章 拦路 Chapter Four Tests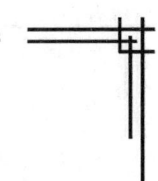

For me to love another one,

the earth would have to fall out from under and the well, go dry!"

15

On hearing this, Zhu Niu Cai Zou
was joyful.
Zha Dong Pi Ran was true to his word
unmoved by temptations three times
and deserving of his good reputation.
The more she thought about this, the happier she became.
Dimples appeared on her smiling cheeks.
Walking up to a secluded place and shaking her body,
she gave out a shiny golden light.
It is the beautiful young Meng Shi Cai Zou,
standing up like a swan.
Opening the colorful umbrella,
she sat there with a smile on her face.
Picking up a Mu-leaf, she played
a wonderful song from her heart:
"Bu li bu li bu li,
Zha Dong Pi Ran, don't worry.
I got up to the Flower Mountain a while ago,
sitting here just to wait for you.
When Zhu Niu Cai Zou said I had died of an illness,
you were weeping while playing the Jin Di.
The sound of it was so sad

我听着心里也悲戚。
你爬花杆摆脱她，
我就暗暗敬佩你。
风刮不到的红椿树呀；
才能成材做桌椅；
水泡不烂的好种子呀，
才能生根长小米；
女色迷不住的男子汉呀，
才算坚贞有出息。
扎董丕冉呀，
我把真情告诉你；
蒙诗彩奏没死去！
快来吧，
我在这里等着你，
快来呀，
蒙诗彩奏在这里！"
扎董丕冉听见木叶声，
感到亲切又熟悉；
声声入耳又入心，
觉得温暖又甜蜜，
他揩干眼泪往下看，
竺妞彩奏早已无踪迹。
他从花杆顶上跳下地，
三步两步跑过去。
跑到蒙诗彩奏的身边，
不知是悲还是喜！

第四章 拦路 Chapter Four Tests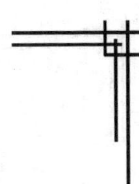

that I felt wretched in my heart.
You climbed up the pole to escape her,
and I admired you for it.
Only the red maple tree that could stand the test of the wind
could be made into chairs and tables;
only the seeds that don't rot soaking in the water
could be used to plant the millet;
only the men who can resist the temptation of women's charm
are staunch and promising.
Zha Dong Pi Ran,
let me tell you the truth:
Meng Shi Cai Zou didn't die!
Come here quickly,
for I'm waiting for you here;
come here quickly,
for Meng Shi Cai Zou is here!"

To Zha Dong Pi Ran, the sound of the Mu-leaf
was endearing and familiar;
it entered into his ear, illuminated his heart,
and was heart-warming and sweet.
Wiping his tears, he looked down,
and Zhu Niu Cai Zou had disappeared without a trace.
He jumped off the pole
and started running.
When he got to the side of Meng Shi Cai Zou,
he couldn't tell it was sad or happy!

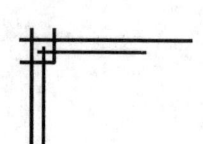

两人并肩罩在伞下，
双双钻进人群里。
一个唱长捎，
一个吟四句。
金声玉嗓来相合，
声声有情又有意。

扎董丕冉对着她，
诉说路上的遭遇。
蒙诗彩奏听完了，
笑得腰也直不起。
她脱下一只金手镯，
戴在扎董丕冉手腕上，
轻轻对他说：
"见了金手镯，
你就想起我。"

扎董丕冉脱下一副银项圈，
挂在蒙诗彩奏脖项上，
低低对她说：
"圈在你项脖上，
我就挂在你心里。"

十六

花山踩了一整天，
情话也说了一整天，

第四章 拦路 Chapter Four Tests

They were both under the umbrella now,
together walking into the crowds.
While one sang in free verse,
the other, four-line poetry.
The golden sound and jade voice matched perfectly,
every line was heart-felt and real.

Zha Dong Pi Ran told her
what he had experienced on the way up the mountain.
Meng Shi Cai Zou listened to the whole story
and laughed so hard that she was bending over.
She took off her gold bracelet
and put it on Zha Dong Pi Ran's wrist,
saying to him softly:
"When you see this gold bracelet,
you will remember me."

Zha Dong Pi Ran took off a silver necklace
and put it around the neck of Meng Shi Cai Zou,
telling her in a low voice,
"With my necklace around your neck,
I will be in your heart."

16

They spent the whole day at the festival climbing the mountain,
the whole day occupied with endless whispers of love.

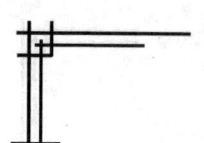

金笛 Jin Di

扎董丕冉沿着羊肠路,
又唱又笑回家转。

檐口挂着的小画眉,
没有他唱得好;
吃饱归家的小牛犊,
没有他跑得欢。
出门时脸上常带笑,
吃饭前还要唱一段。

阿奈坐在堂屋吃草药,
扎董丕冉端水到面前。
她见儿子没戴银项圈,
又见儿子展笑颜。
心想定是找到了好姑娘,
才会这样喜地欢天。
阿奈越想越高兴,
病也好了一大半。
皱紧眉头故意问:
"你的项圈哪去了?
为何不见挂胸前?
拿去街上卖掉了,
还是丢在大路边?
这是我家的传家宝呀,

第四章 拦路 Chapter Four Tests

Zha Dong Pi Ran then walked along the narrow mountain path,

singing and laughinged, to return home.

The little thrush in its abode under the eaves
didn't sing as well as he did;
the well-fed little calves on their way home
didn't run as happily as he did.
He went out of the house with a smile on his face
and sang before each meal.

A Nai was sitting in the main hall taking the herbal medicine,

and Zha Dong Pi Ran brought some water for her to drink with it.

She saw that her son was not wearing the silver necklace
and smiling all the time.
She realized that he must have met a fine young woman
to be so euphoric.
The more she thought about it, the more delighted she became,

and she felt much recovered.
But, frowning, she asked on purpose,
"Where did your necklace go?
How come you're not wearing it?
Did you sell it on the street
or lose it by the roadside?
It is our family's heirloom,

金笛 Jin Di

一代一代传了几百年。
千两黄金也不卖,
万两白银也不换。
我要留着它,
送给儿媳妇。
我一生一世呀,
就是这心愿!
你要把它找回来,
期限给三天。
三天要是找不回来呀,
你就别进家门槛!"

扎董丕冉抿嘴笑,
不禁红了脸。
他取出金笛吹起来,
欢快的笛声响不断:
"布哩布哩布哩噜,
我劝阿奈别发怒。
项圈没卖也没丢,
我为它找到一个好去处。
将它送给一个小姑娘,
她名叫蒙诗彩奏,
就是你的儿媳妇儿!"

这歌正合阿奈的心意,
她越听越喜欢,

第四章 拦路 Chapter Four Tests

passed down from generation to generation for a few hundreds years.

We won't sell it even for thousands of taels of gold,

won't exchange it for tens and thousands of taels of silver.

I want to pass it on

to my daughter-in-law.

My whole life,

I have but this wish!

You find it and bring it back

within three days.

If you cannot bring it back within three days,

don't come back home!"

Zha Dong Pi Ran was beaming with joy

and couldn't help blushing.

He took out the Jin Di and started to play,

with the cheerful sound ringing:

"Bu li bu li bu li bu li lu,

Ai Nai, don't be angry.

The necklace is not sold or lost,

but I have found a good place for it.

I gave it to a young woman,

whose name is Meng Shi Cai Zou,

who will be your daughter-in-law!"

The song was exactly what A Nai wanted to hear,

so the more she listened to it, the more delighted she became.

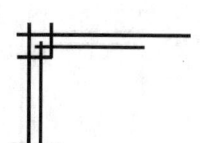

金笛 Jin Di

赶忙拿起纺车来,
高高兴兴纺麻线。

阿支躺在床上干咳,
扎董丕冉给他揉胸口。
他见扎董丕冉哼着歌,
又见他戴着金手镯。
心想儿子定是找到了好姑娘,
才会这样哼不停呀唱不够。

阿支越想越开心,
丝丝笑意挂眉头。
顿觉疾病全消了,
真想起床去喂牛。
收起笑意故意问:
"你这手镯哪里来?
到底是抢还是偷?
家穷也要有志气,
要有一架硬骨头。
别人的手镯决不要,
戴在手上也害羞!"

扎董丕冉暗发笑,
扭扭捏捏低下头。
拿出金笛吹起来,
笛声传遍吊脚楼:
"布哩布哩布哩噜,
我劝阿支莫发怒。
我没去抢也没去偷,

第四章 拦路 Chapter Four Tests

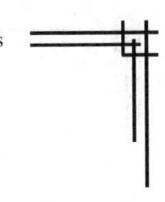

She hastened to take out the spinning wheel
and started to spin the yarn joyously.

A Zhi was in bed, coughing,
so Zha Dong Pi Ran helped to massage his chest.
A Zhi listened to the humming
and also saw the gold bracelet.
He thought that his son must have met a fine young woman
to keep humming and singing so much.

The more A Zhi thought about it, the happier he became,
a glimmer of smile hanging from his eyebrows.
All of a suddenly he completely recovered from his illness
and wanted to go feed the ox right away.
But feigning ignorance, he stopped smiling and asked:
"Where is this bracelet from?
Did you rob someone or steal it from someone?
Destitute as we are,
we must have honor and dignity.
We don't take others' bracelet
and would be ashamed to wear it."

Zha Dong Pi Ran smiled to himself,
as he bashfully lowered his head.
He took out the Jin Di and played,
filling the house with its sound:
"Bu li bu li bu li lu,
A Zhi, don't be angry.
I never robbed or stole from anyone,

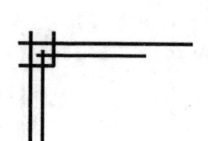

金笛 Jin Di

这只手镯有来路,
是蒙诗彩奏送给我,
她就是你的儿媳妇。"

阿支听罢笑起来,
几步跑出堂屋外。
忙到牛棚去喂牛,
添草上料心自在。

第四章 拦路 Chapter Four Tests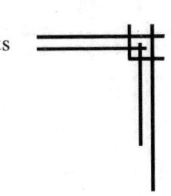

but this bracelet
was given to me by Meng Shi Cai Zou,
who will be your daughter-in-law."

On hearing this, A Zhi was so happy
that in just a few steps he went out of the main hall.
Busily, he was feeding the ox in the shed,
adding fodder and feeling content.

第五章　中计

十七

那次凤凰在山上游玩，
魔虎猛然下山岗。
它将凤凰紧追赶，
眼看很快就追上。
扎董丕冉拿起刀，
跟那魔虎斗一场。
魔虎终于被赶跑，
凤凰才得免祸殃。
躲荫不忘栽树人，
脱险常念救命郎。
为了报答扎董丕冉，
凤凰施法变姑娘。
她就是蒙诗彩奏呀，
美丽又善良。
她跟扎董丕冉结良缘，
二人配成称心的一双。

第五章 中计 Chapter Five The Trap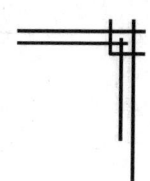

Chapter Five　The Trap

17

　　Previously, when the phoenix was enjoying itself in the mountain,
　　a demon tiger came down the hill.
　　Chasing after the phoenix,
　　the tiger was almost caught up with it.
　　Zha Dong Pi Ran used his machete
　　and fought fiercely with the demon tiger.
　　In the end, the demon tiger was driven away,
　　and the phoenix was saved from a calamity.
　　Just as those who benefit from the shade remember the tree planter,
　　the phoenix kept its benefactor in mind.
　　To repay his kindness,
　　the phoenix magically changed itself into a young woman.
　　This was Meng Shi Cai Zou
　　beautiful and kind-hearted.
　　She and Zha Dong Pi Ran fell in love with each other
　　and became a perfect couple.

金笛 Jin Di

大魔虎没有得到凤凰,
整天把牙咬得咯咯响。
凤凰变成了蒙诗彩奏,
爱上扎董丕冉,
它更是炉火烧胸膛:
"既然凤凰变成了美女,
那就应该抢来做婆娘!"
魔虎打定鬼主意,
只等时机一到又要逞凶狂。

大魔虎共有十兄弟,
虎兄虎弟同住一个洞。
抬牛抓羊拿手戏,
吃人害人是天性,
只要碰上好机会,
它们就一齐倾巢出动。
大魔虎要抢蒙诗彩奏,
九弟兄自然一致赞同。
它们天天出来游串,
奔西又跑东,
只要哪里有动静,
就向大哥报信请功。

十八

就在那年春三月,
扎董丕冉出家门。

第五章　中计　Chapter Five　The Trap

The big demon tiger who didn't get the phoenix
was already so angry that its teeth were grinding loudly.
When the phoenix transformed into to Meng Shi Cai Zou
and fell in love with Zha Dong Pi Ran,
it felt as if fire was burning inside:
"Since the phoenix has turned into a beauty,
I should make her my spouse!"
The demon tiger worked out a plot
and then waited for its opportunity.

The big demon tiger had nine brothers,
and they all lived in the same cave.
Preying on cows and sheep was their specialty,
and killing or attacking humans was their nature.
Whenever they had the opportunity,
they set out together.
Now that the big demond tiger wanted to abduct Meng Shi Cai Zou,
the nine brothers naturally supported the idea unanimously.
Every day they roamed the mountains
from the west to the east.
If there was any sign anywhere,
they ran to report to and seek rewards from their Big Brother.

18

It was the third month of that year
when Zha Dong Pi Ran set off for a trip.

金笛 Jin Di

到了远方寨子里,
去跟吹师学芦笙。
日子过得飞飞快,
一去就是一年整。
二魔虎得知这消息,
笑得浑身抽了筋。
连忙禀告大魔虎,
大魔虎冷冷哼一声:
"上回追扑凤凰没得手,
只因扎董丕冉没归家,
真是老天对我发慈悲,
即刻去把蒙诗彩奏抢,
看有哪个敢救应?"

村头有口大水井,
蒙诗彩奏常到这儿来挑水,
大魔虎抢亲生毒计,
一个红桃丢井内,
然后吩咐虎兄虎弟躲起来,
专等蒙诗彩奏来上钩。

这天天气很阴沉,
蒙诗彩奏心烦闷。
她无心唱歌吹木叶,
也不想拿针绣衣裙。
一年没会情人面,
她没有哪天不伤心。
天天盼着他回转,

第五章 中计 Chapter Five The Trap

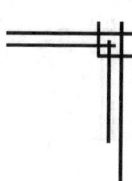

He went to another village far away
to learn from a Lu Sheng master.
Time went by so quickly
that he had spent an entire year there.
When the second demon tiger learned about this,
it laughed so hard that it was having spasms.
Hastily he reported to the big demon tiger,
who snorted drily:
"I failed last time,
but now Zha Dong Pi Ran is not home,
a kindness that heaven is showing towards me.
Who dare to defy that kindness?"

At one end of the village was a well,
and Meng Shi Cai Zou often went there to fetch water.
The big demon tiger itself came up with the venomous scheme
of throwing a ripened peach into the well,
and then having the tiger brothers hide in the area
and wait for Meng Shi Cai Zou to fall into the trap.

One gloomy and humid day,
Meng Shi Cai Zou felt dreary and listless.
She was in no mood to play the Mu-leaf
or to embroider and make clothes.
It had been a year since she saw her beloved,
and there was not a day that went by that she wasn't sad.
Looking forward to his return,

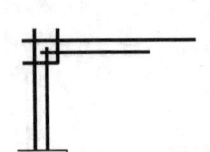

金笛 Jin Di

就是不见他的半个影。
她挑起水桶走到水井边,
假装挑水望情人。

眼睛朝着东边望,
东边有块大乌云;
眼睛朝着西边望,
西边是片大森林;
眼睛朝着南边望,
南边有高高山岭;
眼睛朝着北边望,
北边是个老黑箐。
茫然四顾静悄悄,
要会情人呀到哪里寻?
她本想重新变成凤凰鸟,
天涯海角找情人。
可是自从与扎董丕冉订终身,
她就不再露真形。
她想露了真形不打紧,
会惹得风言风语不安宁。
她住在深山茅屋中,
个个都赞她贤惠,
个个都夸她忠贞。

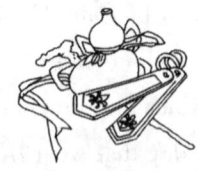

第五章 中计 Chapter Five The Trap

she had not seen any sign of him.

With a bucket, she went to the well,

pretending to fetch water but trying to see if her beloved was coming.

Looking to the east,

she saw a huge patch of the dark clouds;

looking to the west,

she saw a vast expanse of the forests;

looking to the south,

she saw the high mountains;

looking to the north,

she saw the Lao Hei Qing woods.

With stillness all round,

where would she find her beloved?

She had thought of changing back to the phoenix

so that she could go the the edge of the earth to find her love.

But since her engagement with Zha Dong Pi Ran,

she no longer revealed her true nature.

It is not that she couldn't,

but that she didn't want to cause gossip and discord in the village.

As long as she lived in the thatched cottage,

everyone praised her for her virtue,

and everyone commended her for her loyalty.

金笛 Jin Di

蒙诗彩奏走到井口上,
看看井水解愁烦。
忽然见个红桃子,
漂在水面溜溜转。
她越看越有趣,
她越瞧越喜欢。
弯下腰肢伸出手,
想捞起桃子玩一玩。
可是井深手短够不着,
捞了半天难如愿。
她又使劲把腰弯下去,
离那红桃只差一点点。
忽觉背后被谁推一掌,
扑通一声落到井里面。

井水齐腰深,
井帮滑又软,
她左攀右蹬上不来,
泡在水里好为难。
最后她急得没办法,
只好对着井口大声喊。

大魔虎暗地将她推下井,
心想大事已成一半。
此时听她喊救命,
跑到井口出狂言:

第五章 中计 Chapter Five The Trap

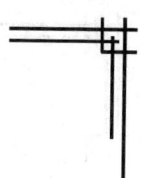

Meng Shi Cai Zou came to the well,
hoping that the water in the well could wash away her worries.
In the well, she saw a red peach,
floating and spinning on the surface of the water.
The more she looked at it, the more she liked it
and the happier she became.
Bending over and reaching her hand out,
she wanted to fetch the peach to play with as a diversion.
But the well was deep and the arm, too short to reach the peach,
so she tried many times in vain.
She tried to bend harder
and was almost getting the peach.
Suddenly, she felt pushed by a hand from behind
and then, plunk, she fell into the well.

The water in the well was waist-deep,
and the wall of the well felt slimy and mushy,
so despite her effort to scale and scramble,
she was still soaked in the water.
Finally, not knowing what else to do,
she shouted up the well for help.

It was the big demon tiger that pushed her down,
and the tiger thought that the mission was half completed.
On hearing her cry for help,
it ran to the well and demanded:

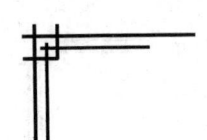

金笛 Jin Di

"我今把你救上来,
你要给我许个愿。
打算怎样报答我,
这话定要说在先!"

"你能救得我的命,
保你全家得平安。
女的活到九十九,
男的活到九十三!"

魔虎听罢哈哈笑,
笑得井水也打战:
"你是这样报答我,
我却一点不喜欢。
要是你不改主意,
要我救你难上难!"

"这个主意怎样改,
还请大哥给指点。
只要大哥说得好,
我就一定照着办。"

"我今把你救上来,
你要跟我结姻缘。
答应给我做老婆,
跟我一起把家还。
如若违背我心愿,
让你小命归西天!"

第五章 中计 Chapter Five The Trap

"I can save you today,
but you must make a pledge.
How you will repay me,
the terms of which must be set before I do it."

"If you can save my life,
I guarantee the safety of your family.
Females will live up till they are ninety-nine years old,
all males will live up till they are ninety-three years old."

On hearing these words, the devilish tiger burst into laughter,
which made even the well-water shiver:
"This kind of repayment
does not interest me in the least.
If you don't change your mind,
it would be impossible for me to save your life."

"How would you want me to change my mind?
Would you please give me some hints, big brother.
As long as your idea is good,
I will follow your advice."

"If I save you today,
you must agree to marry me.
You must promise to be my wife
and go home with me.
If you don't do as I wish,
I will send you to glory!"

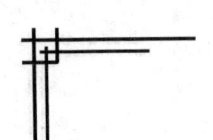

"这事我可不能办,
大哥不要来为难。
我已跟人定了亲,
至今已有整一年。"

蒙诗彩奏说到此,
不禁心中一段酸:
是谁心眼这么狠,
推我落井遭大难?
心想变成凤凰鸟,
展翅飞腾上蓝天,
可是身子泡着水,
再变凤凰难上难。
心中越想越懊恼,
两行泪水挂腮间……

十九

人到绝处不由己,
真是心长舌头短。
要想做的做不成,
不愿干的也得干。
操在别人手里边。
蒙诗彩奏没办法,
只得假意许下愿:
"你若救得我出井,
我就跟你结姻缘,
如今死活这命运。"

第五章 中计　Chapter Five　The Trap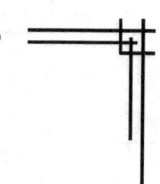

"That is something I can't do,
so please, big brother, do not put me in a hole.
I am enaged to marry someone
and have been for a whole year."

As Meng Shi Cai Zou was talking,
she felt a pang of sadness:
Who could be so cruel
to push her into the well?
She would like to turn into a phoenix,
spreading her wings and flying into the blue sky,
but her body being soaked in the water
it was more than difficulty for her to do so.
The more she thought about this, the more upset she became,
tears running down her cheeks...

19

In desperation, we cannot help ourselves,
unable to say our heart's desire.
Not only cannot we do as we wish,
but we have to go against our heart's desire.
With her life in the hands of another,
Meng Shi Cai Zou had no choice
but to pretend to agree with the terms:
"If you rescue me out of the well,
I will agree to marry you,
as my life and death depends on it today."

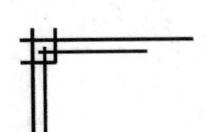

金笛 Jin Di

"这话是真还是假?
诺言出口就不能变!"

蒙诗彩奏暗暗想,
只要出了井,
事情就好办。
又强装笑脸巧周旋:
"这话是真不是假,
你莫多心眼。"

魔虎拿根长竹竿,
一头伸到井里面。
蒙诗彩奏抓住竹竿头,
魔虎将她拖到井外边:
"走吧走吧快走吧,
赶快跟我回家转!"
魔虎一边说话一边笑,
诡计得逞口流涎。

蒙诗彩奏见是一只虎,
吓得心跳腿发软:
"我是人,
你是虎,
人虎怎能结姻缘?
我说死说活也不愿!"

第五章 中计 Chapter Five The Trap

"Do you mean it?

You cannot go back on your word!"

Meng Shi Cai Zou thought to herself,

as long as she was out of the well,

everything would become easier.

Therefore, she forced herself to smile and said,

"Indeed, that's my word,

so do trust me."

The demon tiger picked up a long bamboo pole

dipped one of its end into the well.

Meng Shi Cai Zou got a hold of it,

as the demon tiger pulled her out.

"Come on, come on,

come home with me!"

The demon tiger was laughing while talking.

Its trick having worked, he was unable to wait.

Once seeing it was a tiger, Meng Shi Cai Zou

was so terrified that her pulse was racing and her legs weakened:

"How could I, a human,

and you, a tiger,

ever get married?

I will never marry you even if I have to die!"

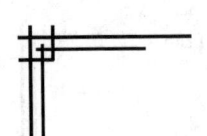

金笛 Jin Di

魔虎听她说"不愿",
咆哮如雷气冲天。
尾巴一翘三丈高,
四脚一纵八丈远。
又将蒙诗彩奏推下井,
龇牙咧嘴唾沫溅:
"叫你吃蜜你不吃,
偏偏要吞苦黄连。
我叫你二次再下井,
让你死在井里面!"

蒙诗彩奏在井里,
不上不下真为难。
无可奈何说了话,
又假意许心愿:
"谁人拉我出水井,
我就跟他结姻缘;
谁人救得我的命,
我就跟他回家转!"

魔虎听了笑哈哈,
开口忙答话:
"只要你不再骗我,
我就再拉你一把;
要是这回再骗我,
我就懒得救你啦。

第五章　中计　Chapter Five　The Trap

On hearing "will never," the demon tiger
let out a thunderous roar.
Its tail raised up three *zhang*① high,
and its four legs were eight *zhang* apart.
It pushed Meng Shi Cai Zou into the well again,
with its fangs bare and its mouth foaming:
"I gave you honey, but you refused
and chose bitterness instead.
Let me send you down the well a second time then
and die there."

Being in the well again Meng Shi Cai Zou
was in a great quandary.
Out of no choice, she spoke,
giving a false promise again:
"Whoever helps me out of this well,
I will get married to him;
whoever saves my life,
I will go home with him!"

The demon tiger laughed heartily
and replied in a hurry,
"As long as you won't fool me again,
I will help you again;
but if you are lying to me again,
I won't lift a finger to help you again.

---

① A Chinese *zhang* is about 11 feet.

金笛 Jin Di

我要死守在井边,
谁人来救也害怕。
哪个敢来搭救你,
我就一口咬死他。
让你泡上一辈子,
泡成一坨烂泥巴!"
蒙诗彩奏心里想,
事到如今也无法。
要是淹死在井里,
不是白白受糟蹋?
扎董丕冉不见我,
定会气死在山洼。
二人都会遭不幸,
落得树死谢了花。
这个结局更悲催,
永世永代难成家。
还是忍辱先答应,
出去再想办法对付它。
于是对着井口说:
"哪有救命不报恩?
这回说话算话。
一定不会再失约,
求你快拉我一把。
只要拉我出水井,
我就跟你转回家。"

第五章 中计 Chapter Five The Trap

I then will guard the well till the day I die,

so that whoever comes to rescue you will be too terrified to try it.

If anyone dares to try it anyway

I will kill him.

Let you rot in the well

until you become a lump of mud!"

Meng Shi Cai Zou thought to herself,

given the circumstances there was no other way.

If she drowned in the well,

what would she have accomplished?

Zha Dong Pi Ran would never see her again

but would rather die of anger in some ditch.

They each would meet an untimely and tragic end

like a tree was dead and its flowers withered with it.

That would be an even more tragic outcome

because neither would have a chance ever to marry the other.

Yet suffering the humiliation now,

she might be able firstly to get out and then to find a way to deal with it.

Realizing this, she shouted up the well,

"How could one not repay the life-saving kindness?

I will keep my word this time.

I won't go back on my word,

so please give me a hand.

As long as you get me out of the well,

I will go home with you."

金笛 Jin Di

魔虎听罢心里乐，
伸下竹竿使劲拖。
一下将她拖出井，
她浑身不住打哆嗦。

魔虎死死拉住她，
逼她答应做老婆。
蒙诗彩奏没办法，
心想这次难逃脱。
只得跟着老虎走，
以后慢慢又再说。

那九只魔虎一齐跳出来，
个个得意洋洋笑颜开。
围着蒙诗彩奏打转转，
前呼后拥扯成一大排。
怪声怪气对她叫"大嫂"，
使她又羞又恼红了腮。
大魔虎不住夸赞三魔虎：
"还是三弟办法好，
让我老婆来得快。
是你叫我丢红桃，
诱她落到网中来；
又叫我朝她背后推一掌，
让她成了缸里泡的水酸菜！"
三魔虎一听很得意：

第五章 中计 Chapter Five　The Trap

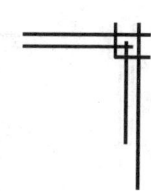

　　On hearing this, the demon tiger was delighted,
dipping the bamboo pole again and then pulling it hard.
With one try, it pulled her out of the well,
and her body couldn't stop shivering all over.

　　The devilish tiger got a hold of her,
forcing her to promise to be its wife.
Meng Shi Cai Zou had no choice,
thinking it would be hard to escape this time.
She went with the tiger,
leaving the rest to the future.

　　The other nine demon tigers jumped out together,
everyone elated and grinning.
Circling around Meng Shi Cai Zou,
they were in front of her and behind her forming a chain.
They creepily addressed her as their big sister-in-law,
　　and she showed a flush of embarrassment and exasperation on her face.
　　The big demon tiger kept praising the third demon tiger:
"Thanks to Third Brother's good trick,
my wife came so quickly.
You told me to throw the peach into the well
to lure her into the trap;
you told me to push her from behind then,
and now she is like a pickle in the vat!"
　　On hearing this, the third demon tiger was very pleased with itself:

151

金笛 Jin Di

"大哥平时待我恩义重,
我为大哥出力也应该!"
二魔虎听着不服气,
嘿嘿一笑发冷语:
"你们的计策倒是好,
可这是脱掉裤子放臭屁,
白白费憨力。
见她来挑水,
一把将她抓住就是了,
何必设计绕圈子?"

大魔虎对它摇摇头,
讲了一番大道理:
"她来挑水抓住她,
看来倒是很省力。
可是她又变成凤凰怎么办?
我哪里还有妻?
那回她是个凤凰鸟,
我想抓她填肚子。

这回她成了个好姑娘,
我要让她跟我拜天地。
古时她们的祖先住在大河边,
大河涨水淹死多少男和女。
后来逃到深山里居住,
总是害怕洪水再侵袭。
将她推进水井里,
就是使她再也不能变把戏。

第五章 中计 Chapter Five The Trap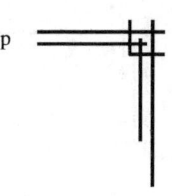

"I have always been indebted to my big brother,
so it is my duty to help you!"
The second demon brother was jealous,
scoffing and sneering:
"Your trick was not bad,
but it was like pulling own the pants just to fart,
silly and unnecessary.
When she came to fetch water,
why didn't you just grab her
and what was the need for the intrigues?"

The big demon tiger shook its head
and then launched into a lecture:
"To grab her when she came to fetch water
might seem to be an easier way.
But what if she changed back to a phoenix?
Would I have still got my wife?
Last time when she was the phoenix,
I just wanted her to be my meal.

Now that she has turned into a fine young woman,
I want her to marry me in front of the altar of Heaven.
In ancient times, her ancestors lived by the big river,
and when the river flooded it killed many of them.
Therefore, they migrated into the mountains,
living forever with the fear for the flood.
Pushing her into the well
prevented her from playing any trick.

153

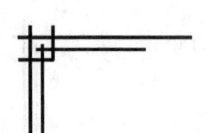

这样可以逼她亲口答应我,
二弟怎懂其中有奥秘。"

二魔虎张口又结舌,
只好在一旁生闷气。

蒙诗彩奏很难过,
急得两眼喷怒火。
受到的侮辱真是比天大,
暗恨魔辱真是比天大,
暗恨魔虎太凶恶。
水泡过身子再也不能变凤凰,
气得她嘴唇都咬破。
半晌她才定住神,
冷冷对着魔虎说:
"我在井里泡久了,
现在肚子有点饿。
那边有棵羊奶树,
树上结满羊奶果。
我去摘些果子吃,
你们好好等着我。"
她想这样哄魔虎,
施个巧计好逃脱。
只要魔虎答应她,
她就可以上山坡。
上了山坡钻深箐,
就到自己的寨子脚。

第五章 中计 Chapter Five The Trap

It was a sure way to force her to give me her word,
but, Second Brother, you could not possibly get all this."

The second demon tiger was struck mute
and could only sulk.

Meng Shi Cai Zou was very upset,
her eyes blazing with fury.
The mount of humiliation she felt surpassed the size of the sky,
and so was her bitterness towards the demon tigers,
their extreme cruelty.
Having been long steeped in the water she could not be a phoenix again,
and she was so angry that she bit her lips blooding.
It took her a while to compose herself
and then said coldly to the demon tiger:
"I was in the water for a long time
and am a little hungry.
Over there is a Yang Nai tree
full of Yang Nai berries.
I go to pick some,
and you wait for me here."
She wanted to fool the demon tigers this way
so that the she could escape.
If the demon tigers let her,
she could run up the hill.
Once she was up on the hill she could dash into the woods
which would take her to the foot of her village.

金笛 Jin Di

大魔虎起初不答应,
怕她跑掉抓不着,
经她再三说了话,
这才准她摘野果:
"吃饱野果就回来,
莫在树上久耽搁。"

三魔虎冷冷哼一声,
阴阳怪气戳大哥:
"大哥心肠倒是好,
鹿子到口还放脱。
什么野果不野果,
这是沙蛆在脱壳。
我劝大哥莫上当,
放走'鹿子'吃不着!"

二魔虎一下跳起来,
张开嘴巴笑呵呵:
"老三也真太过虑,
何必这样心眼多?
谅她长翅飞不了。

真的飞了还有我。
就是飞到天边去,
我也抓来还大哥!"
起先大魔虎夸三魔虎,
二魔虎心中就不乐。
这回它要露一手,
显显本事才快活。

第五章 中计 Chapter Five The Trap

At first the big demon tiger wouldn't agree,
for fear that she would run away,
but after her repeated cajolery,
it relented:
"When you're full, come back right away
without delay."

The third demon tiger snorted
and said sarcastically:
"Big brother, you have a kind heart,
letting go the deer already in your mouth.
This is not about some wild berries,
but it is the maggot escaping by shedding its shell.
I say, big brother, don't fall for it
and lose your 'deer'!"

The second demon tiger jumped up,
laughing with his mouth wide open:
"The third, you worry too much,
but, why overthink this?
She cannot escape even if she had wings.

"Even if she escapes, I am still here.
And even if she could fly to the edge of the sky,
I can catch her for you, big brother!"
When the big demon tiger complimented the third tiger earlier,
the second demon tiger was unhappy.
Now it was trying to show off
and to make itself feel better.

金笛 Jin Di

大魔虎想了好一阵，
便又开口把话说：
"你们两个莫争论，
这事让我来定夺。
既然她的肚子饿，
那就让她摘野果。
不过二弟你要陪她去，
也好防备她逃脱。"
二魔虎大声叫起来，
好像雷声从天落：
"叫我陪她我不去，
别的弟兄也用不着。
就是让她一个去，
要是她真逃脱了，
就砍我的大脑壳！"
大魔虎听它这样讲，
也就不再说什么。

蒙诗彩奏跑去摘野果，
野果结成串，
压弯了枝桠，
她心里乐呵呵。
摘了吃，
吃了摘，
吃饱肚子上山坡。
不走大路走小路，
过深箐，
直奔自己寨子脚。

第五章 中计 Chapter Five The Trap

The big demon tiger thought about it for some time
and then said:
"Don't quarrel about this, you two,
but leave it for me to decide.
Since she is hungry,
let her pick the wild berries.
But, second brother, you must go with her
to prevent her from fleeing."
The second demon tiger started shouting
as loud as the thunder coming down from the sky:
"You ask me to accompany her, but I won't go,
and there is no need to send any other brother either.
Let her go by herself,
and if she escapes successfuly,
you can behead me!"
On hearing these words,
the big demon tiger didn't speak anymore.

Meng Shi Cai Zou ran to pluck the wild berries,
which were in clusters,
weighing down the branches,
and making her happy.
Picking and eating,
eating and picking,
when she was full, she climbed up the hill.
Avoiding the roadways, she walked along the small pathways,
through the woods,
heading to the foot of her village.

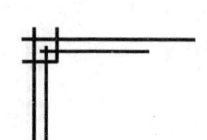

金笛 Jin Di

魔虎们等了大半天,
等得心头冒了火。

总是不见她回来,
大魔虎急得干跺脚。
三魔虎对老二说风凉话:
"二哥的脑壳呀,
到底有几个?
还不赶快砍下来,
还要等什么?"
二魔虎感到很羞愧,
只见它纵身一蹿,
顺着大路追上大山坡。

蒙诗彩奏走的是小路,
二魔虎走的是大路,
任凭它跑得如风快,
哪里追得着?
追了一阵转回来,
不好意思见大哥。
躺在地上就打鼾,
把大魔虎气得直跺脚。

三魔虎看看那小路,
小路印着脚迹窝。
它三纵两跳蹿出去,
没跑远就追着。

第五章 中计 Chapter Five The Trap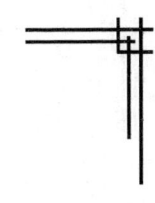

The demon tigers waited for a long time
and then became impatient.

Not seeing her return,
the big demon tiger stamped in anger.
The third demon tiger said to second brother sarcastically,
"Your head, second brother,
how many do you have?
Why don't you cut it off right now,
or are you waiting for something?"
The second demon tiger was ashamed,
and, leaping up,
it chased up the big hill along the main roadway.

Meng Shi Cai Zou took the small pathway,
and the second demon tiger took the main roadway,
so even though it ran as fast as the wind,
how could it possibly catch up to her?
After running for a while, it gave up
and felt ashamed when it came back to its big brother.
It lay down and started to snore right away,
making the big demon tiger so angry that it stamped in anger.

The third demon tiger examined the small pathways
and saw the indented footprints.
It chased by leaps and bounds
and caught up to her very quickly.

161

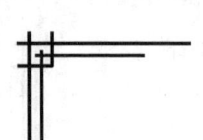

金笛 Jin Di

"老二差点误事,
还是老三心计多。"
大魔虎又夸三魔虎,
三魔虎心中好快活。

蒙诗彩奏很伤心,
势单力薄受折磨。
十只魔虎拖住她,
推推搡搡朝前挪。

走了九山十八洼,
过了十箐百重岭。
不觉来到夺戈底,
蒙诗彩奏更伤情。
那是扎董丕冉家,
触情生情想亲人。
她灵机一动坐地上,
推说走路太多脚杆疼,
要在路边歇一会,
养足力气才好赶路程。
网里的兔子跑不脱,
笼中的斑鸠难飞腾;
魔虎也就没有说什么,
让她歇下养精神。
蒙诗彩奏歇一阵,
摘片木叶吹出声,

第五章 中计 Chapter Five The Trap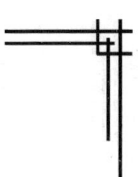

"Second brother almost botched the operation,
and third brother is the smart one."
The big demon tiger complimented the third demon tiger,
who was delighted to hear it.

Meng Shi Cai Zou was distraught,
alone and tormented.
The ten tigers dragged her along.
pushing and shoving her forward.

They walked through many mountains and basins,
passed many woods and hills.
When they came to Duo Ge Di,
Meng Shi Cai Zou became all the sadder.
It was where Zha Dong Pi Ran's family was,
so the sight triggered her memory and made her miss her beloved.
She thought quickly and then sat down on the ground.
She said that the walk had been long and her ankles were sore,
and asked for a break by the roadside,
so as to recharge her energies and keep pressing ahead.
Thinking that the rabbit in the net couldn't run off,
and the turtledove in the cage couldn't fly away,
the demon tiger didn't object
and it let her take a break.
Meng Shi Cai Zou rested for a while,
and then plucking a Mu-leaf, she played it

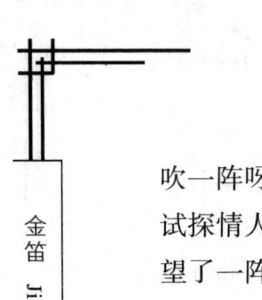

金笛 Jin Di

吹一阵呀望一阵,
试探情人可回村?
望了一阵啊盼一阵,
情人可会来救应?

第五章 中计 Chapter Five The Trap

and then waited, played it again, and waited again:
could her beloved have returned to the village?
She looked and hoped,
would her beloved be able to come to her rescue?

第六章　试刀

二十

扎董丕冉学芦笙，
样样调子学得精。
一年期满别吹师，
高高兴兴回家门。

阿支搁下砍柴斧，
欢天喜地笑向迎：
"自从你去学芦笙，
我在家里做活忙不赢。
又打木床又做柜，
又修房顶又做门。
样样家什备办好，
等你回家来就成婚。"

阿奈停下小纺车，
连忙将儿唤几声：
"自从你离娘出门去，
娘在家中操持受苦辛。

第六章 试刀　Chapter Six　Preparations

Chapter Six   Preparations

20

Zha Dong Pi Ran learned to play the Lu Sheng,
gaining knowledge of expertise on a variety of tunes.
After finishing his one-year apprenticeship,
he returned home full of joy.

A Zhi put down the axe,
greeting him so very happily:
"Ever since you left to learn to play the Lu Sheng,
I've been so busy working at home.
I made the bed and the wardrobe,
and I repaired the roof and the door.
Everything is ready now,
just waiting for you to come home and get married.

A Nai stopped the little spinning wheel,
and quickly called out to her son:
"Ever since you left home,
I worked hard to run the house.

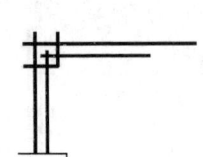

金笛 Jin Di

整日纺麻又织布,
添制被盖和衣裙。
样样穿戴置办好,
等你回来就结亲。"

扎董丕冉抬眼望,
眼前一片好光景:
竹篱房间多别致,
木床柜子多齐整;
碗筷瓢盆换了样,
桌椅板凳样样新。

打开柜子朝里看,
柜中景象更喜人:
新制的被盖绣雀鸟,
才缝的衣裙描花纹。
家中处处有喜气,
扎董丕冉笑盈盈:
"阿支阿奈在家里,
真替孩儿操碎心。
看来万事已齐备,
快请么公定良辰!"
三人正在嘻嘻笑,
远处传来木叶声。
声声低沉又凄婉,

第六章 试刀　Chapter Six　Preparations

Spinning the linen yarn and weaving the cloth all day long,
I made new quilts and clothes,
getting everyting well-prepared
for you to return to get married."

Zha Dong Pi Ran looked up
and saw a most refreshing sight:
The bamboo built room was carefully arranged,
with the wooden bed and wardrobe neatly organized;
the dishes and the cookware were different now,
and the tables and chairs were all new.

Inside the wardrobe
it looked even more pleasant:
The new quilts were embroidered with birds,
and the tailored shirts and skirts had floral patterns on them.
Every thing looked delightful in the house,
and Zha Dong Pi Ran was all smiles:
"A Zhi and A Nai at home,
took so much trouble for me.
It looks like everything is ready,
so let's ask a Me Gong① to find an auspicious day!"
Just as the three of them visited cheerfully,
the sound of the mu-leaf came from afar.
It was somber and melancholy,

---

① Me Gongs are diviners.

金笛　Jin Di

扎董丕冉仔细听。
"布哩布哩布噜哩噜,
我把木叶吹起,
问声扎董丕冉呀,
你可曾回来到家里?
跟你分别一整年,
我天天都在想着你。
你出远门学芦笙,
我俩因此才分离。
我天天走到水井边,
假装挑水来等你。
眼睛望穿不见你回来,
我感到寂寞又孤凄。
今天心里更烦闷,
我又到井边去等你。
为捞一个红桃子,
被虎推落在井里。
魔虎趁机来逼婚,
我已中了它奸计。
如今十只魔虎抓住我,
要将我带到山洞去。
到了山洞就成亲,
我就永远成了魔虎妻。
我若不跟它们去,
定会死在虎口里。
我的扎董丕冉呀,
快来搭救我,
我的扎董丕冉呀,
不要再迟疑!"

第六章 试刀 Chapter Six Preparations

and Zha Dong Pi Ran listened carefully.
"Bu li bu li bu lu li lu,
I am playing the mu-leaf
to ask Zha Dong Pi Ran,
are you home yet?
Having not seen you for a whole year,
I have missed you every day.
You went far away to learn to play the Lu sheng,
the reason we were separated.
Every day I walked to the well,
pretending to fetch water and waiting for you there.
But no matter how much I looked, you never returned,
and I felt alone and miserable.
Feeling bored and listless today,
I waited for you by the well again.
When I tried to fetch a red peach,
the tiger pushed me into the well.
The demon tiger took the opportunity to force me to marry it,
so I realized that I felt into its trap.
Now the ten tigers have captured me,
and they are taking me to their cave.
As soon as we arrive at the cave the wedding will be held,
and I will become the demon tiger's wife forever.
If I didn't go with them,
I would for sure be devoured by them.
My dear Zha Dong Pi Ran,
please come to rescue me;
My dear Zha Dong Pi Ran,
please come without delay!"

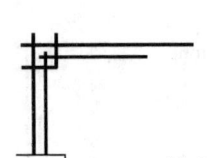

金笛 Jin Di

扎董丕冉在家里，
一字一句听得清。
只觉眼前一片黑，
好像霹雳轰头顶。
蒙诗彩奏遭灾难，
使他气愤又伤心。
生活就像爬山岭，
高高低低路不平。
阿支阿奈也悲痛，
又急又气成泪人。
扎董丕冉抹抹泪，
吹起金笛忙答应：
"布哩布哩布哩噜，
我已知道你受苦。

我的心情很难过，
就像利箭穿胸脯。
只望回到家里来，
跟你相会诉肺腑。
不料祸事从天降，
十只魔虎真狠毒。
趁我不在你身边，
什么坏事都干出。
我的蒙诗彩奏呀，
你不要伤心不要哭。
等我提起大砍刀，
为你报仇杀魔虎。"

第六章 试刀 Chapter Six Preparations

At home Zha Dong Pi Ran
heard every word and every sentence clearly.
Suddenly, he felt like he was blacking out,
as if a thunderbolt struck over his head.
Such catastrophe happening to Meng Shi Cai Zou
made him angry and sad.
Life had been like climbing mountains,
having its ups and downs.
A Zhi and A Nai were also indignant,
anxious, angry, and in tears.
Zha Dong Pi Ran wiped his tears
and began to reply right away by playing the Jin Di:
"Bu li bu li bu li lu,
I now know your suffering.

I am so saddened
that I feel as if sharp arrows were piercing my chest.
I was looking forward to coming home
and having a heart to heart with you.
I didn't expect disaster to strike
and the ten demon tigers to be so atrocious.
Taking advantage of my being away from you,
they have committed an unimaginable crime.
My dear Meng Shi Cai Zou,
don't be sad and don't cry.
Wait for me to come with my machete
to avenge you and slay the demon tigers."

金笛 Jin Di

蒙诗彩奏听到金笛声,
知道扎董丕冉已回村。
她眼前一亮心激动,
紧吹木叶告亲人:
"布哩布哩布噜哩,
你已平安到家里。
我的苦楚你知晓,
你来杀虎要警惕。
十只魔虎凶恶又狡猾,
你要沉着莫性急。
大刀一定要磨快,
杀虎才有力。
如果有闪失,
我俩都会落进虎口里!"

扎董丕冉怒不歇,
又吹金笛答木叶:
"布哩布哩布哩噜,
你的话语我记住。
魔虎凶恶我不怕,
我有心计胆气足。
我就立刻磨大刀,
将刀磨快好杀虎。"

金笛一调接一调,
木叶一声连一声。
金笛木叶传情意,

第六章 试刀　Chapter Six　Preparations

Meng Shi Cai Zou heard the sound of the Jin Di

and knew now that Zha Dong Pi Ran had returned to the village.

Her eyes brightened and felt more hopeful,

so she quickly played the leaf to reply to her beloved:

"Bu li bu li bu lu li,

you have arrived home safely.

You now know my predicment,

but watch out when you come to slay the tigers.

The ten demon tigers are evil and cunning,

and you must be calm and patient.

The machete must be sharpened very well

to defeat the tigers.

Otherwise,

we both will become the meal of the tigers!"

Zha Dong Pi Ran still felt indignant.

and played the Jin Di again to reply to the Mu-leaf:

"Bu li bu li bu li lu,

I will remember your words.

I am not afraid of the demon tigers,

because I am strategic and courageous.

I will go sharpen the machete immediately

to get ready to slay the tigers."

The Jin Di was playing one tune after another,

while the Mu-leaf was playing one song after another.

The Jin Di and the Mu-leaf were expressing their love,

175

一个吹来一个应。
十只魔虎在旁边,
一调一声也不会听,
只得坐在石头上,
闭起双目养精神。

二十一

扎董丕冉不说话,
立刻奔向竹篱笆。
阿支打的大长刀,
正在上面高高挂,
扎董丕冉踮着脚,
伸手忙把刀取下。
又去搬来大磨石,
整天磨个眼不眨。
唰唰唰!
沙沙沙!
磨了三天又三夜,
磨得大刀闪闪放光华。
他拿起大刀晃一晃,
照得竹楼闪闪亮。
到底刀口快不快,
还要试试它。
恰巧就在这时候,
阿支牵牛到院坝。
扎董丕冉又吹笛,

第六章 试刀 Chapter Six Preparations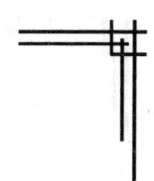

one called and the other responded.
The ten demon devilish tigers were right there,
but they didn't know how to listen to the tune or the song,
so sitting upon stones,
they closed their eyes to catch a break.

21

Zha Dong Pi Ran kept silent
as he quickly ran to the bamboo fence.
The large machete made by A Zhi
was hanging on the fence.
Zha Dong Pi Ran raised his heels
and reached the machete on the fence.
He then brought out the grindstone
and whetted the machete on the stone all day long.
Shiiiing shiiiing shiiiing!
Shashing shashing shashing!
After three days and three nights,
the machete was shining splendedly.
He picked up the large shiny machete,
shook it,
and the bamboo house was brightened up.
But whether the blade was sharp or not
needed to be found out through tests.
Just at this moment,
A Zhi led the ox into the yard.
Zha Dong Pi Ran played the Jin Di

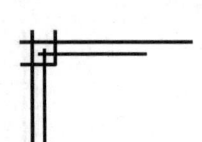

金笛 Jin Di

对着阿支说起话:
"布哩布哩布哩噜,
我正磨刀去杀虎。
不知磨得快不快,
试它一试才有数。
要拿什么来试刀?
就拿这头大黄牯。"

阿支听罢流眼泪,
歌声随着眼泪出:
"儿是爹的心头肉,
牛儿是爹的手中物。
为了搭救蒙诗彩奏呀,
何惜这头大黄牯!"

阿支献牛试大刀,
深明大义心宽阔。
扎董丕冉奔上前,
一刀割断牛鼻索。
他又照准牛屁股,
使劲踢一脚。
黄牯不防挨了这一踢,
猛跳狂奔窜进山窝窝。
踏得满山黄尘滚,
大树小树打哆嗦。
扎董丕冉握起刀,
纵过石坎跨沟壑。
就像一阵狂风卷过去,

第六章 试刀 Chapter Six Preparations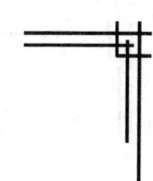

to speak to A Zhi:
"Bu li bu li bu li lu,
I'm sharpening the machete to slay the tigers.
To determine whether it's sharp or not,
I have to try it on something.
What could I use?
Let me use this ox.

Hearing this, A Zhi was in tears,
his tears flowing with the sound of his song:
"My son is the closest to my heart,
and the ox is what I value.
In order to save Meng Shi Cai Zou,
the ox has to be sacrificed!"

A Zhi's offer to sacrifice the ox to test the machete
showed his understanding and generosity.
Zha Dong Pi Ran charged forward
and cut the rope tied to the ox's nose.
He then kicked the ox from behind
very hard.
The ox was caught by surprise
and made a wild dash into the mountains.
It kicked up the dust all over the mountain
and made all trees tremble.
Zha Dong Pi Ran, holding the machete in his hand,
ran across ridges and ravines.
Like a gust of violent wind,

金笛 Jin Di

手一举起刀就落。
一头肥壮的大牯牛呀,
被劈成两截轱轱辘辘滚下坡。
滚到坡下才见流出血,
染红了一片杂草棵。

看来大刀已磨快,
扎董丕冉不禁喜心怀。
可是他深思又细想,
杀虎还得再忍耐。
他又继续磨大刀,
要把大刀磨得飞飞快。
磨了三天零三夜,
磨得大刀能照出影子来。
他拿起大刀晃一晃,
映得山山水水放光彩。

这回又要试试刀,
看看磨得快不快。
要拿什么来试刀?
他半天也想不出主意来。
只见阿奈正在织麻布,
麻布织得细又白。
扎董丕冉拿金笛,
对着阿奈吹起来:

第六章 试刀 Chapter Six Preparations

he raised the machete and struck down hard.
Such a strong ox
was rendered in two rolling down the hillside.
Their blood wasn't seen until they reached the bottom of the hill,
where the plants were stained red.

It seemed that the machete had been sharpened,
and Zha Dong Pi Ran couldn't help feeling glad.
But he thought long and hard
and decided that slaying the tigers would require more patience.
He continued to sharpen his machete
to make it even more sharp.
After another three days and three nights,
the machete was shiny like the light that could throw a shadow.
He picked up the big machete and shook it,
brightening the mountains and rivers brilliantly.

Now he wanted to try it again,
to see whether it was sharp or not.
What should he use to test it?
For a while, he couldn't come up with an idea.
Then he saw that A Nai was weaving the linen,
which was fine and white.
Zha Dong Pi Ran took out the Jin Di
to play it to A Nai:

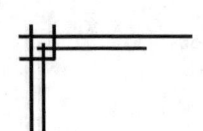

金笛 Jin Di

"布哩布哩布哩噜,
我磨大刀去杀虎。
不知磨得快不快,
试它一试才有数。
要拿什么来试刀?
就拿这匹细麻布。"

阿奈听罢很伤心,
一边唱歌一边哭:
"儿是妈的心头肉,
布是妈的手中物。
为了搭救蒙诗彩奏呀,
何惜这匹细麻布!"
阿奈献布试大刀,
通情达理想得全。
扎董丕冉走上去,
将布一刀就割断。
他将麻布抛上天,
布在天上悠悠转,
布从空中慢慢往下落,
像是降下云一片。
扎董丕冉举刀接住它,
麻布立刻成两段!

大刀磨得飞飞快,
大刀磨得光闪闪。
扎董丕冉摸了又摸,
扎董丕冉看了又看。

第六章 试刀 Chapter Six Preparations

"Bu li bu li bu li lu,

I sharpened the machete for slaying the tigers.

I don't know whether it's sharp or not

and have to test it to find out.

What can I use to do so?

I will use this bolt of fine linen."

A Nai was sad to hear this,

and she started to sing in tears:

"My son is the closest to my heart,

and the cloth is what I value.

In order to save Meng Shi Cai Zuo,

this fine linen has to be sacrificed!"

A Nai offered the linen for testing the machete,

and it showed she was understanding and thoughtful.

Zha Dong Pi Ran walked up,

and cut the cloth.

He tossed up the linen into the sky,

the cloth floating in the sky

and then descending slowly through the air,

like a cloud coming down.

Zha Dong Pi Ran held up the machete to catch it,

and, right away, the linen was cut in half.

The machete was very sharp,

and it was very polished.

Stroking the machete back and forth,

Zha Dong Pi Ran examined it over and over.

金笛 Jin Di

轻轻插进刀鞘里，
用根银链挂在腰间。

扎董丕冉要杀虎，
马上就要离开家。
他用试刀的麻布缝个大口袋，
又用试刀的牯牛烘成香干巴。
他将干巴装进口袋里，
就去告别爹和妈。
阿支说：
"你要杀虎报大仇，
救出亲人快回家！"

阿奈说：
"你在路上多小心，
救出亲人早回家！"

扎董丕冉抹抹泪，
奔出门外去把仇敌杀！

第六章 试刀 Chapter Six Preparations

He then gently put it into the sheath
and, with a silver chain, tied it to his waist.

Zha Dong Pi Ran was ready to slay the tigers
and to leave his home soon.
He sewed a big bag with the linen used to test the machete,
and he dried the jerky with the ox used to test the machete.
He put the jerky into the bag,
and went to say goodbye to his father and mother.
A Zhi said:
"Go slay the tigers, to avenge
your beloved, and then come home quickly!"

A Nai said:
"Be careful on your way,
and rescue your beloved and come home soon!"

Zha Dong Pi Ran wiped his tears
and then ran out of the door to battle his enemy!

第七章　追虎

二十二

穿过苦竹林，
又进东瓜箐；
翻过黄土坡，
又跨红石岭；
涉过山溪水，
再钻茅草丛。
背淌汗，
脚生风。
口里直喘气，
心中恨难平。
扎董丕冉追魔虎，
白天黑夜赶路程。

他快跑紧追到河谷，
见个彩伊在啼哭。
扎董丕冉心难过，
吹起金笛问缘故：
"布哩布哩布哩噜，
问声阿妹为何哭？

第七章 追虎　Chapter Seven　The Putsuit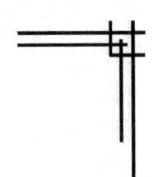

Chapter Seven　The Putsuit

22

He went through the Ku Zhoo grove
and entered the Dong Gua woods;
he went over the Huang Tu slope
and crossed the Hong Shi mountain;
he waded through the streams
and trudged through the marshes of grass.
Sweat ran down his back
and he walked up the stormy wind.
His mouth wanted to catch a breath,
but his heart wanted to seek justice.
Zha Dong Pi Ran was chasing after the demon tigers
hastening forward day and night.

When he hurried to the river valley,
he saw Cai Yi who was crying.
Zha Dong Pi Ran felt sad for her,
so he played the Jin Di to ask why:
"Bu li bu li bu li lu,
May I ask why Little Sister is crying?

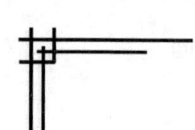

金笛 Jin Di

有仇我来为你报,
有贼我来为你除。
天大疑难我来解,
我劝阿妹莫要哭!"

彩伊伸手擦擦泪,
凄凄切切放悲声:
"前天来了十只虎,
张牙舞爪最吓人。
驮着一个小姑娘,
一下冲进我家门。
吃了我家一头大水牛,
连毛带骨一口吞;
抬走我家两头大母猪,
连儿带崽拖出村。
阿哥呀,
看你是个好心肠,
请你为我除大害,
让我慢慢来报恩!"

扎董丕冉生怒气,
拿起金笛吹几句:
"布哩布哩布哩噜,
我说阿妹你莫急。
魔虎是你的死对头,
也是我的大仇敌。
它背上驮着的那姑娘,
就是我的未婚妻。

第七章 追虎 Chapter Seven The Putsuit

I will avenge you
and bring the scoundrel to justice.
I will help you solve problems, no matter how thorny.
so listen to me and stop crying!"

Cai Yi wiped away her tears
and wailed wretchedly.
"The day before yesterday, ten tigers came,
with long fangs and wielding the paws, very scary.
Carrying a young woman,
they rushed into my house.
They ate our water buffalo
without spitting even the hides or bones;
they robbed us of our two sows
dragged along all the piglets, too, out of the village.
Big Brother,
you look like a kind-hearted man,
so please get rid of those thugs,
and let me repay your kindness little by little in the future!"

Zha Dong Pi Ran was very angry
and took out the Jin Di, playing:
"Bu li bu li bu li lu,
listen to me, young sister, and do not worry.
The demon devilish tigers are your nemeses
and also my mortal enemies.
That young woman on the tiger's back
is my fiancée.

189

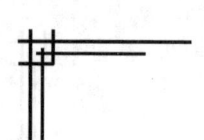

金笛　Jin Di

不管山多高呀路多险,
我定要杀虎来见你!"

扎董丕冉别了那彩伊,
赶到一个大箐旁。
看见一个咪尼娇,
一边啼哭一边嚷。
扎董丕冉心发愁,
又吹金笛问端详:
"布哩布哩布哩噜,
阿弟哭得好凄楚。
是你的蓝靛被糟蹋,
还是死爹或丧母?
阿弟呀,
请你明白告诉我,
我会对你有帮助!"

咪尼娇呀抬起头,
揩干眼泪唱悲歌:
"昨日来了十只虎,
驮着个姑娘进村落。
它们闯进我家里,
又吼又叫太凶恶。
吃了我家枣骝马,
抓走我家鸡和鹅,
阿哥呀,
看你是个有胆有识人,
请你为我除大害,
我的日子才好过!"

第七章 追虎 Chapter Seven The Putsuit

No matter how high the mountains and how dangerous the journey,

I will slay the tigers and then come to see you!"

After Zha Dong Pi Ran said goodbye to Cai Yi,
he came by the large woods.
He met Mi Ni Jiao
who was crying and yelling.
Zha Dong Pi Ran was worried,
so he played the Jin Di again to ask what happened.
"Bu li bu li bu li lu,
young brother, you're crying miserably.
Is it your indigo clothing that was destroyed
or did your father or mother just pass away?
Young brother,
please tell me,
and I can help you!"

Mi Ni Jiao looked up
and dried his tears and sang a sorrowful song:
"Yesterday, ten tigers came,
carrying a young woman and marching into the village.
They budged into my home,
roaring, snarling, and ferocious.
They ate our shiny chestnut-colored horse,
and robbed us of our chickens and geese.
Big brother,
you look like a brave and understanding man,
so please get rid of those thugs
so that I can live in peace!"

金笛 Jin Di

扎董丕冉怒火起,
吹起金笛劝阿弟:
"布哩布哩布哩噜,
我劝阿弟莫心急。
魔虎是你的死对头,
也是我的大仇敌。
它背上驮着的那姑娘,
就是我的未婚妻。
不管河多宽呀水多深,
我定要杀虎来见你!"

扎董丕冉别了咪尼娇,
又追到一条山沟里。
见个佑保坐在荞地头,
呜呜咽咽在哭泣。
扎董丕冉心悲切,
吹起金笛问情由:

"布哩布哩布哩噜,
问声阿佑为何哭?
是你儿孙不孝顺,
还是媳妇受欺侮?
阿佑呀,
请你跟我说清楚,
我会给你解愁苦!"

佑保开口把话答,
满脸挂泪花:
"今早来了十只虎,

第七章 追虎　Chapter Seven　The Putsuit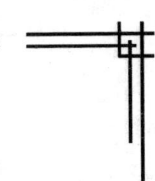

Zha Dong Pi Ran was very angry
and played the Jin Di, saying to him:
"Bu li bu li bu li lu,
listen to me, young brother, and do not worry.
The domon tigers who are your nemeses are also my mortal enemies.
That young woman on the tiger's back
is my fiancée.
No matter how wide the river and how deep its water,
I will slay the tigers and then come to see you!"

Zha Dong Pi Ran said goodbye to Mi Ni Jiao,
and then came to a valley.
He met You Bao who was sitting at the end of the buckwheat field,
crying.
Zha Dong Pi Ran was full of grief
and played the Jin Di to ask why:

"Bu li bu li bu li lu,
may I ask why A You is crying?
Is it that your children are unfilial,
or your wife was taken advantage of?
A You,
please tell me what happened,
for I can help ease your pain!"

A You replied,
with tears running down his cheeks:
"This morning, ten tigers came,

金笛 Jin Di

驮着个姑娘进我家。
又是跳呀又是滚,
个个舞爪又张牙。
咬死我的独儿子,
咬死我的一群鸭。
阿哥呀,
看你是个大智大勇人,
请你为我除大害,
杀死魔虎我死也瞑目啦。"

扎董丕冉怒冲天,
大吼一声震群山。
两眼射出仇和恨,
双手一伸紧握拳。
唰地抽出长刀来,
刀光亮闪闪。
他照准一棵青枫树,
一刀劈下成两段。
他又吹笛劝阿佑,
笛声激昂又威严:

"布哩布哩布哩噜,
我劝阿佑莫着急。
魔虎是你的死对头,
也是我的大仇敌。
它背上驮着的那姑娘就是我的未婚妻。
不管魔虎多凶残,
我定要剥下虎皮来见你!"

第七章 追虎 Chapter Seven The Putsuit

carrying a young woman when they rushed into my home.
Jumping up and down and rolling on the floor,
everyone of them wielding its claws and showing its fangs.
They killed my only son
and a bunch of my ducks.
Young Man,
you look like intelligent and courageous,
so please get rid of those thugs,
so that even if I have to die, I can be in peace."

Zha Dong Pi Ran was in a rage,
shouting so hard that the mountains were echoing.
His eyes blazing with hatred,
he clinched his fists.
Swoosh, he pulled out his long machete,
with the shiny blade gleaming.
Taking aim at a tree,
he hacked it in half.
Again, he played the Jin Di to console A You,
the sound of which was inspired and majestic.

"Bu li bu li bu li lu,
listen to me, A You, and do not worry.
The demon tigers are your nemeses
and are also my mortal enemies.
The young woman carried on their back is my fiancée.
No matter how ferocious the demon tigers are,
I will skin them and come back to see you then!"

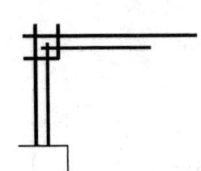

金笛 Jin Di

二十三

天有风会下雨,
人有心事就忧愁。
扎董丕再别了那老人,
来到一个岔路口。
一想起蒙诗彩奏,
他心中就像火上泼了油。
蒙诗彩奏呀,
前天到壮家河边,
昨天到瑶家箐头,
今天到家山沟。
此时此刻呀,
不知又到了哪批梁子,
哪条冲口?

蒙诗彩奏呀,
我的蒙诗彩奏!
魔虎驮着你,
在路上行走,
一定是快如疾风,
决不是慢如老牛。
你在魔虎背上,
要抱紧它的脖子,
不要碰破了头,
不要跌断了手。
饿了,

第七章　追虎　Chapter Seven　The Putsuit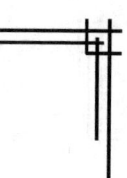

23

Just as the wind ushers in the rain,
distress brings worries.
Zha Dong Pi Ran said goodbye to the old man
and came to where the road forked.
At the thought of Meng Shi Cai Zou,
his heart felt like fire just doused with more oil.
Meng Shi Cai Zou
was at the Zhuangjia river the day before,
the Yaojia woods yesterday,
and the Jiashan village today.
At this moment,
at which ridge has she arrived
or by which river was she now?

Meng Shi Cai Zou,
my dear Meng Shi Cai Zou!
The demon tiger carrying you
must be running as fast as the wind,
not as slow as an old ox.
On the back of the demon tiger,
be sure to hold on to its neck tightly,
not to injure your head
or to fall and fracture your hands.
If you are hungry,
ask for plenty of food;

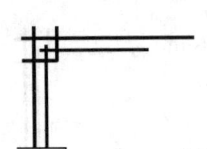

金笛 Jin Di

叫他给你吃个饱；
渴了，
喊它给你喝个够；
手酸了，
你叫它慢慢走；
头晕了，
你喊它且停留。
魔虎的牙齿很尖利，
魔虎的嘴巴脏又臭。
你不要碰着它的牙，
你不要挨近它的口。

他急了，
你不要惹；
它怒了，
你不要去斗。
不管有多少苦楚，
你都暂时忍受。
等我追着了，
你就会得救。
杀虎的日子呀，
不会等很久！

扎董丕冉想了很多，
脚步也走得很快。
翻过黛家山，
又过耆老寨。
为了追魔虎，
大步朝前迈。

第七章 追虎 Chapter Seven The Putsuit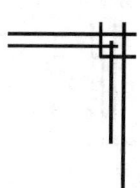

if you are thirsty,
ask for plenty of water;
if your wrists are sore,
ask them to go slowly;
if you are dizzy,
ask them to stop.
The teeth of the demon tigers are sharp,
and their mouths are filthy and stinky.
Do not touch their teeth,
nor get close to their mouths.

When the tiger is irritated,
let it be;
when it is angry,
do not fight it.
No matter how difficult it gets,
withstand it for now.
When I catch up to them,
you will be saved.
The end of the tigers' days
won't be too far away from now.

Zha Dong Pi Ran thought a lot
and he also walked very fast.
He traveled over the Dai Jia mountain
and through the Qi Lao village.
In order to pursue the tigers,
he walked in big strides.

第八章　沉睡

二十四

不知追了多少天，
九双草鞋也磨穿。
不知追了几个月，
三件衣裳也扯烂。
爬到一座高山顶，
石多林又密呀，
道路被隔断。

扎董丕冉抬眼望，
魔虎踪迹看不见；
扎董丕冉侧耳听，
魔虎声音听不见。
他想拿起金笛吹，
探问情人在哪边；
可是肚子饿得慌，
手脚瘫软眼皮酸。

第八章 沉睡 Chapter Eight Deep Sleep

Chapter Eight Deep Sleep

24

He didn't know for how many days he pursued,
only that he worn out nine pairs of straw sandals.
He didn't know for many months he pursued
only that he had three shirts ruined by the prickly tree branches and twigs.
When he climbed up to the top of a mountain,
he saw lots of rocks and dense forests
but the road came to an end.

Zha Dong Pi Ran looked around and far away,
but he saw no traces of the demon tigers.
He listened carefully,
but he heard no sound of the demon tigers.
He wanted to take out the Jin Di and play
to ask his beloved where she was;
but he was so hungry
that his limbs were limp and his eyelid, weary.
He took out the Jin Di but was too exhausted to play it,

金笛 Jin Di

拿起金笛吹不动，
只会喘气淌冷汗。
他在地上坐下来，
想歇一会儿，
再把虎追赶。
可是屁股一落地，
立刻睡倒了，
呼呼就打鼾。

扎董丕冉睡不久，
十只魔虎就走过。
只因他把山路走岔了，
没把虎追着。
这时他在路边睡倒了，
反让魔虎撵上他，
差点碰着他的脚。

大魔虎闻见生人味，
转动眼睛在搜索。
忽见地上躺着一个人，
它就张开大嘴笑呵呵：
"这回走路走得多，
就是铁打的肚子呀，
这时也饥饿。
这人皮嫩肉又厚，
真是打起灯笼难找着。

第八章 沉睡 Chapter Eight Deep Sleep

and found himself breathing heavily and bathed in cold sweat.
He sat on the ground,
hoping to catch his breath
before he would continue to chase after the tigers.
But as soon as his bottom touched the ground
he fell asleep,
snoring away.

Shortly after Dong Zha Pi Ran fell asleep,
the ten demon tigers came along.
He had taken the wrong mountain path
and so didn't catch up to the tigers.
Now that he fell asleep by the roadside,
he became the one who was caught up with by the demon tigers
who almost stepped on his feet.

The big demon tiger smelled the stranger
and rolled its eyes to search for him.
Suddenly spotting a man lying on the ground,
it opened its mouth, laughting:
"We have traveled for such a long time that,
strong as I am,
I am very hungry.
This man has tender skin and plump flesh,
something I would not have found even if I were to look for it.

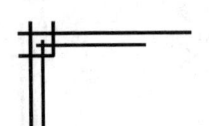

金笛 Jin Di

瞌睡来了遇着花枕头,
这是老天把他送给我!"
它气势汹汹扑过去,
就要去咬他的后颈窝。

蒙诗彩奏仔细看,
不禁吓得心胆寒。
这是扎董丕冉呀,
怎么睡倒在荒山?
眼下自己受苦又受难,
半路遇着情人更心酸。
她从魔虎背上跳下来,
立刻奔到他身边。
伸出双手护住他,
责备魔虎太凶残:
"他跟你们一无仇,
他跟你们二无冤。
如今你们要吃他,
真是害理又伤天!"
大魔虎冷冷笑一声,
瞪起一双铜铃眼:
"我们生来就吃人,
要咬要吃随我意。
这事不要你来管!"

蒙诗彩奏不害怕,
指着魔虎大声骂:
"你们吃了家独儿子,

第八章　沉睡　Chapter Eight　Deep Sleep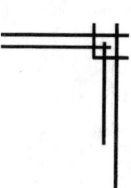

This is like finding a nice pillow when sleepy,
a gift bestowed by heaven!"
It charged forward savagely,
aiming its teeth at the nape of his neck.

Meng Shi Cai Zou took a closer look
and shuddered at what she saw.
This was Zha Dong Pi Ran,
but why was he sleeping in the mountains?
Having endured so much hardship,
meeting her beloved on the way grieved her even more.
She jumped off the back of the demon tiger
and ran to his side at once.
She stretched out her arms to protect him,
scolding the demon tiger for its cruelty:
"He has never hurt you
and has never wronged you.
Yet you are to eat him up,
an act of total senselessness and injustice!"
The demon tiger laughed coldly,
with its copper-bell eyes bulging.
"We were born to eat humans,
so I can bite and eat at will.
It is none of your business!"

Meng Shi Cai Zou was undaunted,
blasting the big demon tiger with her finger pointing at it:
"You have already eaten someone's only son,

如今又要来吃他，
要是你们吃了他，
我就死在大树下。
不再跟着你们走，
你们连我一齐吃了吧！
连肉带骨一齐咽。"

三魔虎生来最狡猾，
立刻开口就问话：
"他是你的什么人，
为何帮他说好话？
你要老实告诉我，
不然就要吃了他！"
蒙诗彩奏最机灵，
振振有词来回答：
"他不是我的什么人，
数遍苗山千万人，
我从来没有见过他。
只因你们太残忍，
我才为他说句话。
害人之心不可有，
对人不可太毒辣。
我说的句句是实话，
你们莫要伤害他！"

大魔虎慢慢鼓起眼，
认真辨认细观察：
"咦，这人像在哪里见过面，

第八章 沉睡 Chapter Eight Deep Sleep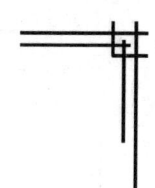

and now you want to eat him.
If you eat him,
I will kill myself under the tree.
I won't go with you any more,
so why don't you just eat me too,
flesh, bone, and all!"

The third demon tigers was the sliest by nature,
and it asked right away:
"Who is he to you
and why do you beg for him?
Tell me the truth,
or I will eat him up!"
Meng Shi Cai Zou, the quickest thinker she was,
replied confidently:
"He is not anyone I know.
There are tens and thousands of people in the Miao villages,
and I have never met him.
But you're too cruel,
the reason I spoke up for him.
One cannot harbour ill-will towards others,
nor treat them with cruelty.
Every word I said is true,
so don't you harm him!"

The big demon tiger strained its eyes
to look at him carefully:
"Whoa, I have seen this man before.

像是那回斗过我的扎董丕冉嘛!
不,不会是扎董丕冉,
扎董丕冉出门没回家。
嘿,不管他是哪一个,
先把他吃了再说话!"

蒙诗彩奏奔到大树下,
哭着喊着要往树上撞:
"你们吃人不眨眼,
我也不想再活啦!
我就撞死在这里,
你们连我也吞下。"

三魔虎见状急上前,
紧紧拖住她:
"要是真的撞死了,
那就丢了一枝花。
大哥没妻我们没嫂,
十个光棍做一家。
操心操肝白费力,
这样就不合算啦。
大哥呀,
不如这就依了她。
肚子饿了忍着点,
这人一定要留下。"

大魔虎听听有道理,
立刻收住爪和牙。

第八章 沉睡　Chapter Eight　Deep Sleep

He looks like Zha Dong Pi Ran who fought me that one time.
But, no, it cannot be Zha dong Pi Ran,
who is on a trip and has not returned home.
Hey, it matters not who he is,
and I can eat first and find out later!"

Meng Shi Cai Zou ran towards the tree,
crying, screaming, and threatening to kill herself:
"You kill people without batting an eyelid,
and what's the point for me to live anymore!
I will die right here,
and you can eat me too."

The third demon tiger quickly caught up to her,
holding her back tightly:
"If she really dies,
a flower will be lost.
Big brother, you will have no wife and we, no sister in-law,
having only us ten bachelors.
All we have accomplished so far will be for nothing,
and that will not be worthwhile.
Big brother,
it may be better to grant her the request.
Let's endure the hunger for now,
but keep the man alive."

The big demon tiger was persuaded,
holding back its claws and teeth.

金笛 Jin Di

蒙诗彩奏一颗心，
啪嗒一声才落下。
扎董丕冉得救了，
全靠蒙诗彩奏几句话。
蒙诗彩奏呀，
看见扎董丕冉正酣睡，
很想大声喊醒他。
跟他诉说离别苦，
向他倾吐贴心话。
多少情意多少话，
尽在心中翻浪花。
但是如果喊醒他，
多少事情就坏啦！
魔虎将他认出来，
定会一口吞掉他。
自己也会遭毒害，
落得双双难归家。
她定下来想一想，
想出一个好办法：
立刻取下银项圈，
悄悄放进石旮旯。
然后跳上魔虎背，
跟着魔虎又出发。

二十五

蒙诗彩奏骑在虎背上，
走了一程又一程。

210

第八章 沉睡 Chapter Eight Deep Sleep

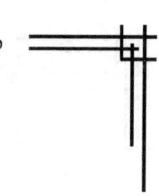

Meng Shi Cai Zou's heart
was finally at ease.
Zha Dong Pi Ran was saved
by the words of Meng Shi Cai Zou.
Meng Shi Cai Zou,
seeing that Zha Dong Pi Ran was deep at sleep,
how she wanted to wake him up.
She wanted to tell him the pain of separation
and have a heart-to-heart with him.
All the love and all the words
were like waves churning in her heart.
But if she woke him up,
it would be the ruin of every thing!
The moment the demon tiger recognized him,
he would be devoured.
She herself would be harmed,
so neither of them would ever return home.
She pulled herself together and thought hard,
and she hit upon a good idea:
She took off her silver necklace
and quietly placed it between the rocks.
She then jumped back onto the back of the demon tiger
and set off again with them.

25

Meng Shi Cai Zou rode on the back of the tiger,
traveling hour after hour.

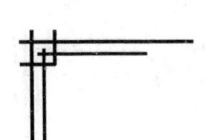

金笛 Jin Di

想起扎董丕冉来，
不觉泪水湿衣襟。
眼泪落在虎背上，
一串一串往下淋。

大魔虎慢慢停下来，
张开嘴巴大声问：
"为何伤心流眼泪，
出了什么大事情？"

蒙诗彩奏有心计，
边哭边答应：
"刚才跳下你的背，
也是怪我不机灵。
丢了一副银项圈，
叫我怎么不伤心？"

大魔虎朝她颈项看，
项圈确实没踪影：
"项圈掉在哪一处，
你可还能记得准？"

"就在那个人身旁，
明明白白记得清。"

大魔虎听了哈哈笑，
笑得眯起大眼睛：
"这有什么了不起，

第八章 沉睡　Chapter Eight　Deep Sleep

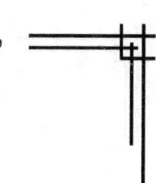

When she thought about Zha Dong Pi Ran,
her tears streamed down and wet her blouse.
Tears fell on the back of the tiger,
rolling down like strings of beads.

The big demon tiger slowed down to a halt
and opened its mouth, asking loudly:
"Why do you grieve, and are you in tears
because some calamity has happened?"

An idea occurred to her,
so she cried as she responded:
"When I jumped off your back just now,
silly me,
I lost my silver necklace,
the reason I am so very sad."

The big demon tiger looked at her neck,
seeing that there was indeed no trace of the necklace:
"Where you lost it,
do you still remember?"

"It was right by that man,
I remember clearly."

On hearing this, the big demon tiger laughed,
his big eyes squinting.
"That's easy,

213

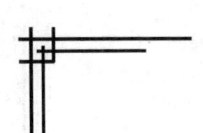

金笛 Jin Di

何必气得泪沾襟。
我去帮你拿回来,
叫你见着就高兴。"

蒙诗彩奏抹抹泪,
假心假意诉苦情:
"要是你去帮我拿,
我也有点不放心。
你的本性难得改,
怕你害了他的命。
看他孤孤单单出远门,
睡在荒山野岭好可怜。
你若害了他的命,
叫我怎忍心?
你们放心等着我,
让我一人去寻,
找着项圈就回来,
一定不会误时辰!"

三魔虎摇头冷冷笑:
"大哥莫听她的话,
她的话语不可信。
前回让她去摘果子吃,
差点误了大事情。
要不是我追得快,
她早就远走高飞无踪影。
还是让我去找项圈吧,
这样事情才把稳。"

第八章 沉睡 Chapter Eight Deep Sleep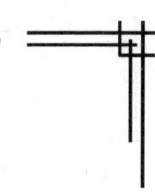

there is no need to cry.
I will go and fetch it for you
to make you happy when you see it."

Meng Shi Cai Zou wiped her tears,
pretending she was still suffering:
"If you go get it for me,
I'm still a little concerned.
I worry that just as leopards can't change their spots,
you will kill him.
He is on a long journey alone
and sadly sleeps in the wilderness in the mountains.
How can I have the heart
to let you kill him?
You rest assured and wait for me here
and let me go find it by myself.
As soon as I find it I will return
without delaying our journey!"

The third demon tiger shook its head with a frosty smile:
"Big brother, don't listen to her,
whose words cannot be believed.
Last time you let her go pick berries,
it almost ruined the whole thing.
If it were not because I ran fast,
she would have disappeared without a trace.
Let me go find the necklace,
a much more sure way to handle this matter."

215

金笛 Jin Di

大魔虎听罢点点头：
"就让三弟去找寻。
可要记住一件事，
莫要伤害那个人。"

三魔虎顺着原路转回去，
为找项圈脚不停。
来到扎董丕冉的身边，
睁大眼睛瞧，
又用鼻子闻。
项圈藏在石旮旯，
左寻右找白费心。

三魔虎垂头丧气跑回来，
蒙诗彩奏好高兴：
"还是让我们去找吧，
你们莫要起疑心。"

二魔虎忙插嘴：
"让她去找也要得，
免得我们费精神。
来到这里离家远，
谅她不敢再逃远。"

大魔虎瞅瞅二魔虎：
"二弟的主意不可靠，
常常坏事情。

第八章 沉睡　Chapter Eight　Deep Sleep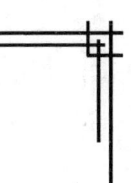

Hearing this, the big demon tiger nodded its head:
"It's decided and, third brother, you go look for it.
But one thing you should keep in mind,
do not harm that man."

The third demon tiger retraced the steps
and looked for the necklace without stopping.
He came up by Zha Dong Pi Ran,
opening his eyes
and sniffing around.
But the necklace was hidden between the rocks,
and such a search was in vain.

The third demon tiger came back in dismay,
and Meng Shi Cai Zou was so happy:
"You have to let me look for it,
and stop being so suspicious."

The second demon tiger interrupted:
"It is okay to let her go find it,
because it will save us energy.
This is so far from her home,
that I dare her to escape again."

The big demon tiger glanced at the second demon tiger:
"Second brother, your ideas cannot be counted on,
and you have often spoiled our efforts.

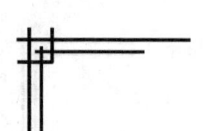

这事由我来安排,
你们莫操心。"
回头又对蒙诗彩奏说:
"让我陪你一同去,
找着项圈就回程。"

蒙诗彩奏暗叫苦:
"这家伙跟我一同去,
麻烦可就多得很。"
她又思量一阵子,
扑哧一下笑出声:
"有你陪我一同去,
我也不觉孤零零。
现在我俩就走吧,
找着项圈就回程。"

蒙诗彩奏带着大魔虎,
停停又走走,
走走又停停。
她故意领它四处转,
转得它四只脚掌酸又疼。

大魔虎说:
"找不着项圈就算了,
莫在这里瞎转圈圈白费劲。"
蒙诗彩奏说:
"就是十天半月也要找,
这项圈是我的命根根。"

第八章 沉睡 Chapter Eight Deep Sleep

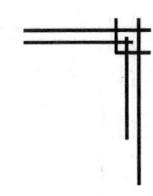

Let me make the arrangements,
so you stop worring about it."
He then looked back at Meng Shi Cai Zou, saying:
"Let me accompany you
and when we find the necklace we will return."

Meng Shi Cai Zou complained in her mind:
"If this fellow goes with me,
there will be too much trouble."
After thinking for a while,
she uttered a laughter.
"If you go with me,
I will not feel lonely.
Let's set off right away,
so that we can find the necklace and come back."

Meng Shi Cai Zou guided the big demon tiger,
stopping and starting,
starting and stopping.
She purposefully let it go here and then there,
making its paws sore.

The big demon tiger said:
"If we can't find it we will give up,
and let's not wander around for nothing."
Meng Shi Cai Zou said:
"Even if it will take a fortnight, we still have to search for it,
because the necklace is my life."

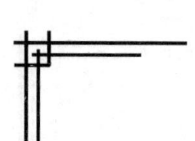

金笛 Jin Di

大魔虎说：
"那你自己去找吧，
我在这棵树脚打个盹。"

蒙诗彩奏心欢喜，
一步并作两步行。
又来到那片草地上，
扎董丕冉还没醒。
这回她也不想再逃跑，
她知道要是自己逃跑了，
扎董丕冉也会没性命。
她想大声喊醒他，
又怕大魔虎暗中观动静。
只好假装兜个大圈子，
又回到大魔虎耳边说了几声：
"这项圈一下难找着，
我怕你等得太焦心。
回来跟你说句话，
也好让你定定神。
你在这里安心等着我，
我再去找找就回程。"

大魔虎也是假装在打盹，
暗中盯着她身影。
它怕她这回又逃跑，
心中总是难平静。
这时见她又回来，

第八章 沉睡 Chapter Eight Deep Sleep

The big demon tiger replied:
"Then you go search by yourself,
and I will take a nap under this tree."

Meng Shi Cai Zou was so happy,
taking steps twice as big as usual.
She returned to the same grassy area
and found that Zha Dong Pi Ran still had not woken up.
This time she didn't want to escape,
because she knew that if she did,
Zha Dong Pi Ran would die.
She wanted to shout at him to wake him up,
but she feared that the big demon tiger was watching her.
She had no choice but to pretend to search in a big circle
and then returned to whisper into the big demon tiger's ear:
"It is hard to find the necklace quickly,
but I don't want you to wait for long and worry.
I came back to let you know,
so that you feel at ease.
Do not worry and just wait for me here,
as I give it another try before we get back."

The big demon tiger was pretending to be dozing off any way,
actually watching her quietly.
It worried that she would escape again
and was unable to keep calm.
Seeing her return,

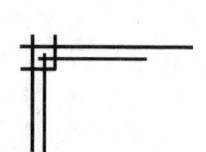

金笛 Jin Di

这才放了心:
"你再回去找找吧,
你的话语我相信。"
说罢慢慢闭起眼,
鼻洞里头打哼哼。

蒙诗彩奏见它睡着了,
赶忙拔脚朝前奔。
跑到扎董丕冉的身边,
又喊又推催他醒:
"阿哥你快睁开眼,
蒙诗彩奏已来临。
快快起来杀魔虎,
救我回去好成亲。"

喊一阵,
推一阵,
哭一阵,
催一阵,
喊得嗓子发了哑,
扎董丕冉还没醒。

那边树下魔虎叫,
催她快快转回程。
一声更比一声高,
一声更比一声紧。

第八章 沉睡 Chapter Eight Deep Sleep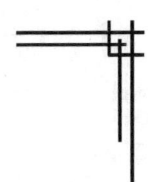

    it felt a little reassured.
"You go ahead and try again,
and I believe what you say."
Then he slowly closed its eyes
and began to snore."

Meng Shi Cai Zou saw that it had fallen asleep,
so she ran without delay.
She came by the side of Zha Dong Pi Ran,
calling, pushing, trying to wake him up.
"My dear, quickly open your eyes,
to see that Meng Shi Cai Zou has come.
Hurry and get up to kill the demon tiger
to rescue me so that we can get married."

She called,
pushed,
cried,
urged
till her voice became hoarse,
but Zha Dong Pi Ran didn't wake up.

    Over there and under the tree the demon tiger was calling her back,
asking her to hurry and return.
The calling became louder and louder
and it became more and more pressing.

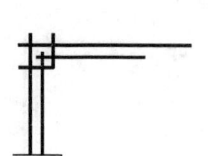

金笛 Jin Di

她忙捡起银项圈,
将它挂在脖子上;
脱下一件花内衣,
流着眼泪盖情人。
又去摘下一兜花,
匆匆忙忙转回程。

大魔虎见她走过来,
扯起嗓子大声问:
"你的项圈可找着?
叫我等得心烦闷。"
她把衣领掀开来,
一副项圈挂脖项。
大魔虎这才没话说,
驮着她又往前奔。

二十六

扎董丕冉睡得甜,
不知睡了多少天。
天上打响闷雷声,
他才醒来揉揉眼。
他想翻身翻不动,
睁大眼睛仔细看:
茅草长起将他盖,
青藤长起将他缠。
盖得严实缠得紧,
叫他怎么能动弹?

第八章 沉睡　Chapter Eight　Deep Sleep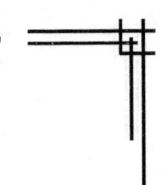

She quickly picked up the silver necklace,
wore it around her neck;
taking off her floral undershirt
and, with tears running, put it on her beloved.
She then went and picked some flowers
and then hurried back.

The demon tiger saw her return
and asked at the top of its voice:
"Did you find the necklace?
The wait made me impatient."
She opened her collar
and showed it the necklace.
That quieted down the demon tiger,
 and soon they set off again with the tiger carrying her on its back.

26

Zha Dong Pi Ran slept a sound sleep,
and he didn't know how many days he had slept.
When the dull thunders rumbled,
he woke up and rubbed his eyes.
He wanted to turn over his body but he couldn't,
and then with his eyes wide open he saw
that the grass was covering him,
and the vine had tied him up.
Covered and bound,
how could he move at all?

金笛 Jin Di

他慢慢抽出长刀来,
上上下下割一遍。
丛丛茅草已割倒,
条条青藤已割断。
他转动身子爬起来,
一件花衣在眼前。
凭着花衣细判断,
蒙诗彩奏来过他身边。
只觉一阵眼睛花,
接着便是泪涟涟。

他怪自己瞌睡大,
睡着就像死一般。
一觉睡得这么久,
不知情人来身边。
如今误了大事情,
怎能杀虎报仇冤?
他捧着那件红内衣,
前后左右转一圈。
踏遍青山找情人,
哪里能见情人面?
他又取下金笛吹,
忙将情人来呼唤:
"布哩布哩布哩噜,
怪我大意又疏忽。
一觉睡去不会醒,
错过良机杀魔虎。
我的蒙诗彩奏呀,

第八章 沉睡 Chapter Eight Deep Sleep

Slowly, he pulled out the long machete
and cut through the grass and the vine.
Clumps of grass were mowed down,
and stems of vine were cut loose.
When he turned himself over, picked himself up
he saw the floral shirt in front of his eyes.
Judging by the shirt,
he knew Meng Shi Cai Zou had been there by his side.
Suddenly, his vision became blurry,
and tears came down.

He blamed himself for the sound sleep,
so sound that he was completely out of it all.
He slept so long
that he didn't realize her beloved had come by.
With this serious delay,
how would he revenge the tiger?
With the red undershirt in his hand,
he surveyed around in a circle.
His beloved could be anywhere in the entire green mountain,
and where would he find her?
He took out the Jin Di again and started to play,
calling to his beloved:
"Bu li bu li bu li lu,
it was my fault to be so careless.
Sleeping so soundly,
I missed the opportunity to kill the demon tigers.
My dear Meng Shi Cai Zou,

金笛 Jin Di

你究竟到了哪一处?
你若听到金笛声,
赶忙回答莫迟误!
看见你的红内衣,
我的心中就痛苦。
只见衣裳不见人,
叫我怎能不啼哭?"
吹罢金笛仔细听,
深山处处无回音。
只有风吹草动呼呼响,
只有鸟叫虫鸣唧唧声。
扎董丕冉心焦急,
睁大一双亮眼睛。
扒开草棵细细看,
沿着小路慢慢行。
魔虎脚迹一个连一个,
一直伸进大森林。
脚迹窝里浸满水,
长出青苔一层层。
扎董丕冉很失望,
心头罩上一团云。
他从脚迹来判断,
魔虎远去难追寻。
到了这个时候呀,
就要忍耐受艰辛。
难得追呀也要追,
难得寻呀也要寻!

第八章 沉睡　Chapter Eight　Deep Sleep

where are you now?
If you hear the sound of the Jin Di,
reply without delay!
When I look at your red undershirt,
my heart aches.
When I see the shirt but not the person,
how could I not be crying?"
He stopped playing and then listened carefully,
but he heard no reply from the mountains.
There was only wind soughing,
birds chirping, and insects buzzing.
Zha Dong Pi Ran was worried
and opened his bright eyes wide.
Pushing the grass aside, he scanned the area
and then walked slowly along the path.
He saw the footprints of the demon tiger one after another,
that were leading all the way into the forest.
The footprints had turned into puddles of water,
with layers of the moss growing.
Zha Dong Pi Ran was disappointed,
feeling like the cloud were shrouding his heart.
Judging by the footprints,
he thought the demon tigers had gone too far to be found.
But in times like this
the endurance for hardship was tested.
Even though it was hard to pursue, he must keep pursuing,
and even it was hard to find, he must keep searching.

二十七

顺着魔虎脚迹走，
日夜兼程往前赶。
跨过浑水河，
翻过太阳山；
穿过刺竹坝，
绕过烂泥潭；
钻过大黑箐，
越过要命寨。
越是往前赶，
魔虎脚迹越新鲜。

不知走了多少路，
登上一座大山岭。
看见路边有堆灰，
扎董丕冉很高兴。
赶忙取出牛干巴，
放进灰堆焐一阵。
这时肚子饿得慌，
烧块干巴吃一顿。
可是干巴烧不熟，
想吃也是吃不成。
伸手进去摸一摸，
灰堆已经冷冰冰。
魔虎还在离得远，
收起干巴赶路程。

第八章　沉睡　Chapter Eight　Deep Sleep

27

Following the demon tigers' footprints,
Zha Dong Pi Ran kept going day and night.
He crossed the Hun Shui river
and over the Tai Yang mountain;
he went through the Ci Zhu dam,
and skirted around the Lan Ni marsh;
he cut through the Da Hei woods
and passed the Yao Ming post.
The farther he went,
the fresher the footprints.

He didn't know how long he had walked,
when he came up to the top of a mountain ridge.
He saw a heap of ashes by the roadside,
which made Zha Dong Pi Ran happy.
Quickly, he took out his beef jerky
and pushed it under the ashes.
At that moment, he felt the pangs of hunger
and wanted to have his meal of jerky.
But the jerky could not be cooked
and he couldn't have his meal.
He used his hand to feel the ashes
and found out that they were already icy cold.
He realized that the demon tigers were still far away,
so he gathered his jerky and went back on the road.

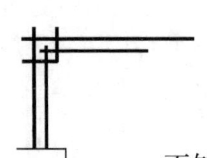

金笛 Jin Di

不知走了多少天,
来到一条大河边。
河边又有一堆灰,
扎董丕冉心喜欢。
他又取出牛干巴,
放进灰堆焐半天。
肚子饿得难忍受,
烧块干巴吃一餐。
可是干巴烧不熟,
又冷又硬难得咽。
伸手进去试一试,
炭熄灰冷无火烟。
魔虎还在离得远,
收起干巴把路赶。

扎董丕冉呀,
为了搭救蒙诗彩奏,
不知翻过多少大山头。
白天顶着烈日行,
晚上戴着月亮走。
不怕山高水又长,
不惧林密和坡陡。
这天刚过晌午后,
他钻进一条大山沟。
又见树脚有堆灰,
扎董丕冉心甜透。
他又取出牛干巴,
赶忙焐进灰里头。

第八章 沉睡　Chapter Eight　Deep Sleep

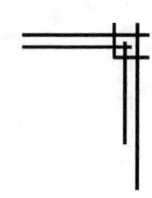

He didn't know how many days had gone by

when he came by a river.

There was another pile of ashes,

which delighted Zha Dong Pi Ran.

He took out his beef jerky again

and left it under the ashes for some time.

He felt the unbearable hunger pangs

and would like to have his meal of jerky.

But the jerky could not be cooked,

so cold and hard that it was difficult to swallow.

Testing with his hand,

he realized that the ashes were cold.

The demon tigers were still far away,

so he gathered his jerky and returned to his journey.

Zha Dong Pi Ran,

to rescue Meng Shi Cai Zou, didn't know how many mountains he crossed.

During the day he walked under the scotching sun,

and at night he walked along the moon.

He had no fear of the high mountains and long rivers,

or dense forests and steep slopes.

Shortly after noon one day,

he walked into a mountain gully.

He saw yet another pile of ashes under a tree,

which made Zha Dong Pi Ran happy.

Again, taking out the beef jerky,

he quickly pushed it into the ashes.

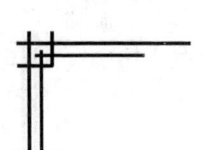

金笛 Jin Di

他在旁边等一阵，
掏出干巴咬一口。
干巴焐得热乎乎，
也还勉强咽下喉。
伸手进去探一探，
灰堆冒烟正烫手。

他想魔虎已不远，
信心百倍朝前走。

跨过一座天生桥，
登上一个小山包。
扎董丕冉擦把汗，
放开眼睛四处瞧。
路边又有一堆灰，
扎董丕冉呵呵笑：
"这灰堆定然有来历，
定是情人设下的指路标！"
心头高兴手脚快，
赶忙打开麻布包。
拿出一块干巴来，
把它放在灰上烤。
灰里火炭还发红，
烤得青烟往外冒。
这块干巴肥又大，
又宽又厚难得烤。
可是因为火炭红，
咂袋辣烟就熟了。

第八章 沉睡 Chapter Eight Deep Sleep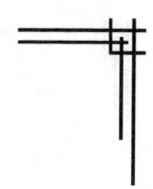

After standing by for a while,
he took it out and had a bite.
The jerky was hot,
but with some effort Zha Dong Pi Ran ate it.
Reaching out his hand to get a feel,
he saw smoke from the ashes and felt his hand burning.

He knew that the tigers were not far away
and confidently marched forward.

After crossing a natural bridge,
he reached the top of a small hill.
Zha Dong Pi Ran wiped the sweat
and looked around.
There was another a pile of ashes,
which made Zha Dong Pi Ran smile:
"The piles of ashes must have their story,
must be the road posts left by my beloved!"
Elated, he acted quickly as well
to unpack his burlap bag.
He took out a piece of jerky
and warmed it up on the ashes.
The charcoal in the ashes was still burning,
and the jerky was smoking.
This piece of jerky was big,
broad and thick and hard to cook.
But the burning charcoal
got it ready in the time of a pipe of smoke.

金笛 Jin Di

又香又软很好吃,
越吃越觉得有味道。
大口嚼来大口咽,
津津有味吃个饱。
灰堆旁边布满虎脚迹,
魔虎定然离得很近了。
吃完干巴赶路程,
杀虎的日子快到了!

扎董丕冉呀,
抽出那把大长刀,
迈开双脚大步跑。
步步踩着虎脚迹,
沿着小路上山腰。
穿过芭蕉林,
走过黑猪坳,
来到魔虎山,
山高岩陡峭。
千个石峰拔地起,
巍巍峨峨冲云霄;
万棵树木倚天立,
摇摇晃晃起林涛。
听见一声吼,
呼呼啦啦似虎啸;
看见一堆火,
噼里啪啦在燃烧。
扎董丕冉心里想,
魔虎刚刚过山腰。

第八章 沉睡 Chapter Eight Deep Sleep

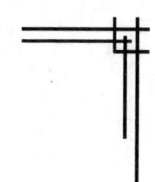

It was soft and delicious
and the more he ate the tastier it became.
He downed one mouthful after another,
relished his meal, and soon had a full stomach.
All around the ash pile were many tigers' footprints,
so he knew the demon tigers were not far away.
He finished his jerky and continued his pursuit,
the date to slay the tigers getting near.

Zha Dong Pi Ran
pulled out his long machete
and ran with large strides.
He followed the tigers' footprints
and went up the mountain along its winding paths.
He went through the Ba Jiao forest
and passed the Hei Zhu gorge.
He came to the demon tiger mountain,
which was immense and precipitous.
Thousands of bluffs rose from the ground
and soared into the sky;
tens and thousands of trees leaned against the sky
and swayed like waves of timber.
He heard a roar,
like the howling of the tigers;
he saw a bonfire burning,
crackling and glowing.
Zha Dong Pi Ran thought to himself,
the tigers just passed the mountainside,

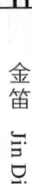

附近深山密林里，
定是它们的窝巢。

二十八

扎董丕冉呀，
爬上一棵大古树，
取出金笛吹起来，
笛声阵阵绕山谷：
"布哩布哩布哩噜，
我恨透那十只虎。
抢我情人进深山，
不知藏在哪一处。
幸好灰堆来指路，
我爬山过水不迷途。
只因我疏忽又大意，
贪睡竟把良机误。
蒙诗彩奏呀，
我的笛声你可听清楚？
请你快快回答我，
好把魔虎尽铲除！"

笛声飞过高山岭，
满山满谷起回音。
林中传为木叶响，
声音悠扬听得清：

第八章 沉睡　Chapter Eight　Deep Sleep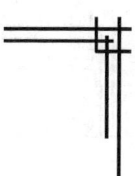

so somewhere around here deep in the dense forest

must be their cave.

28

Zha Dong Pi Ran

climbed up an ancient tree,

taking out the Jin Di and played,

the sound of which floating around the valley:

"Bu li bu li bu li lu,

I detest those ten tigers.

They abducted my beloved

and are in hiding somewhere.

Luckily, with the ash piles leading the way,

I crossed the mountains and wade the rivers without getting

lost.

Due to my carelessness,

I missed a good opportunity.

Meng Shi Cai Zou,

can you hear my Jin Di clearly?

Please reply to me soon,

so that the demon tigers will be eliminated soon.

The sound of the Jin Di rang over the hills,

resonating with the mountains and filling the valleys.

Then from the depth of the woods came the sound of the Mu-

leaf,

melodious and clear:

金笛　Jin Di

"布哩布哩布哩，
误失良机不怪你。
我拿灰堆给你指方向，
你来到虎山路不迷。
现在杀魔虎，
也还来得及。
沿着花路来找我，
我在山洞等着你。
十只魔虎太凶恶，
将我困在山洞里。
快来呀快来吧，
莫再失良机！"

扎董丕冉听到木叶声，
心中焦急如火焚。
虽说情人有下落，
可是被虎缠了身。
抬眼顺着山上望，
小路伸进半山中。
路上撒满小红花，
这是情人把路引。
他从树上跳下来，
踏着花路往前行。

第八章 沉睡 Chapter Eight Deep Sleep

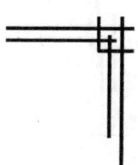

"Bu li bu li bu li,
it was not your fault that the opportunity was missed.
I left the ash piles to guide you,
and you found your way to the tiger mountain.
To kill the demon tigers now
it is not too late.
Follow the flowers on the road to find me,
and I am awaiting you in the cave.
The ten tigers are ferocious,
and they have imprisoned me in the cave.
Hurry up, hurry up,
hurry so that a good opportunity won't be missed again."

Zha Dong Pi Ran listened to the sound of the Mu-leaf,
so worried that he felt his heart was on fire.
Even though he knew where his beloved was,
she was in the midst of tigers.
Looking up at the mountain,
he saw a small path leading up to the mountainside.
Little red blossoms were strewn along the roadside,
the way his beloved was guiding him.
He jumped off the tree
and continued to walk along the flower-strewn road.

第九章　血溅魔窟

二十九

花路左盘右转，
一直通到山巅。
你看扎董丕冉呀，
顺着花路猛追赶。
当他爬到山顶上，
花路突然就中断。
来到这里没有路，
眼前尽是荒草滩。
"蒙诗彩奏在哪处？
蒙诗彩奏在哪边？"
扎董丕冉问苍天，
苍天泛起云片片；
扎董丕冉问大地，
大地默默不开言。
问遍四方无回应，
扎董丕冉心烦乱。
就在路断心急时，
一个奇迹突然现：

第九章 血溅魔窟　Chapter Nine　The Bloody Fight

Chapter Nine　The Bloody Fight

29

The flowery-road zigzaged
all the way up to the top of the mountain.
Behold, Zha Dong Pi Ran
raced along the flowery road.
When he reached the top,
the road with flowers ended abruptly.
There was no road
but marshes as far as his eyes could see.
"Where is Meng Shi Cai Zou?
Where is Meng Shi Cai Zou?"
Zha Dong Pi Ran asked the sky,
but it gave him only the clouds;
Zha Dong Pi Ran asked the earth,
but it gave him only silence.
Having asked to no avail,
Zha Dong Pi Ran became worried.
Just at this moment of desperation,
something marvelous happened:

金笛 Jin Di

一只小蜜蜂,
飞到面前打转转;
一只蝴蝶,
飞到身边绕圈圈。
蜜蜂蝴蝶说了话,
句句话语赛蜜甜:
"扎董丕冉别忧愁,
有心杀虎莫怕难。
请你扒开苦刺棵,
跟着我们上高山。
等到爬上悬岩头,
定会见你情人面。"

蜜蜂蝴蝶前面飞,
扎董丕冉在后撵。
钻过刺棵一丛丛,
攀过藤萝一串串。
看两手,
十个指头都划烂;
摸脸上,
满脸戳得血斑斑。
浑身上下是伤痕,
忍痛赶路咬牙关。
为了杀魔虎,
不怕受苦难;
为了救情人,

第九章 血溅魔窟　Chapter Nine　The Bloody Fight

A little bee
came and started to spin in front of him;
a butterfly
came and started to circle around him.
The bee and the butterfly then started speaking
words so sweet:
"Dong Zha Pi Ran, don't worry,
because if you have the will you can overcome the difficulties.
Please push aside the prickly shrubs
and follow us up the mountain.
When you reach the top of the cliff,
you will see your beloved."

The bee and the butterfly were leading the way,
and Zha Dong Pi Ran kept up closely behind them.
He went through bushes and bushes of prickly shrubs
and climbed a sinewy vine after another.
Looking at his hands,
he saw all ten fingers cut;
touching his face,
he felt the face covered with scratches.
He had wounds all over his body,
but he endured the pain, marched forward, and clenched his teeth.
For killing the demon tigers,
he was not afraid of hardship;
for saving his beloved,

金笛 Jin Di

敢去闯龙潭。
可是道路不平坦,
忽明忽灭多变幻。
来到一座悬岩上,
蜜蜂蝴蝶已不见。

扎董丕冉喊蜜蜂,
不知蜜蜂在何处;
扎董丕冉唤蝴蝶,
不知蝴蝶在哪边。
千声喊来万声唤,
蜜蜂蝴蝶不露面。

扎董丕冉站在岩顶上,
举目四处看。
向左看,
绵绵大山一架接一架,
灰灰蒙蒙连着天;
向右看,
莽莽林海一片连一片,
一眼难得望到边;
向后看,
万丈峭崖一层叠一层,
叫人头晕眼又眩;
向前看,
照妖河里一浪推一浪,
波光粼粼亮闪闪。

第九章 血溅魔窟 Chapter Nine The Bloody Fight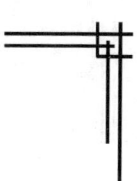

he dared to venture the dragon's lake.
But the road was rugged,
through light, darkness, and vicissitudes.
When he reached the top of an overhanging cliff,
the bee and the butterfly disappeared.

Zha Dong Pi Ran called out to the bee,
but the bee was nowhere to be found;
Zha Dong Pi Ran called out to the butterfly,
but the butterfly was nowhere to be found.
He called again and again,
but the bee and the butterfly never reappeared.

Zha Dong Pi Ran stood on the top of the cliff
and looked round.
He looked to his left
and saw continuous mountains one after another
connecting to the horizon;
he looked to his right
and saw a sea of forests one after another
stretching as far as the eye could see;
he looked behind him
and saw the bottomless canyon with layer upon layer of rocks,
that made people dizzy;
he looked ahead
and saw the Zhao Yao river with its choppy waves
gleaming in the sunlight.

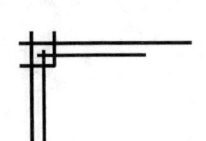

金笛 Jin Di

顺着岩石往下看，
一个大洞悬在半岩间。

蒙诗彩奏坐在岩洞口，
低头绣花手不闲。
扎董丕冉见了她，
又惊又喜又心酸。
路行千里历艰险，
终于见着情人面。
一股激情涌心头，
不觉两眼泪涟涟。
滴滴泪水往下落，
一直落到岩洞前。
正好落在花帕上，
打湿花帕一片片。

蒙诗彩奏很奇怪，
赶忙丢下针和线。
提起花帕抖一抖，
满心狐疑独自言：
"今天是个大晴天，
为何半空落雨点？
淋湿我的摆喳喳，
叫我心中很不安！"
说完又坐下绣花帕，
绣的花帕更鲜艳。

第九章　血溅魔窟　Chapter Nine　The Bloody Fight

Looking down the rock,

he saw a large cave standing in the midsection of the cliff.

Meng Shi Cia Zou was sitting in front of the cave,

with her head down busy embroidering.

Zha Dong Pi Ran, on seeing her,

felt surprised, happy, but also sorrowful.

After a long perilous journey,

he finally saw his beloved.

He felt a surge of emotions

and his eyes were brimmed with tears.

The tears fell drop by drop,

dropping all the way to the front of the cave.

They fell on her embroidery

making it spotty with wet stains.

Meng Shi Cai Zou was surprised

and quickly put down the needle and thread.

Shaking the floral embroidery,

she was confused and said to herself:

"It is sunny today,

so whence came the raindrops?

It rains on my bai zha zha

and makes me feel uneasy!"

Then she sat down again and continued with her floral embroidery,

and its color now became brighter.

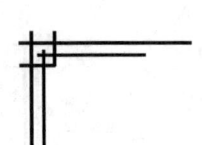

金笛 Jin Di

扎董丕冉有心计,
摘兜野花撒下去。
一把撒在岩洞口,
一把撒在她的衣兜里。
一把一把往下撒,
花朵纷纷落满地。

她看着花朵落下来,
心中不禁又猜疑:
"今天没有刮大风,
为何花朵飞满地?
究竟花朵从哪来?
这事看来很稀奇!"
说完抬头往上看,
心中顿觉惊又喜。
在那高高岩顶上,
扎董丕冉在站立,
向她点头微笑,
向她挥手示意。

蒙诗彩奏呀,
丢下手中的活,
对着岩顶轻轻唱起歌:
"抬头见亲人,
心里真快乐。
多少贴心话,
不知从何说。
魔虎出外去找食,

第九章 血溅魔窟 Chapter Nine The Bloody Fight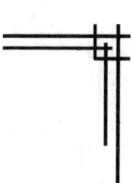

Zha Dong Pi Ran got an idea,
so he plucked some flowers and threw them down.
He threw a handful to the front of the cave
and a handful into her pocket.
One handful after another,
the ground was dusted with flowers.

She saw the falling flowers
and wondered:
"It isn't windy today,
so why are flowers falling to the ground?
Where really are the flowers from?
It seems very odd indeed!"
Having said this, she looked up
and was surprised and happy.
On the top of the cliff,
Zha Dong Pi Ran stood,
nodding and smiling
and waving at her.

Meng Shi Cai Zou
dropped what she was doing
and sang softly towards the top of the cliff:
"Looking up, I saw my beloved,
and my heart is filled with joy.
I have so much to say to you,
but I don't know where to start.
The demon tigers went pillaging for food

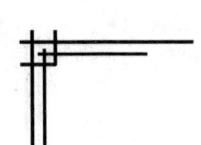

金笛 Jin Di

要到天黑才回窝。
请你快点下山岩,
商量办法斩妖魔!"

扎董丕冉听见这歌声,
心绪如潮猛翻腾。
恨不得身上长翅膀,
立刻飞下悬岩去。
可是眼前没有路,
怪石林立好吓人。
刀削斧劈大岩子,
真是寸步也难行!
他对着岩下轻轻唱,
唱出忧伤和苦闷:
"找到阿妹我高兴,
追上魔虎我痛恨。
只是脚下无路走,
难与阿妹在一起!"

蒙诗彩奏忙回答,
句句话语寄深情:
"岩上有根葛麻藤,
一直挂到石洞门。
顺着藤子梭下来,
就可杀死魔虎雪仇恨。"

扎董丕冉仔细瞧,
果然有根葛麻藤。

第九章 血溅魔窟 Chapter Nine The Bloody Fight

and won't be back to the cave until dark.
Please come down quickly
so that we can talk about the way to slay the tigers!"

Zha Dong Pi Ran listened to the song,
his heart feeling like the rising tide.
He wished he had wings
and could fly down the cliff.
But there was not a road,
but the threatening rocky forests.
The rocks were like knifes and axes,
making it hard for him take a single step!
He sang softly facing the cave,
with sadness and anguish:
"Finding you makes me happy,
and I have caught up to the demon tigers I despise.
But there is not a road I can take,
so it is hard for me to come to you!"

Meng Shi Cai Zou replied quickly,
every word sending her deep feelings:
"There is a Ge Ma vine up there
that can take you all the way to the front of the cave.
Slide down through the vine,
and then you can revenge the demon tigers."

Zha Dong Pi Ran looked carefully
and found that there was indeed a Ge Ma vine.

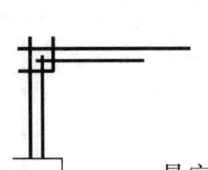

金笛 Jin Di

悬空挂在陡岩上，
随着微风在摆动。
这藤足有九丈长，
叶子长得翠生生；
这藤只有拇指粗，
无权无蔓孤零零。
要想顺藤往下梭，
前后左右无路径。
望着葛藤想一阵，
下岩只有梭葛藤。
为了杀虎报仇恨，
哪管伤身不伤身！

他抓住藤子一蹬脚，
身子下滑像藤云。
离地还有三丈高，
葛藤咔嚓响一声。
蒙诗彩奏抬头望，
真是吃了一大惊。
扎董丕冉往下落，
好像鹞子在翻身。
要是高高摔下地，
定会折骨又断筋。
蒙诗彩奏心一急，
连忙扯开长褶裙。
长裙张开像把伞，

第九章　血溅魔窟　Chapter Nine　The Bloody Fight

Hanging from the steep cliff edge,
it swayed in the breeze.
The vine was at least *nine zhang*① long
with bright green leaves;
it was only as thick as a thumb,
with no branching or twining and all by itself.
To climb down through the vine,
he would have nothing else to help him.
He looked at the vine and thought for a while,
realizing the vine was the only way to the cave.
For slaying the tigers and avenging his beloved,
he didn't care whether he would be hurt!

Holding tight to the vine, he kicked back hard
and started glided down quickly like a vine cloud.
When he was still three *zhang* above the ground,
the vine sanpped with a clicking sound.
Meng Shi Cai Zou looked up
and was startled by what she saw.
Zha Dong Pi Ran was falling
like a sparrow hawk somersaulting in the air.
If he fell to the ground,
he would be in pieces.
Meng Shi Cai Zou was worried
and quickly opened her long skirt.
The skirt opened like an umbrella,

---

① zhang: a unit of length (= 3 1/3 metres).

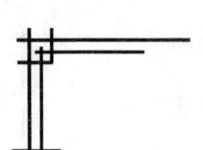

金笛 Jin Di

她把两边抓得紧。
稳稳撑在地面上，
情急生智救情人。
说时迟呀那时快，
一团黑影晃眼睛。
扎董丕冉落下来，
正好落在长裙里。
长裙将他接住了，
没伤骨头没伤筋。

扎董丕冉走下地，
蒙诗彩奏放了心。
情人相逢惊又喜，
哽哽咽咽诉苦情。
她对着他细讲述，
被虎侮辱仇恨深。
他向着她细诉说，
追赶魔虎受苦辛。
哭一阵啊讲一阵，
越讲越觉更伤情。
大树听了垂下头，
小河听了放悲声。
这时魔虎没回来，
洞里显得很寂静。
他俩走进石洞里，
又仔仔细细来谈心。
蒙诗彩奏瘪瘪嘴，
痛哭流涕不成声：

第九章 血溅魔窟　Chapter Nine The Bloody Fight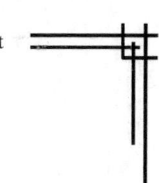

and she held on tight to the two sides.
She set it up steadily on the ground,
her love and worry giving rise to quick thinking.
Quick as a wink,
a black shadowy bundle of black zoomed down in front of her eyes.
Zha Dong Pi Ran fell
right into the long-skirt tent.
Caught by the long skirt,
he broke no bones and hurt no joints.

Zha Dong Pi Ran walked out of the skirt and to the ground,
and Meng Shi Cai Zuo was relieved.
The reunited lovers were both shocked and happy,
sobbing as they told each other their hardships.
She told him in detail
the humiliation by the demon tigers and her hatred for them.
He told her in detail
his pursuit of the demon tigers that was fraught with peril.
They cried and they chatted,
both feeling more and more sorrowful.
On hearing their stories, big trees bowed their heads,
and smaller rivers groaned dolefully.
Since the demon tigers had not returned,
the cave felt very quiet.
They walked into the cave
and continued to talk with each other heart to heart.
Meng Shi Cai Zou pouted
and cried so hard that she could hardly talk:

金笛 Jin Di

"魔虎施计我落井,
从此落进虎掌中。
起先我也曾逃走,
魔虎奸诈没逃成。
后来想逃没有逃,
山高水远路难认。
又怕你来不见我,
误了杀虎大事情。
忍辱含悲过日子,
等你杀虎雪大恨。
顺从魔虎是假意,
等你报仇是真心。
这事你别错怪我,
我说的话是真情。"

扎董丕冉听完话,
心中更觉痛难忍:
"你的遭遇最悲惨,
木叶声里已知情。
是你叫我磨大刀,
磨快大刀除祸根。
我将大刀磨快了,
立刻追虎赶路程。
这事怎能怪罪你,
只怪魔虎太凶狠。
如今我俩得相会,
正好商量大事情。"

第九章　血溅魔窟　Chapter Nine　The Bloody Fight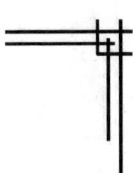

"I fell into the trap set by the demon tigers,
and have been in captivity ever since.
Initially, I did try to escape,
but the demon tigers were so crafty that I failed.
Later I wanted to escape but didn't,
because the mountains were too high and rivers, too long.
I also feared that if you came and I wasn't here,
we would not be able to slay the tigers.
I endured loneliness and resentment,
just to wait for you to slay the tigers and to get even.
I pretended to cooperate with the tigers,
and my heart was waiting for you to fight for justice.
Please do not blame me,
because what I say is true."

Zha Dong Pi Ran listened
and felt more wretched than before.
"You have suffered most miserably,
an experience I have learned from the sound of the Mu-leaf.
It was you who asked me to sharpen the machete
so as to deal with the disaster from its roots.
As soon as the machete was sharpend,
I set out to chase after the tigers day after day.
No one should blame you for what happened,
but only the atrocious demon tigers.
We have reunited now,
a perfect opportunity for us to discuss the next key step."

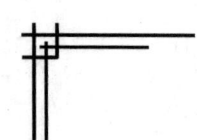

金笛　Jin Di

贴心的话说不完，
离别的苦难诉尽。
你一言呀我一语，
不觉太阳落山顶。
扎董丕冉摘朵花，
放在鼻尖闻一闻。
然后插在她鬓旁，
脉脉向她表深情。

蒙诗彩奏抬头看，
照妖河里现魔影。
十只魔虎排成队，
吼吼叫叫转回程。
魔虎虽然离得远，
照妖河里看得真。
这条河叫照妖河，
能使魔虎现身形。
蒙诗彩奏观动静。
魔虎出门瞧得准，
魔虎回来看得清。
魔虎背上驮牲口，
一定又去糟害人！
扎董丕冉也来看，
越看心中越愤恨。
唰啦抽出那金笛，
凑到嘴边吹几声：
"布哩布哩布哩布哩，

第九章　血溅魔窟　Chapter Nine　The Bloody Fight

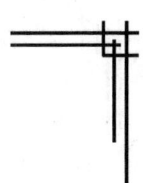

They could talk endlessly
about their sufferings while they were apart.
They talked and listened to each other
and without realizing it the sun already touched the mountain top.
Zha Dong Pi Ran plucked a flower
and smelled it.
He then put it in her hair and by her ear
to show his love for her.

Meng Shi Cai Zou looked up
and saw the demonic reflection in the Zhao Yao river.
The ten demon tigers were in a line,
howling and roaring on their way back.
Even though they were still far away,
they could be seen clearly in the Zhao Yao river.
The river was called Zhao Yao
because it revealed their true demonic shape.
Meng Shi Cai Zou watched closely.
She could always see when they went out,
and when they returned.
They now were carrying animals on their backs
so they must have just robbed more people!
Zha Dong Pi Ran also came over to look,
but the more he saw, the angrier he became.
Whoosh, he took out his Jin Di,
put it close to his mouth, and played:
"Bu li bu li bu li bu li,

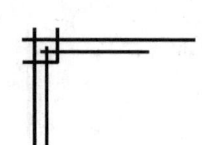

金笛 Jin Di

看见魔虎我愤恨。
它们扰乱村和寨,
抬走牛马又吃猪。
糟害牲口又伤人,
蒙诗彩奏受侮辱。
为救阿妹我今入虎穴,
历尽人间千般苦。
今天我要拼一场,
杀死十只大魔虎!
我要剥它们的皮,
我要吃它们的肉!"

扎董丕冉一吹完,
抽出大刀舞起来。
大刀舞得呼呼响,
好像蛟龙闹大海。
只见刀光不见人,
蒙诗彩奏看着发了呆。
两只眼睛眨不下,
半天她才醒过来。
赶紧拿起木叶吹,
对着阿哥表心怀:

"布哩布哩布哩布哩,
魔虎作乱人焦急。
叫声阿哥听我讲,
阿妹有话告诉你。
十只魔虎威力大,

第九章 血溅魔窟 Chapter Nine The Bloody Fight

the sight of the demon tigers makes me angry.
They loot villages
and rob villagers of their animals.
They hurt animals and people,
and they violated Meng Shi Cai Zou.
To save my beloved, I entered into the tiger's den today
and have endured all kinds of torment.
Today is the time for the showdown,
and I will slay the ten demon tigers!
I will skin them
and eat their flesh!"

As soon as Zha Dong Pi Ran was done playing
he swung his big machete.
The machete sounded like wind
and like the dragon was stirring up the sea.
All that could be seen was the shiny blade, not him,
and Meng Shi Cai Zou was transfixed by the sight of this.
Her eyes were not blinking,
and it took her a while to recover.
Quickly, she picked up the Mu-leaf
and to express her feelings to her beloved.

"Bu li bu li bu li bu li,
the disturbance by the demon tigers is worrisome.
My dear, please listen to me,
for I have a few words to tell you.
The ten tigers are so powerful

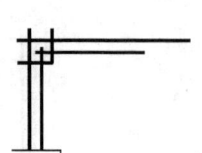

金笛 Jin Di

四方猎人也难敌。
多少猎人来打虎,
个个死在虎口里。
单人独手难对付,
杀虎还需施巧计。"

"四方猎人没本事,
个个死在虎口里。
我的本事最高强,
不杀魔虎不见你!"

"你的本事我知晓,
千人万人不如你。
可是魔虎法力大,
不可粗心大意。

我也有点小本事,
也想设法逃出去。
怎奈魔虎太凶恶,
只得忍下这口气。"

吹完就往前面看,
魔虎已经过小溪。
眼看魔虎要回窝,
蒙诗彩奏拿主意。
事事赶紧准备好,
慢了一步来不及。
夺下阿哥手中刀,

第九章 血溅魔窟 Chapter Nine　The Bloody Fight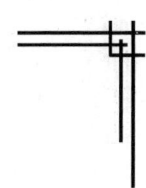

that even hunters found them a handful.
So many hunters have come to hunt the tigers,
but all lost their lives to the tigers.
You're all by yourself,
so to slay them requires strategy."

"Those hunters were incompetent,
the reason they lost their lives to the tigers.
I am the most competent,
and I won't see you until I kill all of them."

"I know you're competent,
more so than many, many others.
But the demon tigers have demonic power,
so do not take them lightly.

"I, too, am competent in my way
and also tried to escape.
But the demon tigers were so atrocious
that I had to wait."

When she finished playing, she looked ahead
and saw that the demon tigers had crossed the stream.
At any moment now they would be back at the den,
so Meng Shi Cai Zou must act.
She must quickly get everything ready
without a moment's delay.
She snatched the sword from the hand of his beloved

将它插进刀鞘里。
把嘴凑在他耳边,
悄悄讲了好几句。
扎董丕冉点点头,
暗夸阿妹有心计。

三十

蒙诗彩奏的话呀,
扎董丕冉记心上。
瞧他一点不作声,
蹲在岩洞石壁旁。
蒙诗彩奏拿长裙,
紧紧盖在他身上。
她又搬块大石头,
支在石洞正中央。
坐在石上绣花帕,
一针一线绣得忙。
洞里显得很平静,
她也显得很安详。

只听一阵嗷嗷叫,
叫声震山冈。
大魔虎一纵进了洞,
驮来一匹青骠马。
它拿鼻子四处闻了闻,
张开大口说了话:
"怎么有股甜酒味?
你吃了甜酒才绣花?"

第九章 血溅魔窟 Chapter Nine The Bloody Fight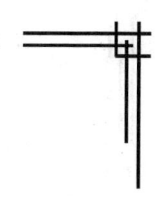

and put it into the sheath.
She whispereed into his ears
for a while.
Zha Dong Pi Ran nodded,
impressed with the smarts of his beloved.

30

Meng Shi Cai Zou's words
Zha Dong Pi Ran kept in mind.
He was silent,
squatting by the sidewall of the cave.
Meng Shi Cai Zou took out the long skirt
and covered him tightly head to toe.
She then put a large stone
in the middle of the cave.
Sitting on the stone and embroidering,
she was busy working one stitch at a time.
The cave felt very calm,
and she seemed very peaceful.

Suddenly came the howling
that shook the mountians.
The big demon tiger leaped into the cave
carrying a horse on its back.
It sniffed around
and then opened its mouth asking:
"Why is there the smell of the sweet wine?
Did you have some of it before you started to embroider?

金笛 Jin Di

蒙诗彩奏不惊慌,
若无其事把话答:
"你在外面吃甜酒,
吃得满嘴冒油花。
你把鼻孔张大点,
闻闻你的大嘴巴。
我在家里不出门,
哪有甜酒来吃呀?"

大魔虎放下青骡马,
喘着粗气又说话:
"就算你没有吃甜酒,
总是有人来过啦。
满洞都是生人味,
我说的话不会假。"

"劝你莫要瞎猜想,
这个洞里只有我,
你说哪个来过嘛?"

"要是没有人来过,
你又为何戴朵花?"

蒙诗彩奏吃一惊,
想起头上有朵花。
但她立刻就镇静,
冷言冷语回答它:
"我的脾气有点怪,

第九章　血溅魔窟　Chapter Nine　The Bloody Fight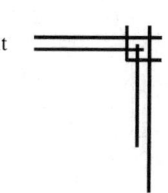

Meng Shi Cai Zou didn't panic
and replied nonchanllantly:
"You had the sweet wine yourself while outside
with oil still on your mouth.
Open your nostrils wider
and smell your own mouth.
I stay at home and do not go anywhere,
and where would I get the sweet wine?"

The big demon tiger put down the horse,
caught its breath, and said again:
"Even if you didn't have the sweet wine,
somebody must have been here.
The cave smell a stranger's smell,
and I cannot be wrong about that."

"Don't think too much,
and I was the only one in this cave.
Who would you say have come?"

"If nobody came,
why are you wearing a flower?"

Meng Shi Cai Zou was taken aback,
remembering now the flower in her hair.
But she quickly recovered
and replied coolly:
"I am a little different from everyone else

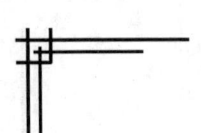

金笛 Jin Di

生来就是爱戴花。
风一吹来花就落。
你看满地都是花。
其中一朵最鲜艳,
我就捡来戴上啦!"

大魔虎听了没话说,
倒在一旁就睡下。

忽听一阵树叶响,
条条树枝在发抖。
二魔虎唰地跳进洞,
驮来一头大牯牛。
它向四周看了看,
粗声粗气问情由:
"甜酒味道这么香,
莫非大嫂吃甜酒?"

蒙诗彩奏不惊慌,
大大方方又开口:
"二弟你别说昏话,
你到外面吃甜酒,
吃进肚子里,
香在鼻洞头。
我在家中坐,
不到外面走,
白酒难吃上,
哪能吃甜酒?"

第九章 血溅魔窟 Chapter Nine The Bloody Fight

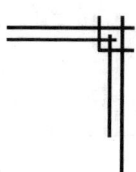

and have always liked to wear flowers.
When the wind blows, the flowers fall,
and that's why the ground is covered with flowers.
One of them was the most beautiful,
the one I put in my hair."

On hearing this, the big demon tiger had no more to say,
and it lay down by the side to sleep.

Suddenly, the tree leaves rustled,
and the tree branches trembled.
The second demon tiger jumped into the cave
with an ox on its back.
It looked around,
and spoke roughly,
"The sweet wine smells so good,
and does this mean my sister-in-law had some?"

Meng Shi Cai Zou kept her cool
and said again confidently:
"Second brother, don't speak nonsense,
when you are the one who had the sweet wine outside.
It went into your belly
and smell good in your nose.
I stayed at home,
never left it,
and could hardly ever have regular wine,
so where could I get the sweet wine?

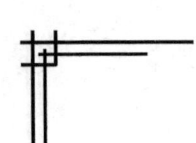

金笛 Jin Di

二魔虎放下大牯牛,
瞅着地面不肯走:
"满地都是人脚印,
这事一定有来头。
就算你没吃甜酒,
也引生人来洞头。"

蒙诗彩奏冷冷笑,
说话滴水也不漏:
"我整天都在洞里走,
我的脚迹处处留。
疑心疑肝生暗鬼,
二弟真是没理由!"

二魔虎一听没话说,
只得讨个没趣头。
倒在地上睡着了,
鼾声呼呼响不休。

又听刮起一阵风,
山间四处如响雷。
三魔虎倏地蹿进洞,
背上驮着一个人。
这人已经被咬死,
浑身上下血淋淋。
三魔虎一进洞里来,

第九章　血溅魔窟　Chapter Nine　The Bloody Fight

The second demon tiger put down the ox,
but staring at the ground he would not leave:
"There are people's footprints all over
and that cannot be right.
Let's say you didn't have the sweet wine,
but you must have had someone here."

Meng Shi Cai Zou gave it a frosty smile
and replied with a perfect answer:
"I move around all day long in the cave,
so of course my footprints are everywhere.
You're overly suspicious, are hallucinating,
Second brother, and are making no sense!"

On hearing this, the second demon tiger had nothing more to say,
only feeling it had just embarrassed itself.
It lay down to the ground and fell asleep quickly,
snoring loudly.

Another gust of wind was blowing,
like thunders striking and echoing everywhere.
The third demon tiger dashed into the cave,
with a person on its back.
The person had already been bitten to death
with blood all over the body.
As soon as the third demon tiger came into the cave,

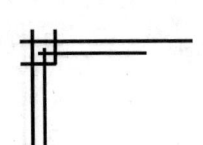

金笛 Jin Di

就用鼻子四处闻,
阴阳怪气大哼哼:
"大嫂在家有福气,
吃了甜酒香喷喷。
咋不留点给我呀,
让我也来开开荤?"

蒙诗彩奏盯住它,
直起嗓子骂出声:
"三弟背上驮着人,
满洞甜酒味正浓。
你吃了甜酒不认账,
还要血口来喷人!
你不说话我不气,
你一说话我生恨。
世间数你无道理,
吃人害人没良心!"

扎董丕冉在裙下,
听说魔虎又吃人。
牙齿咬得格格响,
一腔怒火胆边生。
气得伸手抽长刀,
要跟魔虎来厮拼。

蒙诗彩奏好机灵,
听见裙下有响动,
轻轻咳了一声嗽,

第九章　血溅魔窟　Chapter Nine　The Bloody Fight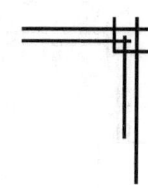

it sniffed around with its nose
and then groaned sarcastically:
"My sister-in-law is fortunate
to stay at home and have the sweet wine that smells so good.
Why didn't you leave some for me
to let me satisfy my craving for the delicacy?"

Meng Shi Cai Zou looked at it in the eye,
scolding it loudly:
"Third brother, you carry a person on your back
and filled the cave with the strong fragrance of the sweet wine.
You yourself had the sweet wine, are denying it,
and are now smearing me as having had it.
I don't get angry when you're quiet,
but as soon as you open your mouth you make me mad.
You're the most unreasonable,
ruthless, and ungrateful!"

Zha Dong Pi Ran, under the skirt,
overheard that the demon tiger killed a person again.
His teeth were grinding,
and he was enraged.
Drawing out the long machete,
he was ready to confront the demon tigers.

Meng Shi Cai Zou was very quick,
and as soon as she perceived the noise under the skirt,

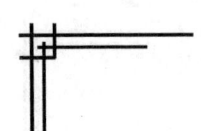

又去按按长褶裙。
暗示阿哥别动手，
免得坏了大事情。
扎董丕冉忍住性，
强压怒火不吱声。

三魔虎生性最狡猾，
看见长裙起疑心：
"大嫂洗的长褶裙，
常常晾在洞外小树丛；
今天却是有点怪，
为何晾在石洞中？
大嫂不要再瞒我，
长裙底下定有人！"
说罢就要掀长裙，
蒙诗彩奏好心惊，
火焰舔着眼眉毛，
急中生智解危境。
她忙丢下针和线，
哎哟哎哟叫几声。
三魔虎赶紧缩回爪，
"大嫂为何叫出声？"

"绣花针儿戳手掌，
赶快找药来止疼！"
说着伸出左手来，

第九章　血溅魔窟　Chapter Nine　The Bloody Fight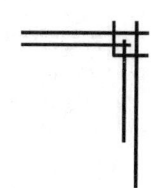

    she coughed slightly

and then pressed on the long pleated skirt.

She was hinting at him not yet to start,

so as not to ruin the plan.

Zha Dong Pi Ran restrained himself,

suppressed his anger, and kept quiet.

    The third demon tiger was the most cunning by nature,

so it became suspicious at the sight of the long skirt:

"Sister-in-law, when you wash the long pleated skirt,

you often dry it on the bushes outside the cave;

isn't it odd that today

you let it dry inside the cave?

My sister-in-law, don't lie to me,

and admit that there is someone under that skirt!"

As soon as it was done talking, it went up to lift the long skirt,

shocking Meng Shi Cai Zou,

who at this extremely critical moment

came up with a way to prevent a crisis.

She put down the needle and thread quickly,

shouting ouch, ouch.

The third demon tiger quickly retracted its claws,

"What are you shouting about?"

    "The needle poked my hand,

so hurry and find some medicine to relieve my pain!"

As she spoke, she showed her left hand,

277

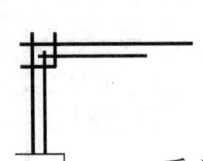

金笛 Jin Di

手心果然有血印。
那血滴滴往下落,
落在地上红殷殷。

三魔虎用力耸耸肩,
放下背上那个人。
张着嘴巴喘口气,
几步蹿出石洞门。
钻进草棵去找药,
找了半晌无音信。

蒙诗彩奏手脚快,
赶紧掀开长褶裙。
示意阿哥进后洞,
大石背后暂藏身。
扎董丕冉跳起来,
闪身跳进后洞中。
蒙诗彩奏真伶俐,
顺手抓个大竹笼,
将笼放在裙底下,
就跟原来一个样。

三魔虎找药进洞来,
看着长裙没变动。
裙下究竟有何人?
疑团还在填心胸。
它一纵身蹿过去,

第九章　血溅魔窟　Chapter Nine　The Bloody Fight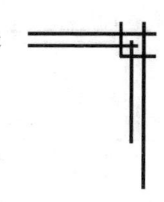

and the palm was indeed blooding.
The blood dropped to the ground,
reddening it.

The third demon tiger shruged its shoulders
and then put person on its back down.
Taking a deep breath,
it ran out in a few steps.
It went into the field to look for medicine,
and wouldn't return for a while.

Now Meng Shi Cai Zou acted quickly
and lifted the the long skirt.
She signaled to her beloved to go into the cave in the back
and to hide behind the large stone for the time being.
Zha Dong Pi Ran jumped up
and dashed into the cave in the back.
Meng Shi Cai Zou was so quick
that she grabed a big bamboo cage,
put it under the skirt,
and made it look just like before.

The third demon tiger returned to the cave from its search for medicine
and noted that the long skirt looked the same as before.
Who was under the skirt?
It had to resolve the suspecion.
Suddenly, it made a dash for it

金笛 Jin Di

用爪扒开长褶裙。
裙下是个竹笼子,
这时它才放了心。

蒙诗彩奏包好手,
假意对它谢大恩:
"三弟心肠最慈善,
愿你多福添寿命!"
她的话是风凉话,
一字一句说得重,
哪是多福添寿命?
分明叫它命归阴!
三魔虎狡猾又愚蠢,
听了反而很开心。
四脚一伸倒下地,
躺在洞里入梦境。

蒙诗彩奏咳声轻,
扎董丕冉出后洞。
重又躲在长裙下,
等待时机报仇恨。

还有其他七只虎,
也跟着陆续回洞里。
个个背上驮牲口,
尽是羊狗猪鸭鸡。

第九章 血溅魔窟 Chapter Nine The Bloody Fight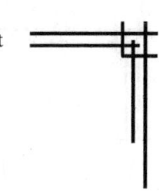

and clawed aside the long pleated skirt.
It was a bamboo cage,
which finally put him at ease.

Meng Shi Cai Zou bandaged her hand
and then feigned her gratitude, saying:
"Third Brother, you are the most charitable,
so may you be happy and live a long life!"
She was sarcastic,
stressing every word,
and how could she really wish it happiness or a long life?
It was a curse!
The third demon tiger was sly but also so thick
that it was happy to hear those words.
With its four feet stretched, it lay down on the ground,
having its dreams in the cave.

Meng Shi Cai Zou coughs lightly again,
and Zha Dong Pi Rang walked out of the cave in the back.
He hid under the long skirt again,
awaiting the opportunity for vengeance.

There were seven other tigers
who, by and by, also returned to the cave.
All carried animals on their backs,
mainly sheep, dogs, pigs, ducks, and chickens.

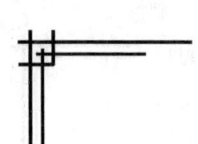

都说洞里来生人,
个个心中犯猜疑。
蒙诗彩奏巧回答,
将虎一一哄出去。
七只魔虎没话说,
个个伸腰躺下地。

三十一

月亮升到东山顶,
茫茫林海多寂静。
十只魔虎睡着了,
洞里处处起鼾声。

蒙诗彩奏坐在石头上,
细听细看察动静;
扎董丕冉躲群下,
紧紧握住长刀柄。
黄昏过后夜深沉,
蛐蛐蛤蟆歇了声。
虎影斑斑满石洞,
石洞里头阴森森。
扎董丕冉举起刀,
猛然掀开长褶裙。
呼地一声站起来,
瞪着一双大眼睛。

第九章 血溅魔窟 Chapter Nine　The Bloody Fight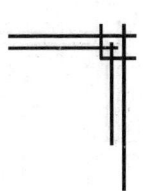

They all said some stranger had been to the cave,
and all were suspicious.
Meng Shi Cai Zou gave each of them a neat reply
and convinced them otherwise.
The seven demon tigers had nothing else to say
and, one by one, they all stretched out and lay on the ground.

31

The moon rose to the top of the Dong mountain,
and the vast forests were silent.
The ten demon tigers fell asleep,
and the sound of snoring filled the cave.

Meng Shi Cai Zou sat on the stone,
carefully listening, watching, observing;
Zha Dong Pi Ran hid under the skirt,
holding tight the handle of the long machete.
After the dusk the night came,
and the crickets stopped chirping and frogs stopped croaking.
The shadowy tigers dotted the cave,
where it was horrid and dark.
Zha dong Pi Ran raised the machete
and suddenly threw off the long pleated skirt.
Zoom, he stood up
with his two big eyes wide open.

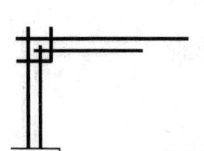

金笛 Jin Di

蒙诗彩奏心一动,
想到这事要冷静。
要是莽撞来行事,
魔虎定然杀不成。
杀虎不成不打紧,
惹来灾祸无穷尽。
赶忙将他强按下,
叫他耐心等时辰。
扎董丕冉没奈何,
只得躲进长褶裙。
大约夜已到三更,
石洞门口月亮明。
蒙诗彩奏站起来,
试探老虎醒没醒。
她拿一个大竹筒,
高高举起过头顶,
然后使劲砸下来,
嘭嘭咚咚发响声。

大魔虎睡得像死猪,
没有听见竹筒声,
二魔虎听了哼一哼,
翻个身就无动静;
三魔虎听了嚷起来,
粗声粗气最难听:
"这是哪样东西响,
吵得叫我睡不成!
半夜三更瞎胡闹,
莫非大嫂生歹心?"

第九章　血溅魔窟　Chapter Nine　The Bloody Fight

Meng Shi Cai Zou thought quickly
and decided they needed to proceed prudently.
If they acted recklessly,
slaying the demon tiger would surely fail.
Failure to slay the tigers would not matter that much,
but its disastrous consequences would be countless.
Hurriedly, she pushed him down
and told him to wait patiently for the right moment.
Zha Dong Pi ran had no choice
but to hide under the long pleated skirt.
By about the midnight,
the moon lit up the entrance of the cave.
Meng Shi Cai Zou stood up,
ready to test if the tigers were awake.
She held a big bamboo barrel,
raised it above her head,
and then threw it down hard,
making the big noise of a bang.

The big demon tiger remained asleep like a dead pig,
not hearing the sound of the bamboo barrel at all.
The second demon tiger made some noise,
turned over, and continued to sleep.
The third demon tiger cried out
with a rough and ugly voice:
"Whatever it is that made such noise,
making it impossible for me to sleep!
Making such noise in the middle of the night,
is the sister-in-law scheming against us?"

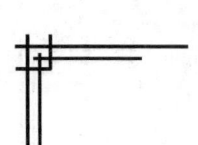

金笛 Jin Di

蒙诗彩奏冷冷笑,
伶牙俐齿说原因:
"我拿竹筒去打水,
竹筒落地发响声。
三弟不必生疑惑,
怪我做事不小心!"
三魔虎听罢呱呱嘴,
闭起眼睛入梦境。

过了一阵夜更静,
蒙诗彩奏又起身。
拿个土罐摔在地,
叭的一声碎片飞。
十只魔虎都没醒,
呼呼大睡没吱声。
看来魔虎已睡熟,
可是她仍不放心。
这个时候最要紧,
更须沉着又冷静。
要是稍稍有疏忽,
横生岔事理不清。
凝神沉思好一会,
她又拿起绣花针。
先去戳戳大魔虎,
看它会醒不会醒。
大魔虎接连挨两针,
也不听它哼一哼。
看来它是睡熟了,

第九章　血溅魔窟　Chapter Nine　The Bloody Fight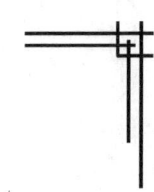

Meng Shi Cai Zou laughed coldly
and offered a ready explanation:
"I took the bamboo barrel to go fetch some water
but dropped it and made some noise.
Third Brother, you don't need to be suspicious,
because it was just my carelessness!"
On hearing this, the third demon tiger clicked its tongue,
closed its eyes, and went back to sleep.

After another while, the night was even quieter,
and Meng Shi Cai Zou got up again,
She threw a clay jar to the ground,
and, with a sudden crash of the jar, its fragments were shattered all over.
None of the ten tigers woke up or made any sound.
It seemed that they were all in a deep sleep,
but she was still unsure.
This was the most crucial moment
and required most calm and clearest-thinking.
One misstep
could lead to unresolvable disasters.
Contemplating for another long while,
she picked up an embroidering needle.
First, she poked the big demon tiger
to see whether it would wake up.
The big demon tiger was poked twice,
but it didn't utter a sound.
It seemed to be in a deep sleep,

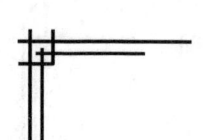

金笛 Jin Di

蒙诗彩奏放了心。
再去戳戳二魔虎,
二魔虎只是翻个身。
看来它也不会醒,
蒙诗彩奏又放心。
又去戳戳三魔虎,
三魔虎嗷地吼一声,
骨碌翻身跳起来,
瞪着一双蓝眼睛:

"大嫂为何来捣乱,
可是出了大事情?
我才刚刚睡着了,
你又将我来吵醒!"
说着张开血盆口,
样子凶恶又狰狞。

蒙诗彩奏忙回答,
假装跟它献殷勤:
"三弟也真太小气,
何必发怒吓唬人。
我跟你们来这里,
一无戚来二无亲。
你们整天出门去,
我在洞里孤零零。
要想说话没说处,
要想唱歌没人听。
整天低头绣花朵,

第九章 血溅魔窟 Chapter Nine The Bloody Fight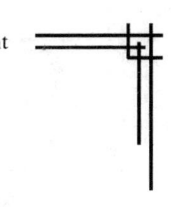

and Meng Shi Cai Zou felt good.
She then poked the second demon tiger,
who only turned over once.
It did seem like it would wake up,
and Meng Shi Cai Zou felt good.
She then poked the third demon tiger,
who gave a loud roar,
turned over, jumped up,
and opened wide its blue eyes.

"Sister-in-law, why do you bother me?
Did something bad happen?
I just fell asleep,
but you woke me up again!"
With its bloody mouth open and shouting,
it looked ferocious.

Meng Shi Cai Zou quickly replied,
pretending to try to please it:
"Third Brother, don't be so petty,
with such anger that frightens me.
I came here with all of you
and do not have a relative.
You go out for a whole day,
but I am lonely in the cave.
When I want to talk to someone, no one can be found,
and if I want to sing, no one listens.
With my head down, I embroider all day long,

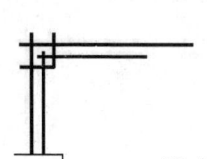

没有趣头心烦闷。
现在看你没睡着,
跟你说话散散心。
谁知你竟不通情,
发威逞凶现兽性!"

蒙诗彩奏一番话,
三魔虎听了很高兴:
"叫声大嫂莫见怪,
我的脾气生来愣。
得罪大嫂好多回,
还望大嫂莫认真。
大嫂好意我认得,
怪我身子太疲困。
整天串村又串寨,
累得腰酸脚又疼。
无力跟你款百话,
有话明天再慢叙。"
说完倒下又睡着,
戳它几下不会醒。

三十二

十只魔虎都戳过,
戳弯一根绣花针。
有的被戳醒来了,
有的再戳也不醒。
不会醒的别管它,

第九章 血溅魔窟 Chapter Nine The Bloody Fight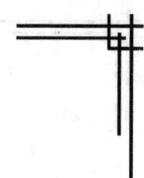

feeling bored and listless.
Now that you are still awake,
I thought I could talk with you to relax a little.
Who knew you are so mean,
irritable, belligerent, showing your bestial nature!"

Those words by Meng Shi Cai Zou
made the third demon tiger feel flattered.
"My dear Sister-in-law, don't be cross with me,
I was born a straight-shooter.
Many times have I offended you,
but I hope you don't mind.
I know your kindness,
but it is just that I am too tired.
Ransacking village after village every day,
I am exhausted with a sore back and aching paws.
I have no energy left to chat with you,
so let's visit tomorrow."
Once done talking, it went back to sleep,
and didn't wake up even after several pokes.

32

Now that all ten tigers had been poked,
the embroidery needle was bent.
Some of them woke up,
and others did not.
Those that didn't wake up were left alone

金笛 Jin Di

让它各自去做梦。
对于醒的怎么办?
就用巧语将它哄。
等到过了许多时,
她又挨个戳几针。
魔虎睡得更昏沉,
从大到小戳不醒。

杀虎时机来到了,
赶忙掀开长褶裙。
扎董丕冉跳起来,
站在洞里抖抖身。
长刀舞得像闪电,
双脚跳得旋风生。

像进地里砍南瓜,
像上山去割麻秆,
左砍右剁呼呼响,
杀得魔虎遍地滚。
地上淌满魔虎血,
石壁溅满虎脑髓。
钢刀捅出虎肠子,
手指抠烂虎眼睛。
刀光闪闪石岩抖,
血肉横飞天地惊。
一刀捅死十魔虎,

第九章 血溅魔窟 Chapter Nine The Bloody Fight

in their dreamland.
But what did she do to those who did wake up?
She coaxed them with clever words back to sleep.
After a long while,
she poked them again one by one.
The demon tigers were sleeping even more soundly now,
and none of them was poked awake.

The time to slay the tigers had arrived,
so she quickly lifted the long pleated skirt.
Zha Dong Pi Ran jumped out
and shook himself a couple of times.
Then his long machete was swung like lightning,
and his feet were twirling like a tornado.

It was like harvesting the pumpkins in the field,
or cutting the flax stalks in the mountains.
Hacking left and hewing right, thwack, thwack, thwack,
he slayed the demon tigers who were rolling all over the ground.
The ground was covered with the tigers' blood,
and the cave wall was splattered with the tigers' gory brain.
He ripped out the tigers' insides with his machete,
and dug out their eyes with his fingers.
The machete was flashing, and the rocks were shivering;
the blood and flesh were flying, and heaven and earth were astounded.
He killed the tenth demon tiger with one stab

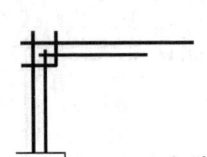

金笛 Jin Di

九魔虎又丧了命。
刚刚剁了八魔虎，
七魔虎又归阴。
从小到大杀过来，
一刀一个不落空。
当他杀死四魔虎，
不慎绊着长褶裙。
连人带刀跌在地，
正好把三魔虎碰醒。
它嗖地一下跳起来，
气势汹汹要拼命。
扎董丕冉不惊慌，
故意躺着不动身。
等到魔虎扑过来，
他才使出好本领。
刀把支在地面上，
刀尖直指虎喉咙。
任这魔虎再狡猾，
也难逃脱这一招。
三魔虎朝他一扑下，
脖颈戳个大窟窿。
它仰天伸伸脚，
滚在一旁丧了命。

大魔虎和二魔虎，
这时一齐被惊醒。
它们弹脚翻起身，
一只左边扑，

第九章 血溅魔窟 Chapter Nine The Bloody Fight

and next killed the ninth demon tiger.
Right after he chopped up the eighth demon tiger,
he sent the seventh demon tiger to the underworld.
From the younger to the older,
each was done with one single strike.
But when he slayed the fourth tiger,
he tripped on the long pleated skirt.
Falling on the ground with his machete,
he woke up the third demon tiger.
Whiz, it jumped up,
truculent and desperate.
Zha Dong Pi Ran kept his calm,
deliberately lying on the ground motionless.
Just when the demon tiger was about to pounce,
he showed his expert skill.
With the handle of the machete propped against the ground,
the tip of it aimed right at the throat of the tiger.
Even though the tiger was sly,
It could not outmaneuver this ploy.
Pouncing, the third demon tiger
ended up with a big hole in its neck.
Stretching out its feet and lying on its back,
it then rolled over to the side and died.

The big and second demon tigers
were then startled to wide-awakeness.
They kicked their feet, flipped over, and jumped up,
one lunging from the left,

金笛 Jin Di

一只右面攻，
齐向扎董丕冉扑过来，
又吼又咬又撕蹬。
扎董丕冉沉住气，
力敌二虎显威风。
大刀舞得团团转，
前三后四使劲挡，
左五右六奋力拼，
两只魔虎难招架，
被杀得遍地乱打滚。
扎董丕冉一弹脚，
身子腾在半空中，
奋力一刀劈下来，
二魔虎刀光闪处丧了命。

大魔虎见十个弟兄死九个，
气得头发晕。
眼睛鼓得像尿泡，
大吼一声如雷鸣。
大口张得像铜盆，
牙齿尖得像铁钉。
拼着老命撞过来，
扎董丕冉一时站不稳，
右脚一滑扑下地，
躺在地上打个滚。
他不立刻爬起来，

第九章 血溅魔窟 Chapter Nine The Bloody Fight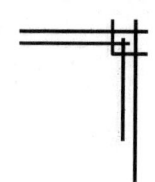

the other attacking from the right,
both charging at Zha Dong Pi Ran,
roaring, biting, tearing, and kicking.
Zha Dong Pi Ran kept his cool,
fearless and ready to take on both of them.
The machete was swinging,
three and four strikes warding off the tigers,
five and six strikes charging at the tigers,
who, being no match,
were rolling on the ground.
Zha Dong Pi Ran kicked the ground hard,
bounced up in midair,
then hacked down with a hard strike,

and finished the second demon tiger with a flash of his machete.

The big demon tiger saw that nine of the ten siblings were dead
and became dizzy with anger.
With its eyes bulging like two full bladders,
It roared like a thunderclap.
Opened up its mouth big like a copper pot,
it showed its fangs that were sharp like iron nails.
When it lunged desperately,
Zha Dong Pi Ran lost his footing,
as his right foot slipped
and he rolled once on the ground.
He didn't get up right away,

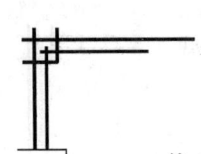

金笛 Jin Di

伏在地上养精神。
大魔虎以为得手了,
张开嘴巴想咬他的后脖颈。
这时扎董丕冉一躬腰,
来个岩鹰巧翻身。
呼的一声跃起来,
一步窜出石洞门。
大魔虎一嘴咬下去,
咬着那个大石墩。
嘴巴哪有石头硬,
磕得满嘴血淋淋。
这下蒙羞更恼怒,
四脚一纵出洞追。
扎董丕冉不慌乱,
舞起长刀又来拼,
忽左忽右进又退,
忽高忽低捷如飞。
瞧他越斗越勇猛,
各路刀法学得精。
头上三刀光闪闪,
脚下三刀冒火星;
身前三刀龙现爪,
身后三刀凤翻身;
东西三刀鬼也哭,

第九章 血溅魔窟 Chapter Nine The Bloody Fight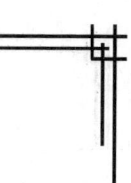

lying on the ground to ready himself.

The big demon tiger thought it won,

opened its mouth, and went for the nape of his neck.

At that time, Zha Dong Pi Ran pulled the four limbs up

and turned over like an eagle.

With a flutter, he jumped up

and then bolted out of the mouth of the cave.

The big demon tiger bit a big bite

of the rock.

Being no match for the rock,

its fangs were knocked out and its maw was dripping with blood.

Humiliated, it became even more exasperated,

and kicking back its four feet, it chased out of the cave.

Zha Dong Pi Ran was very calm,

swinging his long machete to fight again,

now left, now right, now charging, now guarding,

now high, now low, like a bird flying.

Behold, the more he fought, the braver and harder he fought,

using all the techniques he had mastered.

Three strikes upward, his machete was gleaming,

and three strikes downward, his machete was sparkling;

three strikes in front of him, he did the dragon claw,

and three strikes behind him, he did the phoenix somersault;

three strikes to the east and west, he did the cry of the ghosts,

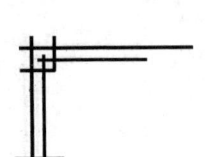

金笛 Jin Di

南北三刀神也哼。
大魔虎哪里能招架？
跌跌撞撞乱扑通。
死到临头心不甘，
狠命一扑山压顶。
扎董丕冉被压着，
只觉眼花头发晕。
因他连杀九只虎，
力气也就减几分。
他想挺胸鼓鼓劲，
可是双脚站不稳。
身子一晃要跌下，
刀法也就不严谨。
魔虎看到这空隙，
拼命一扑力千钧。
蒙诗彩奏心一震，
急得冷汗湿手心。
危急之中强镇定，
连忙抓起长褶裙。
她把长裙甩过去，
紧紧罩住魔虎身。
魔虎被罩动不得，
晕头转向乱打滚。
扎董丕冉举起刀，
照准虎心狠使劲，
只听魔虎一声嚎，
褶裙下面血水喷。

第九章 血溅魔窟 Chapter Nine The Bloody Fight

and three strikes to the south and north, he did the moaning
of the deities.

How could the big demon tiger be the match for all this?
Stumbling around, it was struggling like it was drowning.
But it would not give up on giving a last try
and pounced again from the top down.
Under the tiger, Zha Dong Pi Ran
felt dizzy and saw stars in front of his eyes.
Since he had killed nine tigers without a break,
he wasn't as strong as before.
He wanted to raise his chest and stand firm,
but he was losing his footing.
This body swaying to one side,
he wasn't as accurate at aiming his machete.
The tiger seized this moment
and used all it had to overpower him.
Meng Shi Cai Zou was terrified,
so worried that her hands were wet with cold sweat.
Facing another possible crisis, she forced herself to keep calm
and snatched up the long pleated skirt.
Whipping it,
she tightly netted the demon tiger.
The tiger couldn't move,
rolling aimlessly in circles.
Zha Dong Pi Ran raised his machete,
aimed at its heart, and stabbed very hard.
A howling of the demon tiger was heard,
and the blood was sprouting under the pleated skirt.

第十章　苦守坟台

三十三

十只魔虎被斩除。
灾难过去得幸福；
黑夜之后是黎明，
朝霞朵朵映山林。
扎董丕冉拿起刀，
将十只虎皮全剥尽。
再拿虎肉做干巴，
又把虎心虎肝烧熟吃一顿。
挑起干巴和虎皮，
双双爬上悬岩顶。

蒙诗彩奏前边走，
扎董丕冉后面跟。
有说有笑回家转，
顺着山路结伴行。
走了一程又一程，

第十章　苦守坟台　Chapter Ten　The Tomb Guard

Chapter Ten   The Tomb Guard

33

The ten demon tigers were eradicated.
After adversity was happiness,
just like after the dark night was the dawn,
with the morning clouds deflecting the sunlight on mountains and forests.
Zha Dong Pi Ran picked up the machete
and skinned all ten tigers.
He used the flesh to make the tiger jerky
and had a meal of tiger livers and hearts.
Carrying the jerky and the tiger skin,
they climbed up to the top of the cliff together.

Meng Shi Cai Zou was walking in front,
and Zha Dong Pi Ran was following behind.
Talking and laughing,
they travelled along the mountain paths in each other's company.
After they walked for a long way,

金笛 Jin Di

忽然天上起乌云。
蒙诗彩奏越走越缓慢,
嘴皮发紫脸发青。
泪水不住往下淌,
点点滴滴湿衣襟。
扎董丕冉问她为哪样,
她只是叹气不出声。
来到扎董丕冉睡觉处,
她的双脚再也迈不起。
啪地昏倒在地上,
口吐白沫四肢冷。
扎董丕冉心焦急,
将她抱进草丛中。
又是嚎哭又是喊,
再哭再喊也不应。
一会她才睁开眼,
喘着粗气哼出声:

"我的阿哥哟,
听我说原因。
魔虎欺侮我,
心中积仇恨。
身陷魔洞里,
灾难无穷尽。
天天想念你,
夜夜噩梦生。
思念太过分,
早已成了病。

第十章 苦守坟台　Chapter Ten　The Tomb Guard

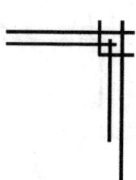

suddenly a dark cloud gathered in the sky.
Meng Shi Cai Zou was walking more and more slowly,
her lips turning purple and her face, blue.
Tears poured down without stopping,
and drop after drop soaked the front of her blouse.
Zha Dong Pi Ran asked her what happened,
but she sighed without uttering a word.
By the time they reached where Zha Dong Pi Ran slept,
she couldn't take another step.
Flop, she slumped down onto the ground,
her mouth foaming and her limbs cold.
Zha Dong Pi Ran was worried
and carried her into a grassy area.
He cried and called her,
but no crying and calling brought him a response.
After a while, she opened her eyes,
and breathing heavily, she murmured:

"My dear,
let me explain.
The tigers abused me,
and hatred was built in my heart.
Trapped in the cave,
I suffered endless injustice.
I missed you every day.
and had nightmares every night,
Suffering from melancholy of longing for you,
I had been sick for a long time.

金笛 Jin Di

杀死十只虎,
阿妹最高兴。
本该得幸福,
共度好光景。
回到家里去,
正好结婚姻。
可是如今我病重,
难得跟你度光阴。
过了一难又一难,
患难夫妻又离分。
这时我心中最难过,
眼睛发花头发晕。
恐怕难得过午时,
阿哥呀,
望你好自奔前程!"

扎董丕冉放声哭:
"我的阿妹呀,
怎能说跟我又离分!
为了你,
我踏遍山和岭;
为了你,
我历尽饥寒和苦辛;
为了你,
我只身闯虎穴;
为了你,
我九死又逢生。
我俩的情意呀,

第十章 苦守坟台 Chapter Ten The Tomb Guard

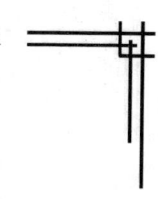

Ridding off the ten tigers
delighted me the most.
We should be happy
and enjoy a good time.
We should go home
and get married.
But now I am too ill
to accompany you any more.
After all the trials and tributlations,
you and I have to part again.
I feel so heartbroken
that I am sick and dizzy.
I am afraid I won't live past noon,
and, my dear,
take care and have a good future."

Zha Dong Pi Ran burst out crying:
"My dear,
how can you talk about parting with me!
For you,
I travelled across mountains and hills;
for you,
I suffered hunger and cold;
for you,
I ventured into the tigers' den alone;
for you,
I survived nine brushes with death.
You and I are destined to be together,

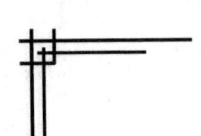

金笛 Jin Di

比路长来比海深。
如今要是没有你,
阿哥我也活不成!"

蒙诗彩奏缓缓说,
声音细得难听真:
"我的阿哥哟,
如今你还正年轻。
一定不能为我死,
不要随便就轻生。
多看几回菜花黄,
多瞧几次荞叶青;
多望几回蜂蝶舞,
多听几次百鸟鸣;
多吹几回芦笙调,
多爬几次花杆顶。
人间快乐都享尽,
也不枉活这一生!
红花绿柳我都爱,
命到尽头爱不成。
眼看午时已快到,
分离就在这时辰!"

第十章　苦守坟台　Chapter Ten　The Tomb Guard

the destiny that is longer than the road and deeper than the sea.

Without you,

I won't last!"

Meng shi cai zou said slowly,

in a voice so feeble that it was barely audible:

"My dear,

you are still young.

You cannot die because of me

and shouldn't take life lightly.

Year after year, watch the greens bear seeds

and look for the buckwheat-scallions turn green;

time after time, appreciate the dance of the butterflies

and listen to the sound of hundreds of the birds;

over and over, play the Lu Sheng music

and climb to the top of the decorated pole.

Enjoy all the happiness of life,

not short-changing yourself!

I love red blossoms and green branches,

but I have reached the end of my road and cannot love them anymore.

It's almost noon,

and I must bid you adieu now!

金笛 Jin Di

"阿哥呀,
我本不愿离开你,
要想跟你度终生。
你若是棵常青树,
我愿做条小青藤,
青藤缠着常青树,
树繁叶茂绿茵茵;
你若是个圆月亮,
我愿做颗小星星,
星星跟着月亮转,
天长地久不离分;
你若是汪池塘水,
我愿做片小浮萍,
浮萍漂在水面上,
追风逐浪紧相偎;
你若是只画眉鸟,
我愿做个小白灵,
百灵画眉共啼鸣,
一唱一合最动听。
可是这些难如愿,
你阳我阴两离分。
我俩若要再团聚,
要看你心真不真。

第十章 苦守坟台 Chapter Ten The Tomb Guard

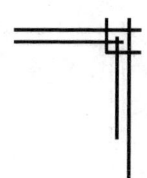

"My dear,

I don't want part with you,

and want to accompany you for the rest of my life.

If you were an evergreen tree,

I will be the small vine

that winds around the evergreen tree,

the strong tree, the luxuriant foliage, and abundance of green;

if you were moon,

I will be the little star

that orbits with the moon,

always together and never apart;

if you were a pond of water,

I will be the common duckweed

that floats on the surface of the pond,

rising and falling as one with the waves;

if you were a thrush,

I will be the little lark

that sings together with the thrush

in chorus and most movingly.

But it's hard for these dreams to come true now,

and you're the *yang*①, and I am the *yin*②, so we are parting our ways.

The reunion of you and me

will depend on how true your love is.

---

① yang: on earth
② yin: in heaven

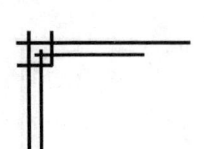

金笛 Jin Di

你若真心爱着我,
将我埋在花丛中。
然后砍根小金竹,
插在我的墓门顶。
你就睡在墓旁边,
天天为我守坟茔。
若是金竹发新芽,
你就刨开我的坟。
将我轻轻扶起来,
连续将我喊几声。
你的喊声惊醒我,
我就重又得生命。
不管三年和五载,
还有指望成婚姻。
要是金竹枯死了,
我就永远不还魂。
你就干净忘记我,
另找姑娘去成亲。"

蒙诗彩奏说完话,
躺在地上不出声。
扎董丕冉大声喊,
再喊她也不答应。
只听天空炸雷响,
大雨哗哗下不停。
蒙诗彩奏真的死掉了,
静静躺着任雨淋。
扎董丕冉拿起魔虎皮,

第十章 苦守坟台　Chapter Ten　The Tomb Guard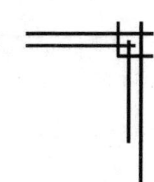

If you truly love me,
bury me among the flower bushes.
Then chop a small golden bamboo
and put it on top of my grave.
You sleep by the grave
and guard it everyday.
If the golden bamboo sprouts,
you dig open my grave.
Gently prop me up,
and call me by my name a few times.
Once your calling wakes me up,
my life returns to me.
It does not matter if it will take three or five years,
there is still hope for us to get married.
But if the golden bamboo withers and dies,
my life will never return to me.
In that case, you should forget about me completely,
and find another young woman to marry."

When Meng Shi Cai Zou finished speaking,
she lay on the ground quietly.
Zha Dong Pi Ran called her,
but no matter how much he called she didn't respond.
Then with an explosive thunderclap in the sky,
rain started to pour down nonstop.
Meng Shi Cai Zou died,
lying peacefully in the rain.
Zha Dong Pi Ran picked up the demon tiger skin

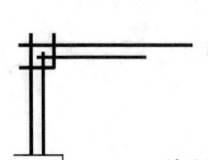

金笛 Jin Di

将她裹了一层又一层。
十张虎皮裹完了,
又拿藤子细细捆。
然后就在花丛中,
冒着大雨刨个坑。
将她埋进土坑里,
又用石头砌座坟。
砍根金竹插在坟头上,
守在坟地不离身。
这时他才放声哭,
山谷四面传悲音。
眼泪打湿坟边草,
山上岩石也伤心!

三十四

守坟五个月,
干巴已吃完。
桃树开了花,
金竹没发芽。

守坟一年多,
野果已摘完。
桃树又开花,
金竹没发芽。

守坟三年整,
草根已挖完。

第十章 苦守坟台 Chapter Ten The Tomb Guard

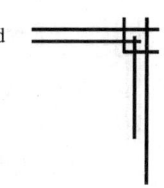

and wrapped her up one layer after another.
He used all the ten pieces of the tiger skin
and then used the vine to tie it up carefully.
Then in the middle of the flower bushes
and in the pouring rain, he dug a grave.
He buried her in the grave
and used the rocks to make the tombstone.
He cut a golden bamboo, stuck it to the top of the grave,
and he started guarding it day and night.
Only then did he burst into crying,
the mournful sound spreading throughout the valley.
His tears watered the grass by the grave
and saddened the mountain rocks!

34

After guarding the grave for five months,
he had eaten up all the jerky.
The peach trees had blossomed,
but the golden bamboo didn't sprout.

Having guarded the grave for a year,
he had picked all the wild berries in the area.
The peach trees blossomed again,
but the golden bamboo didn't sprout.

Having guarded the grave for three years,
he had dug up all the grassroots in the area.

金笛 Jin Di

扎董丕冉看金竹，
金竹仍旧没发芽。

守了三年整，
尝尽苦与辣。
太阳晒金竹，
他拿树叶遮；
大风刮金竹，
他拿衣裳拦；
大雪压金竹，
他忙抖雪花；
可是金竹不发芽，
扎董丕冉呀，
心痛如刀扎。

想起蒙诗彩奏赠手镯，
手捧金镯泪水如雨下，
本说二人结下百年好，
只落得你阴我阳不成家。
如今镯在人不在，
铁打的心肝也碎啦！
扎董丕冉好灰心，
他没心思吹金笛，
也无闲情采野花。
扎董丕冉正伤心，
一对蜜蜂来传话：
"小米种在坡地上，
不到节令不结籽；

第十章 苦守坟台 Chapter Ten The Tomb Guard

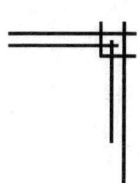

Zha Dong Pi Ran looked at the golden bamboo again,
but it still didn't sprout.

Guarding for three years,
he suffered all kinds of pain and hardship possible.
When the sun would shine upon the golden bamboo,
he shaded it with tree leaves;
when the wind could blow the golden bamboo,
he protected it with his clothes;
when the snow crushed down on the golden bamboo,
he shook off the snowflakes;
but the golden bamboo didn't sprout,
and Zha Dong Pi Ran
felt the pain in his heart.

He remembered when Meng Shi Cai Zou gave him the bracelet,
and with it in his hand he broke into tears.
They promised each other to be together forever,
but now they were *yin-yang* apart from each other.
Now that there was only the bracelet without her,
and it was sad enough to break an ironclad heart!
Zha Dong Pi Ran was so discouraged,
that he was in no mood to play the Jin Di
or to gather the wild flowers.
Just when Zha Dong Pi Ran was the most wretched,
a pair of bees brought words to him:
"The millet that is planted on the hillside
does not bear fruit before its season;

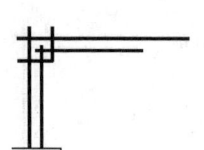

金笛 Jin Di

桃树栽在大路边,
不到时候不开花。
要叫金竹发新芽,
你要耐心侍护它。
金笛你要吹,
野花你要采。
诚心能使天睁眼,
再守十年也不怕!"

扎董丕冉听完话,
摘把野花供坟前。
他又拿起金笛吹,
笛声悠悠四处传:

"布哩布哩布哩布哩,
吹起金笛把情诉。
守坟守了三年整,
金竹越来越干枯。
要到几时才发芽?
要到哪天叶才绿?
蜜蜂使者来安慰,
我才丢开悲和苦。
我要死守在坟前,
誓跟阿妹共堆土。
活着不能在一起,
死了也要埋一处。
哪怕地旋天倒转,
也要守到春色染金竹!"

第十章 苦守坟台 Chapter Ten The Tomb Guard

the peach tree planted by the road
does not blossom before its time.
For the golden bamboo to sprout,
you must care for it patiently.
You must also play the Jin Di
and gather the wild flowers.
True love can open heaven's eye,
so even another ten years can be overcome!"

Zha Dong Pi Ran listened to the bees
and then picked a bundle of the wild flowers and put it in front of the grave.
He then picked up the Jin Di and played,
its sad sound drifting everywhere:

"Bu li bu li bu li bu li,
I play the Jin Di to tell our story.
I have guarded the grave for three years,
but the golden bamboo has been withering away.
When will it sprout?
When will its leaves turn green?
The envoy bee came to comfort me,
and I finally put aside sorrow and pain.
I will guard here in front of the grave till I die
and to be buried with my beloved.
If we can't be together when we are alive,
we will be buried together after we die.
Even if I have to wait till the end of time,
I must guard till the golded bamboo sprouts!"

金笛 Jin Di

扎董丕冉刚吹完,
云间传来木叶声:
"布哩布哩布哩布哩,
叫声阿哥莫焦急。
劝你仔细听我说,
我是山间凤凰女。
见你勤劳又善良,
心中暗暗爱慕你。
知你上山来砍柴,
走出树林来会你。
不幸遇到大魔虎,
穷追猛扑将我欺。
危急之中你救我,
我把金笛送给你。
你在坡上种下米,
我又赶来帮助你。
当你寨上踩花山,
你我想会是良机。
可是我施仙家法,
变成三个小幺女。
将你拦在大路上,
三次纠缠考验你。
考你三次有结果,
知道你果真有诚意。
你只爱着蒙诗彩奏呀,
眼不乱来心不迷!
我又变成蒙诗彩奏哟,

第十章 苦守坟台 Chapter Ten The Tomb Guard

As soon as Zha Dong Pi Ran stopped playing,
the sound of the Mu-leaf came from behind the clouds:
"Bu li bu li bu li bu li,
my dear, do not be anxious.
Listen to me carefully,
a young phoenix-woman from the mountains.
I saw you were diligent and kind
and I fell in love with you.
I knew you would come up to the mountains to cut the firewood,
so I waited and then came out of the forest to meet you.
Unfortunately, I ran into the big demon tiger,
who chased and attacked me.
It was you who rescued me,
so I gave you the Jin Di as a gift.
When you planted the millet on the hillside,
I came again to help you.
The Mountain Treading festival in your village
was a good time for us to meet.
But I used my magical power
and changed into three young women.
Stopping you halfway,
they tested you three times.
After the three tests,
I knew your feelings for me were true.
You loved only Meng Shi Cai Zou,
clear-eyed and single-minded.
I changed back to Meng Shi Cai Zou,

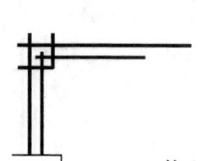

金笛 Jin Di

你见了我多亲昵。
我就跟你把情定，
拿只手镯送给你。
你把项圈送给我，
我的心中也欢喜。
我俩合心又合意，
只愿到老不分离。
谁知你去学芦笙，
魔虎又来将我逼。
魔虎实在太凶恶，
将我抢到山洞里。
你来追杀十只虎，
我俩终于得团聚。
哪知我忧心过了头，
又遭残害成了疾。
死在半路野坝中，
埋在路边花丛里。
你守坟守了三年整，
你的诚心动天地。
你对我的情意真，
你不忍心离开我。
这个地方你睡过，
地上还在冒热气。
我俩的热气润金竹，
金竹发芽我喘息。
如今我已活转来，

第十章 苦守坟台 Chapter Ten The Tomb Guard

and you were so affectionate when you saw me again.

We were engaged,

and I gave a bracelet to you.

When you gave me the necklace,

I was so happy.

You and I were such a perfect match,

that we hoped that we never had to be apart.

Little did we know that when you went to learn to play the Lu Sheng,

the demon tigers came to harass me again.

The demon tigers were so heinous

that they abducted me and took me back to their cave.

You chased and slayed the ten tigers,

and we finally reunited.

But again I didn't know that I was sad for so long

and was abused so much that I fell ill.

I died in the wilderness halfway on our way home

and was buried among the flowers by the roadside.

You've been guarding the grave for three years,

and your love moves heaven and earth.

You love me truly

and could not bear to leave me.

This is the place you've slept in,

and it is still warm.

The warmth from both you and me moistens the golden bamboo,

and when the golden bamboo sprouts, I breathe.

Now I have come to live

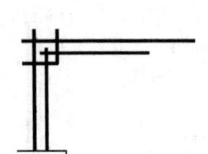

金笛 Jin Di

听见你在吹金笛。
请你抬头看金竹,
青枝绿叶多稀奇。
请你快快刨开坟,
我俩回家成夫妻!"

三十五

扎董丕冉听见木叶声,
像从梦中醒过来。
越听心里越高兴,
眼前突然添异彩:

山更青呀水更绿,
青山绿水更可爱。
抬起头来看金竹,
一看不禁喜心怀。
金竹果然发新芽,
绿叶丛丛像伞盖。
他一下扑到坟头上,
将层层黄土全刨开。

虎皮已经沤烂了,
化成一摊细土块。
他开口高声喊阿妹,
又将她轻轻抬出来。
睁大眼睛看阿妹,
一看他就发了呆。

第十章 苦守坟台 Chapter Ten The Tomb Guard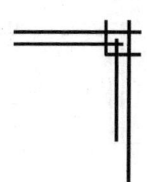

and have heard the Jin Di that you play.
Please look up at the golden bamboo,
whose green branches and leaves are such a wonder.
Please quickly dig open the grave,
so that you and I can go home and get married!"

35

Zha Dong Pi Ran heard the sound of the Mu-leaf,
feeling as if he woke up from a dream.
The more he listened, the happier he felt,
everything in front of him becoming brighter all of a sudden.

The mountains were greener and the rivers, clearer,
and green mountains and clear rivers were lovelier.
Looking up at the golden bamboo,
he couldn't help feeling so very happy.
It really had sprouted
with luxuriant leaves like umbrellas.
He rushed to the top of the grave
and dug away the dirt.

The tiger skin had already rotted
into a clump of fine soil.
He called out for her beloved
and then gently lifted her out.
Opening his eyes wide, he looked closely at his sweetheart
and was stunned by what he saw.

金笛 Jin Di

头发更比原来长,
牙齿更比原来白,
眉毛更比原来弯,
眼睛更加有光彩。
阿妹变得更漂亮,
叫他越看越喜爱。

蒙诗彩奏伸伸腰,
打个哈欠站起来。
她像刚刚才睡醒,
抖抖长裙摸摸腮。
哭泣变成了欢笑呀,
幸福撵走了悲哀!
扎董丕冉拉着她,
翩翩起舞好自在。
一边跳舞一边唱,
歌声传到青山外。
树木听了齐叫好,
小河听了也喝彩。
沿着小路转回家,
翻山越岭多轻快。

来到彝家山,
找到老佑保。
扎董丕冉说:
"我杀死魔虎来见你,
三年前的话我没忘记!"

第十章 苦守坟台 Chapter Ten The Tomb Guard

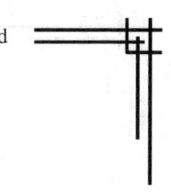

Her hair was longer than before,
and her teeth were whiter than before,
and her eyebrows were curvier than before,
and her eyes were shinier than before.
She had become more beautiful,
and the more he looked at her, the happier he became.

Meng Shi Cai Zou stretched
and yawned before she stood up.
As if just waking up,
she shook her long skirt and touched her chin.
Tears turned into laughters,
and happiness drove away sorrow!
Zha Dong Pi Ran held her hands,
and they danced so happily.
They sang as they danced,
and the song spread beyond the mountains.
On hearing the song, the trees celebrated,
and the rivers cheered.
They walked along the small path to go home,
and they climbed the mountains with a spring in their steps.

They came to the Yi mountain
and found the old You Bao.
Zha Dong Pi Ran said:
"I've killed the demon tigers and come to see you,
and I never forgot what I said three years ago!"

金笛 Jin Di

来到瑶家山，
找着咪尼娇。
扎董丕冉说：
"我杀魔虎来见你，
三年前的话我没忘掉！"

来到壮家大河边，
又去找彩伊。
扎董丕冉说：
"我杀死魔虎来见你，
三年前的话我牢记在心底！"

三年的时光多漫长，
像是隔了千万代；
阴间阳间离得远，
隔着两个大世界。

扎董丕冉最真诚，
含辛茹苦守坟台。
沉沉黑夜过去了，
东方白天地开。

第十章 苦守坟台 Chapter Ten The Tomb Guard

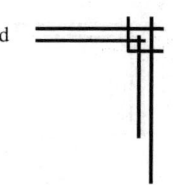

They came to the Yao Jia Mountain
and found Min Ni Jiao.
Zha Dong Pi Ran said:
"I've killed the demon tigers and come to see you,
and I never forgot what I said three years ago!"

They came to the Zhuang village by the river
and went to see Cai Yi again.
Zha Dong Pi Ran said:
"I've killed the demon tigers and come to see you,
and I remember what I said three years ago!"

Three years felt like a long time,
like tens and thousands of generations;
the living and the dead were far apart,
separated into two worlds.

Zha Dong Pi Ran's love was the most true,
and he endured harrowing experience in guarding the grave.
Now the dark night had passed,
and the sun was rising in the eastern sky.

第十一章　悲去喜来

三十六

蒙诗彩奏前边走，
扎董丕冉后面跟。
不觉来到寨子边，
忽听寨里起闹声。
他俩走进寨子里，
看见房前站满人。
家里打响牛皮鼓，
屋里吹响大芦笙？
为啥要打牛皮鼓？
为啥要吹大芦笙？
大鼓咚咚能传话，
芦笙呜呜能传情。
扎董丕冉最懂事，
蒙诗彩奏也聪明。
知道大鼓传话召亲戚，
明白芦笙传情唤寨邻。
亲戚朋友一齐来，
正在办丧悼亲人。

第十一章 悲去喜来 Chapter Eleven New Beginning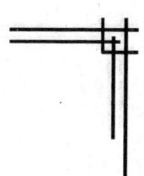

Chapter Eleven　New Beginning

36

Meng Shi Cai Zou walked in front,
and Zha Dong Pi Ran was behind her.
By and by, they came to the edge of his home village
where it was noisy.
They went into the village
and saw many people standing in front of a house.
Inside the house, the drum was playing
and so was the Lu Sheng.
Why did they play the drum?
Why did they play the Lu Sheng?
The drum could tell a story,
and the Lu Sheng could express feelings.
Zha Dong Pi Ran understood,
and Meng Shi Cai Zou also knew,
The drum was spreading the word to the relatives,
and the Lu Sheng was spreading the feelings to adjacent villages.
Relatives and friends came together
to commemorate and mourn the dead.

金笛 Jin Di

你看吧，
那边人有人擤鼻涕，
这边有人擦眼睛。
哭哭啼啼真凄惨，
嘘嘘叹叹好伤心。
扎董丕冉很奇怪，
蒙诗彩奏也吃惊。
心想莫非阿支过了世？
又想莫非阿奈归了阴？
二人不禁心酸难忍耐，
哇地一下哭出声。
呼天唤地肝肠断，
串串珠泪往下滚。

扎董丕冉拉阿妹，
一步一步往前行。
上前没有走几步，
又见场上挤满人。
有的跳芦笙，
有的招灵魂，
有的刮牛头，
有的剁牛筋，
有的切牛肉，
有的抱柴薪，
有的忙接客，
有的搬桌凳。
闹闹嚷嚷好排场，
烟雾腾腾好阴森。

第十一章 悲去喜来 Chapter Eleven New Beginning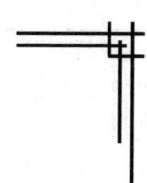

Behold,

some were blowing their nose over there,

and others were wiping tears over here.

They cried so mournfully,

and they sighed so sorrowfully.

Zha Dong Pi Ran was wondering

and Meng Shi Cai Zou was surprised.

Could it be that A Zhi had passed away?

Could it be that A Nai had died?

They couldn't help feeling grieved

and burst into crying.

They called to heaven and they called to earth,

with tears falling down.

Zha Dong Pi Ran held Meng Shi Cai Zou's hand,

going forward step by step.

Before long,

they came to a yard packed with people.

Some were dancing to the Lu sheng,

while others were calling out to the souls,

or shaving the ox heads,

or chopping the beef tendons,

or hashing the beef,

or transporting the firewood,

or greeting the new arrivals

or getting ready the tables and chairs.

What a noisy display,

and what a smoky and gloomy scene.

金笛 Jin Di

二人抬头往前看，
墙角又有巡逻人。
有的吹牛角，
有的拿弯弓，
有的提大刀，
有的喊出声：
"我们在为死者巡逻呀，
要让死者能安心。
白天巡逻三回得清静，
夜晚巡逻三次得太平！"
到底死了什么人？
二人心里更纳闷。
扎董丕冉带阿妹，
两步跨进自家门。
堂前不见大棺材，
只有两个大簸箕在屋厅。
簸箕上面插篾圈，
看着篾圈好吓人！
一个篾圈在左边，
套着男人新衣裤；
一个篾圈在右边，
套着女人新褶裙。
还有两对小竹卦，
合拢放在簸箕中。
堂中栽根大竹竿，
大鼓挂在竹竿顶。
一人站着打大鼓，
一人绕竿吹芦笙。

第十一章 悲去喜来　Chapter Eleven　New Beginning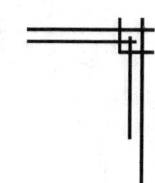

They looked ahead

and found some watchmen in the corner.

Some of them blew the ox-horns,

and others held the bows,

and others had big machetes,

and still others shouted:

"We're patrolling for the dead,

so that they could rest at ease.

We patrol three times during the day for peace,

and three times during the night for quiet!"

Who on earth died?

The two of them became more puzzled.

Zha Dong Pi Ran brought his beloved

into his own home.

No big coffin was seen on the front of the big hall,

but only two big shallow baskets there.

On the baskets were the splinted memorial wreaths,

which looked eerie!

The splint on the wreath to the left

wore the new jacket and pants for a man;

the splint on the wreath to the right wore a new pleated skirt

for a woman.

There were two pairs of bamboo strips,

and each pair was together and placed in one basket.

In the middle of the hall was a big bamboo pole,

from the top of which hung a drum.

One man stood to play the drum,

while another played the Lu Sheng pacing around the pole.

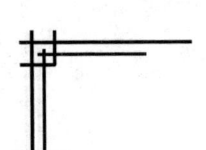

金笛 Jin Di

鼓点伴着芦笙曲,
曲曲调调撕人心。
满屋的人在啼哭,
眼睛哭得红通通。
他们一边揩眼泪,
一边忙着做事情。
有的忙烧香,
有的忙念经,
有的忙磕头,
有的忙烧灵,
有的忙把丧歌唱,
有的忙着收礼金。
只见么公拿着小竹卦,
丢在地上问吉凶。
反复丢了好几次,
直到竹卦一翻一扑手才停。
这卦是个吉利卦,
表示死者活者都安宁。

么公提起一只公鸡,
对着篾圈念几声。
然后活活捏死那公鸡,
剖开鸡肚取鸡心。
再把鸡心拿到火上烤,
烤得满屋香喷喷。
一个鸡心分两半,

第十一章 悲去喜来 Chapter Eleven New Beginning

The drumbeats were accompanied by the sound of the Lu Sheng,
and every tune was heart-wrenching.
Everyone in the room was crying,
eyes red.
They wiped their tears,
as they were busy working.
Some were busy burning the incense,
others chanting,
others kowtowing,
others burning the spiritual-money,
others singing the mourning songs,
and others receiving the monetary donations.
A Me Gong held the small bamboo strips
and then threw them on the ground to divine the future.
He did it several times
and stopped when one bamboo strip was facing up and the other, down.
This was an auspicious sign,
showing that the living and the dead would have peace.

Picking up a rooster,
the Me Gong said a few words to the wreaths.
He then choked the rooster to death
and then cut the chicken belly open and took out its heart.
He then roasted the heart,
and the room was filled with the roasting fragrance.
He cut the roasted chicken heart in half

放在两个簸箕中。
接着倒了两杯酒,
一边一杯摆得正。
口里唱起"指路歌",
慢声慢气听得清:
"鸡是人的伴,
人和鸡同心。
你们吃了这鸡心,
跟这公鸡结伴行。
然后再喝一杯酒,
路行千里有精神。
你们骑在鸡背上,
走起路来快如风。
太阳出来天气热,
翅膀底下好躲荫;
要是老天下大雨,
尾巴下面好藏身。
走到毛虫坡,
鸡会啄完小毛虫;
遇到大灰狼,
鸡会啄瞎狼眼睛;
走到岔路口,
公鸡自会辨西东。
你们的鸡叫起来,
人家的鸡不打鸣,
那就不是你们的亲奶爷,
你们不要去相认;
你们的鸡叫起来,

第十一章 悲去喜来　Chapter Eleven　New Beginning

and then placed each half in one basket.
He then poured two small cups of wine
and placed each straight in front of each basket.
Singing the *Directional Song*,
he sounded deliberate and clear:
"The chicken is the companion of people,
and people's hearts are one with the chicken.
Once you eat this chicken heart,
you will be accompanied by this rooster.
And once you drink the cup of wine,
you can walk a thousand miles energetically.
Riding on the back of this rooster,
you will go fast like the wind.
When the sun rises and heats up the day,
you will find shade under its wings;
if it rains heavily,
you can hide under its tail.
When you get to the slope of the caterpillars,
the rooster will eat all the little caterpillars for you;
when you run into the big gray wolf,
the rooster will peck the wolf blind;
when the road folks,
the rooster knows the way.
If your rooster crows
but others don't respond,
then you haven't found your grandparents,
so do not greet them as if they were;
if your rooster crows,

金笛 Jin Di

人家的鸡也答应，
那才是你们的亲奶爷，
你们就要去相认。
我劝你们莫着急，
我还有话要说明；
要是奶爷出来看你们，
只是站在远处看，
那是别家的奶爷，
你们不要去相认；
要是奶爷出来看你们，
站在近处看，
那是你们的堂奶爷，
你们可以喊一声；
要是奶爷跑过来，
伸开双手搂你们，
那才是你们的亲奶爷，
你们就要去相认。
奶爷住在浑水河那边，
有田有地好耕种。
牛也杀给你们了，
你们安心带着牛去种庄稼；
狗也杀给你们了，
你们好好领着狗去看家门。
我的"指路歌"，
句句唱得清。
顺着我指的大路走，
回到老家找先人！"

第十一章 悲去喜来 Chapter Eleven New Beginning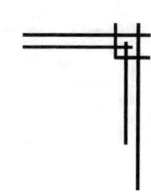

and others' do respond,

then they are grandparents,

so greet them as such.

But I urge you not to be hasty,

because I have something else to tell you;

if the grantparents come out to see you

but only look at you at a distance,

then they are others' grandparents,

and you do not greet them as if they were your own;

if the grandparents come out to see you

and looking at you up close,

then they are your grandparents' relatives,

and you can greet them and call them as such;

if the grandparents run towards you

with open arms and give you a hug,

then they are truly your grandparents,

and you should greet them as such.

They live by the Hun Shui river

and have their own field.

The ox has already been butchered for you,

so be assured that you will have an ox for growing crops there;

a dog has also been killed for you two,

so take it with you to guard the house.

Every word of my *Directions Song* is clear.

Now you walk along the main road I've pointed out for you

and go back to your hometown to find your ancestors!"

金笛 Jin Di

扎董丕冉听罢伤情,
心想家里定是死了两个人。
莫非阿支阿奈双双去世了?
可又不见棺材停在堂屋中。
只有左边篾圈套的男人衣,
还有右边篾圈套的女人裙。
到底死了什么人?
可要细细问分明。
扎董丕冉刚想问,
吹师又吹芦笙来招魂。
扎董丕冉一边抹眼泪,
一边侧耳仔细听。
听出曲曲芦笙调,
吹的都是自己的事情:

"嘀啦哒,嘀啦哒,
啦哒伦罗啦嘀啦,
啦哒伦罗啦嘀啦,
嘀罗伦啦嘀罗啦。
太阳已经落了山,
亲人远去不回家。
月亮出来没有光,
亲友个个把泪洒。
不幸的人儿遭灾难,
山水也在闪泪花。
'蒙嘎祝、蒙嘎老',
哭丧的调子不断吹,

第十一章 悲去喜来 Chapter Eleven New Beginning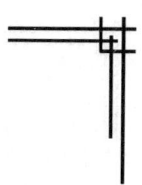

Zha Dong Pi Ran listened

and became more sad because two people in his family must have died.

Could it be that A Zhi and A Nai had both passed away?

But then there should be coffins in the hall.

There were only the man's clothes on the wreath to the left

and the woman's skirt, to the right.

Whoever did pass away?

I have to ask and find out.

Just when Zha dong pi Ran was about to ask,

the Lu Sheng player started again to summon the souls.

Zha Dong Piran wiped his tears

and listened carefully.

He found out that the Lu Sheng song

was about his own experience:

"Di la da, di la da,

la da lun luo la di la,

la da lun luo la di la,

di luo lun la di luo la.

The sun is set behind the mountain,

but our loved ones travelled afar and don't come home.

The moon comes out without the shine,

and all the relatives and friends shed tears.

The unfortunate persons suffered calamities,

and the mountains and rivers are also shimmering with tears.

'Meng ga zhu, meng ga lao,'

the mourning tune kept playing,

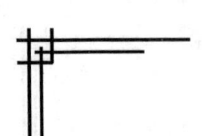

金笛 Jin Di

吹得人心乱如麻。
悲悲戚戚来办丧,
不是祭奠爹和妈。
只因扎董丕冉到远方,
为救妻子去把虎追杀。
蒙诗彩奏救不回,
他俩反被虎糟蹋。
扎董丕冉变成魔虎屎
早被屙进山旮旯,
蒙诗彩奏变成魔虎尿,
也被撒在山垭巴。
他俩双双把命丧,
寨邻亲友来超拔。
男人眼泪像水淌,
女人眼泪如雨下。

"嘀啦哒,嘀啦哒,
拉哒伦罗啦嘀啦。
哭声阵阵不停息,
哭得头昏眼发花;
丧歌声声不间断,
唱得心疼如刀扎。
芦笙吹出'招魂调',
大香烧了好几把,
纸钱化了好几捆,
要将他俩的魂魄招回家。
不幸的扎董丕冉呀,
可怜的蒙诗彩奏呀,

第十一章 悲去喜来 Chapter Eleven New Beginning

making everyone feel restless.
Sad and weeping, they came to pay tribute
but not to the parents.
They came because Zha Dong Pi Ran travelled afar
to rescue his beloved and to kill the tigers.
Meng Shi Cai Zou wasn't saved,
but rather the two of them lost their lives to the tigers.
Zha Dong Pi Ran turned into the demon tigers' feces,
discharged in some pit a long time ago.
Meng shi cai zou became the demon tigers' urine,
also scattered somewhere in Mount Ya Ba.
They both died,
and their relatives and friends have come to pray for them.
Men's tears are running like streams,
and women's tears are falling like the rain.

"Di la da, di la da.
la da lun luo la di la.
Bursts of crying went on continually,
and people became dizzy with tears;
the songs of mourning went on continuously,
and people felt their hearts aching as if pierced by knifes.
The Lu Sheng was playing the *Soul Summoning Tune*,
and a few big bundles of incense have been burnt,
and several bundles of paper money have been burnt,
just to call their souls home.
Unlucky Zha Dong Pi Ran,
and poor Meng Shi Cai Zou,

金笛 Jin Di

路头路脑莫停留，
三魂七魄回来吧！
山间莫摘果，
岭上莫采花，
林里莫打鸟，
水边莫捞虾。

"回来啦，回来啦，
三魂七魄回来啦！
蛇缠就拿竹鞭抽，
豹攥就用铁猫夹，
蜂叮就拿火烟熏，
狗咬给它扔粑粑。

"回来啦，回来啦，
三魂七魄回来啦！
撑起花伞遮太阳，
披起蓑衣挡风沙，
缠起裹腿脚不疼，
穿起草鞋路不滑。

"回来啦，回来啦，
三魂七魄回来啦！
跌倒赶紧爬起来，
淌汗就拿花帕擦，

第十一章 悲去喜来　Chapter Eleven　New Beginning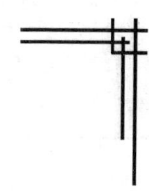

do not delay on the way;

your souls, come back!

Do not pick fruits in the mountains,

or pick flowers on the hills,

or catch birds in the forests,

or fish for shrimp in the river.

"Come back, come back,

come back the souls!

If the snake winds up on you, whip it with a bamboo whip;

if the leopard chases you, snap it with an iron cat-snapper,

if the bee stings you, smokes it away with fire,

and if the dog bites you, throw feces at it.

"Come back, come back,

come back the souls!

Open the floral umbrella to shade the sun;

put on the *suo*-coat① to block the wind and sand;

wrap your legs and feet up with cloth to avoid the pain;

and wear the straw sandals not to slip and fall.

"Come back, come back,

come back the souls!

When you fall, pick yourselves up;

when you sweat, wipe it away with the embroidered cloth;

---

① suo-coat: straw or palm-bark raincoat

金笛 Jin Di

渴了就喝山泉水,
饿了就吃荞疙瘩。

"回来啦,回来啦,
三魂七魄回来啦!
我吹'招魂曲',
吹得嘴发麻。
吹了好几回,
要催你们转回家。
不让你们受孤苦,
魂魄落在荒山和野坝。
你们回到家里来,
立刻拜见爹和妈。
顺着公公指的路,
赶快回老家!
回到老家见祖先,
祖先定会乐哈哈。

"么公在唱'指路歌',
唱得嗓子哑。
路已指明白,
一点也不差。
就等你们来,
骑马上路啦。

"回来吧,回来吧,
三魂七魄回来吧!

第十一章 悲去喜来 Chapter Eleven New Beginning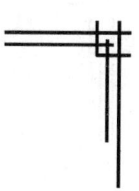

when you're thirsty, drink from the mountain springs;
when you're hungry, eat buckwheat heads.

"Come back, come back,
come back the souls!
I play the *Soul Summoning Song*
till my mouth is numb,
I've played it many times
to urge you to come home.
I do not want you to suffer loninesss
and become the souls roaming the barren mountains and wild fields.
When you come home,
go see Mom and Dad at once.
Along the path that the Gong Gong has pointed at,
return to your hometown right away!
There you go see your ancestors
who will be happy to see you.

"Gong Gong sang the *Directions Song*,
his voice already hoarse.
The road is pointed out clearly
and accurately.
It is just waiting for you to come
to mount the horse and set off.

"Come back, come back,
come back the souls!

金笛 Jin Di

嘀啦哒,嘀啦哒,
啦哒伦罗啦嘀啦,
啦哒伦罗啦嘀啦,
嘀罗伦啦嘀罗啦。"

三十七

扎董丕冉听完了,
哭笑不得难回答。
原来是为这回事,
解开一个大疙瘩。
事到此时真相明,
顿时心里乐开花。
转悲为喜热泪滚,
对着吹师忙说话:

"你的芦笙吹得妙,
婉转悠扬真热闹。
招魂调子动人心,
将我吹得心欢笑。
我看你已吹累了,
让我替你吹一调。"

吹师一听怔住了,
不知这是什么话?
个个痛哭他发笑,

第十一章 悲去喜来　Chapter Eleven　New Beginning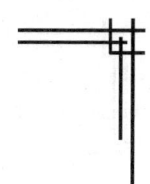

Di La da, di la da,
la da lun luo la di la,
la da lun luo la di la,
di luo lun la di luo la."

37

Zha Dong Pi Ran finished listening to it
and he didn't know if he should respond by crying or laughing.
This was what it was all about,
and he finally resolved the puzzle.
Now it had all become clear,
he became very happy.
Sadness turned into happiness, and Zha Dong Pi Ran began to tear up
and quickly said to the player:

"You played the Lu sheng wonderfully,
with complexity, melody, and liveliness.
Your soul-calling tune was very moving,
and it made me very happy.
I see that you are tired,
so please let me play a tune."

The player was surprised:
did he hear this person right?
Everyone was crying but he laughed:

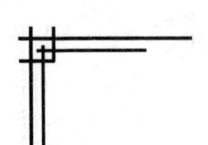

金笛 Jin Di

莫非他是疯子吗？
看他吹的什么调，
且把芦笙交给他。

扎董丕冉接过芦笙来，
吹出一番真情话：
"嘀啦哒，嘀啦哒，
啦哒伦罗啦嘀啦，
啦哒伦罗啦嘀啦，
嘀罗伦啦嘀罗啦。
西边太阳映晚霞，
东边月亮往上爬。

"亲戚呀，朋友呀，
大家莫把眼泪洒。
吹哪曲，唱哪调？
哭调悲调不吹它。
吹起一曲团圆调，
哥弟姐妹来玩耍！

"嘀啦哒，嘀啦哒，
啦哒伦罗啦嘀啦。
那个扎董丕冉呀，
为救妻子走天涯。
历尽千难和万险，
终于把那魔虎杀。
扎董丕冉没有死，
如今他已回到家！

第十一章 悲去喜来 Chapter Eleven New Beginning

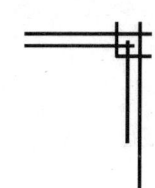

was this person crazy?
To find out what tune he would play,
the player handed over the Lu sheng.

Having taken over the Lu Sheng,
Zha Dong Pi Ran played to tell the real story:
"Di la da, di la da,
la da lun luo la di la,
la da lun luo la di la,
di luo lun la di luo la.
The sun in the west stains the evening clouds,
and the moon in the east is rising.

"Relatives and friends,
do not shed tears.
Which tune should be played and which song should be sung?
Let's not play the sad tunes and sing the sad songs.
Let's play a tune of reunification,
so that brothers and sisters can come and have fun!

"Di la da, di la da,
la da lun luo la di la.
That Zha Dong Pi Ran
went to the edge of the earth to save his beloved.
After so many trails and tributions,
he slayed the demon tigers.
Zha Dong Pi Ran did not die,
and he has just returned home!

353

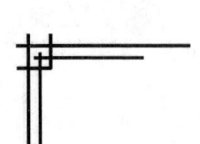

金笛 Jin Di

"嘀啦哒，嘀啦哒，
啦哒伦罗啦嘀啦。
蒙诗彩奏没喂虎，
堂屋里面就是她。
快把簸箕收起来，
快把大鼓也放下！

"嘀啦哒，嘀啦嘀，
啦嘀伦罗嘀啦嘀。
扎董丕冉还活着，
他已站在堂屋里。
快把香火扫出去，
快把灵堂也收起！

"嘀啦哒，嘀啦嘀，
啦嘀伦罗嘀啦嘀。
寨邻亲友莫悲伤，
哥弟姐妹莫哭泣。
远方亲人已归家，
快把衣裙都藏起。
要是他们真死了，
你再超拔也无益！"

扎董丕冉吹的欢乐调，
吹师觉得很惊奇。
唱出扎董丕冉已归家，
又唱蒙诗彩奏在屋里。
个个高兴又心疼，
人人将信又将疑：

第十一章 悲去喜来 Chapter Eleven New Beginning

"Di la da, di la da,
la da lun luo la di la.
Meng Shi Cai Zou wasn't eaten by the tigers,
and the one inside of the hall is just she.
Hurry and put away the shallow baskets
and hurry and put down the drums!

"Di la da, di la di,
la di lun luo di la di.
Zha Dong Pi Ran is still alive,
and he is already standing in the hall.
Hurry and sweep out the burning incense,
and hurry to put away the memorial altar!

"Di la da, di la di,
la di lun luo di la di.
Relatives and friends, do not be sad,
and brothers and sisters, do not cry.
Your loved ones have returned from their long journey,
so hide your clothes and skirts quickly.
If they really had died,
no amount of praying can be useful to them!"

Zha Dong Pi Ran's joyous tune
surprised the player.
He said that Dong Pi Ran had returned home
and Meng Shi Cai Zou was in the house.
Everyone was happy but also concerned,
both believed it but were also skeptical:

金笛 Jin Di

"扎董丕冉在哪里?
蒙诗彩奏在哪里?"
人们纷纷来询问,
都想搞清这秘密。
扎董丕冉微微笑,
忙向大家作个揖:
"扎董丕冉就是我,
莫非你们已忘记?"

蒙诗彩奏扯扯裙,
忙向大家行个礼:
"蒙诗彩奏就是我,
我是头回来这里!"
人们一齐围拢来,
老人使劲往前挤:
"扎董丕冉出门已多年,
变了模样难记忆。
胡子长了没有刮,
头发长了没有剃,
衣裳烂了没有补,
裤子脏了没有洗。
好像变成两个人,
哪里还能记得起?
如今见面不相识,
莫怪乡亲不讲礼!"

第十一章　悲去喜来　Chapter Eleven　New Beginning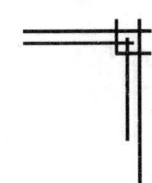

"Where is Zha Dong Pi Ran,
and where is Meng Shi Cai Zou?"
People all came to ask
and wanted to find out about the mystery.
Zha Dong Pi Ran smiled
and put both of his hands together to greet them:
"I am Zha Dong Pi Ran,
whom you haven't forgotten, have you?"

Meng Shi Cai Zou curtsied
to greet everyone:
"I am Meng Shi Cai Zou,
It is the first time I have come here!"
People gathered together,
with the elderlies coming to the front:
"Zha Dong Pi Ran, you have left home for several years,
and it is hard for us to remember your looks because you have changed.
Your beard is long because you haven't shaved;
you hair is messy because you haven't had a haircut;
your clothes are torn because you haven't mended them;
and your pants are dirty because you haven't washed them.
You look like a different person,
so how could you have reminded us of you?
That's why we didn't recognize you,
so do not think of us as being rude!"

扎董丕冉唱起歌,
亲亲热热答亲戚:
"乡邻亲友我不怪,
只怪魔虎施奸计。
害我离乡好几年,
春去冬来无归期。
如今大害已除尽,
亲人才能得团聚!"

屋里屋外是欢歌,
房前房后是笑语。
阿支躲在竹楼上,
伤伤心心在哭泣。
听说儿子回到家,
揩干眼泪下楼梯。

阿奈坐在墙角落,
哭得腰也直不起。
听说媳妇也来了,
抹把眼泪笑嘻嘻。

三十八

阿支阿奈欢笑着,
跑到儿子的身边。
摸着他的宽肩膀,
从头到脚仔细看:

第十一章 悲去喜来　Chapter Eleven　New Beginning

Zha Dong Pi Ran sang again,
warmly addressing the relatives:
"I do not blame my relatives and friends,
and only blame the demon tigers' tricks.
They were the reason I was forced to leave my hometown for years,
season after season not knowing when I would return.
Now that the demon tigers have all been eradicated,
the loved ones are able to reunite!"

Cheerful songs rang inside and outside of the hall,
and happy talks were in front of and behind the house.
A Zhi was hiding upstairs in the bamboo house,
crying sadly.
When he learned that his son had returned home,
he wiped his tears and came downstairs.

A Nai was sitting at the corner of the house,
crying so hard that she could barely stand up.
When she heard that her daughter-in-law came too,
she wiped her tears and smiled.

38

Laughing, A Zhi and A Nai
ran towards their son.
Touching his broad shoulders,
they carefully looked at him from head to toe:

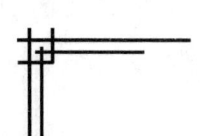

金笛 Jin Di

"孩儿呀,
都说你们被虎吃,
早已离开人世间。
今天办丧来超度,
希望你们早升天。
如今你们回来了,
莫非是在梦里见?"

扎董丕冉微微笑,
蒙诗彩奏眨眨眼。
双双站在爹眼前,
双双站在妈面前,
向着爹妈躬躬腰,
异口同声齐开言:

"阿支阿奈在家里,
挂儿挂媳好几年。
如今我们回来了,
从此全家得团圆!
叫声阿支阿奈,
莫难过呀莫心酸!"

管事寨老一声喊,
人们一起拥上前。
放下牛皮鼓,
拔去长竹竿,
取走篾圈和衣裙,
扫尽香火和纸钱,

第十一章　悲去喜来　Chapter Eleven　New Beginning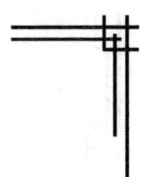

"Son,
they all said that you were eaten by the tigers
and had left this world for a long time.
Today we held the funeral to release your soul from suffering
and hoped you would go to heaven early.
Now you're back,
but it is not a dream, is it?"

Zha Dong Pi Ran smiled,
and Meng Shi Cai Zou blinked her eyes.
They both stood in front of A Zhi,
and they both stood in front of A Nai,
and they bowed to their parents,
speaking in unison:

"A Zhi and A Nai at home
have worried about us for several years.
Now that we're back,
the whole family has reunited!
A Zhi and A Nai,
do not be distressed and do not be sad!"

The old man in charge gave the order in a loud voice
and the villagers thronged the room and the yard.
They put down the ox-skin drum,
pulled up the long bamboo pole,
removed the splinted wreathes and the clothes,
swept away the burning incense and the paper money,

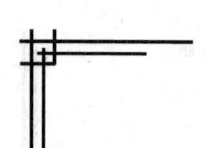

金笛 Jin Di

收起簸箕和灵堂,
撕掉祭幛和挽联。
重新换上喜酒席,
丧事转成喜事办。

管事提调各套人,
点起红烛和油灯,
贴上纸花和喜对,
摆好碗碟和果品,
布置新房和新床,
唱起喜歌来迎亲。

蒙诗彩奏巧梳妆,
活像一个仙女样:
长裙轻轻在摇摆,
手镯闪闪在发亮,
双颊微微在泛红,
两眼熠熠在生光。

扎董丕冉细穿戴,
活像一个王子样:
布褂软软贴在身,
腰带悠悠在飘荡,
金笛横插在腰间,
长刀斜挎在肩上。

寨中一位老婆婆,
抱着一只大公鸡,

第十一章 悲去喜来 Chapter Eleven New Beginning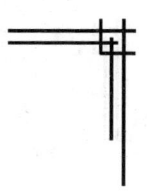

put away the baskets and the altar,
and tore off the streamers inscribed with elegiac couplets.
They changed the occasion into a wedding reception,
turning the sad event into a happy one.

The man in charge was making the arrangements,
so some lighted the red candles and the oil lamps,
some put up the window paper cuts and celebratory couplets,
some set up the dishes and fruits,
some decorated the bridal room and bed,
and some sang welcoming songs to receive the bride.

Meng Shi Cai Zou was good at making herself up
to look just like a living fairy:
She put on a long skirt that swayed gently,
wore a bracelet that sparkled,
applied just enough blush to her cheeks,
and made up her eyes so they shined.

Zha Dong Pi Ran was caregully dressed,
just like a prince:
he put on a soft cotton shirt that fit him comfortably,
wore a waistband that was floating with the breeze,
had the Jin Di set across his waist,
and carried the long machete across his shoulders.

An old woman in the village,
holding a rooster,

金笛 Jin Di

领着新郎出门去，
带着新娘出门去。

新郎身后有陪宾，
新娘身后有福女。
吹吹打打往前走，
一直走到树林里。

大家坐在树荫下，
说笑唱歌表情意。
生火烤肉吃晌午，
边吃边闹多有趣。
新郎夹起一块肉，
放进新娘饭碗里；
新娘夹起一块肉，
放进新郎饭碗里。
肉香饭热吃得甜，
你敬我让多亲密。

陪宾夹起一块肉，
举在面前笑嘻嘻：
"我这块肉烤得香，
要叫新郎新娘一起吃！
你们吃了这块吉祥肉，
永远得过好日子。"

新郎对着新娘眨眨眼，
慢慢把嘴凑过去；

第十一章 悲去喜来　Chapter Eleven　New Beginning

guided the bride to walk out of the door,
and guided the groom to walk out of the door.

The groom was followed by the best men,
and the bride was followed by her bridesmaids.
Walking forward with music playing,
they came to the woods.

Sitting in the shade under the trees,
they were chatting, laughing, singing, and mingling.
They set up the bonfire to roast the meats,
eating, playing, and having much fun.
The groom picked up a piece of meat
and put it into the bride's bowl;
the bride picked up a piece of meat
and put it into the groom's bowl.
They enjoyed the delicious meat and hot dishes,
respectful, cordial, and intimate.

A best man picked up a piece of meat,
holding it with a smile:
"This piece of meat is roasted so well,
it is for the bridegroom and the bride to eat together!
After eating this lucky meat,
you will lead a good life together forever."

The groom made eye contact with the bride
and then slowly turned towards the meat;

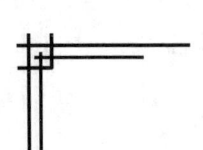

金笛 Jin Di

新娘对着新郎点点头，
轻轻把嘴凑过去。
两人同时咬断那块肉，
嘴唇相碰在一起。
逗得众人哈哈笑，
雀鸟也跟着叫叽叽。
新郎激动得手发抖，
新娘害羞得把头低。

闹一阵又笑一阵，
不觉太阳已偏西。
大家顺着寨子绕一圈，
要让整个山寨添喜气。
又叫新郎新娘肩挨肩，
双双走进堂屋里。
表示迎接新人进家里，
说是这样才吉利。

福女拿起一把伞，
罩住新郎和新娘。
老婆婆抱起大公鸡，
举到新娘头顶上，
转去转来绕三圈，
然后夫妻才拜堂。

先拜天和地，

第十一章 悲去喜来　Chapter Eleven　New Beginning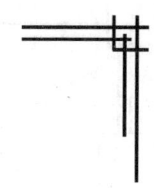

the bride nodded at the groom,
and then gently turned towards the meat.
They bit the piece at the same time and severed it in half,
their lips touching each other.
The crowd was amused and started laughing,
and the birds joined in and chattering.
The groom's hands were trembling with excitement,
and the bride lowered her head out of shyness.

They played and laughed,
and before they knew it the sun moved to the west.
They walked around the village once
to let the whole village share the happiness with them.
Then the groom and the bride walked into the house shoulder by shoulder,
walking into the main hall together.
This symbolized that they were welcomed home as a new couple,
the welcome that would bring them good luck.

A bridesmaid opened up an umbrella
to cover the groom and the bride.
The old woman lifted up the rooster,
held it above the bride's head,
and circled three times,
readying the husband and wife for the marriage ceremony.

They first saluted heaven and earth,

金笛 Jin Di

再拜众先人，
又拜爹和妈，
还拜亲友和寨邻。
亲疏远近都拜过，
夫妻互拜最真诚。

临时又找四个老公公，
换上新衣做媒人。
四位媒公坐上席，
饮酒对歌来贺喜。
你一杯呀我一盏，
一杯一盏甜如蜜：
"他们二人自相爱，
历尽艰险成夫妻。
有情的人得幸福，
我们做媒也欢喜。

"我们做的现成媒，
没费口舌没出力。
定要多喝一碗酒，
不怕酒醉爬不起！"

大家唱起"祝酒歌"，
喝一口酒唱一句。
酒香歌甜心里乐，
三杯两碗醉如泥。

第十一章 悲去喜来 Chapter Eleven New Beginning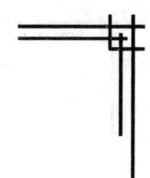

then the ancestors

then their father and mother,

and then their relatives, friends, and neighbors.

After saluting everyone else,

the husband and wife salute each other most sincerely.

They then found four elderly men

and gave them change of clothes and asked them to be the matchmakers.

The four matchmakers sat at the most important position at the table.

Drinking and singing responsorial songs to congratulate the newly wed.

One cup for you, one for me,

every cup was sweet as honey:

"They fell in love on their own

and went through so many difficulties to become a couple.

They are meant to be together and do get together,

and we matchmakers are happy, too.

"The match was made before we came in,

so we didn't have to work or make any effort.

We must then drink an extra cut of wine to you

and fear not of getting drunk!"

Everyone sang the *Drinking Song*,

drinking and singing, drinking and singing.

The fragrant wine, the sweet songs, and the delightful people,

after a few cups everyone was immersed in the intoxicating present.

金笛 Jin Di

四位接亲老长辈，
喜上心头笑在眉。
夸赞新娘人品好，
跟这新郎正相配：

"看这新娘懂礼节，
又像天仙一样美。
扎董丕冉跟她在一起，
就像一对鸳鸯比翼飞。

"今天迎亲日子好，
愿他俩情意如同长流水。
来年生个胖娃娃，
像金竹一样越长越青翠！"

他们高唱"迎亲调"，
唱了一回又一回。
歌声入耳酒入心，
喝酒不多也会醉。

陪郎阿哥最爱玩，
拉着新郎跳得欢。
姑娘一齐来伴唱，
跳通了地呀唱翻了天！

陪嫁姑娘了不起，

第十一章 悲去喜来 Chapter Eleven New Beginning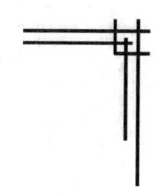

The four elderlies who welcomed them home
were delighted at heart, smiling ear to ear.
They praised the bride for having excellent character
and being a perfect match to the groom:

"What a well-mannered bride,
and she is also beautiful like a fairy.
Zha Dong Pi Ran and she
are like a pair of mandarin ducks flying together."

"Today is an audpicious day,
and we wish their love last forever.
Have a chubby adorable baby next year,
who is like the golden bamboo: the more it grows, the fresher it becomes!"

They sang the *Welcoming Song* several more times,
over and over.
The song entered the ears, and the wine entered the heart,
and it didn't take too much wine for one to feel intoxicated.

The young men liked to have fun
and they danced with the groom.
The young women liked to sing together, and they
danced so hard that the earth could cave, sang so hard the sky could fall!

The bridemaids were so great,

金笛 Jin Di

唱起山歌醉倒你。
伴着新娘唱主角,
歌声传遍几十里。
姑娘小伙肩挨肩,
围成几个大圈圈。
圈圈转去又转来,
轻歌曼舞乐无边。
腰带飘飞裙子摆,
犹如身临彩云间。

帮忙的人不简单,
抱柴挑水当厨倌。
烧水煮饭磨豆腐,
摆碗理筷抬盘盘。
来来往往如穿梭,
脚不停歇手不闲。

桌椅碗筷摆满场,
宾客欢笑聚一堂。
桌桌都有八碗菜,
旁边还有牛肉汤。
一缸喜酒放桌下,
满场尽是米酒香。

三十九

蒙诗彩奏抬金碗,

第十一章 悲去喜来 Chapter Eleven New Beginning

their mountain songs could get one drunk.
Accompaning the bride who led the singing,
they could be heard miles away.
The young women and men were side by side,
forming a few big circles.
The circles moved in one direction and then the other,
merry songs, graceful dances, and boundless happinesses.
With the waistbands floating and the skirt fluttering,
they all felt like being in the midst of colored clouds.

Those in the kitchen were truly great,
carrying the firewood and fetching the water.
They boiled the water, cooked the rice, and ground the bean-curds,
arranged the table, and served the dishes.
They came and went like the weaving shuttles,
their feet always moving and their hands always working.

The tables were set and they filled the yard,
and all the guests gathered together with laughters.
Every table had eight dishes,
and by each table was the beef soup.
A big earthen jar of the wedding wine was under each table,
the fragrance of which permeated the air.

39

Meng Shi Cai Zou raised the golden bowl,

金笛 Jin Di

扎董丕冉抱酒缸。
挨一挨二来敬酒,
喜气盈门心欢畅。
一碗喜酒喝下肚,
调子唱得更响亮。

新郎唱起"谢媒歌",
字字句句表衷肠:
"多谢媒公来操持,
我俩才得结成双。
敬请媒公多喝一杯酒,
祝你添福添寿永安康!"

新娘唱起"谢厨调",
感谢厨师来帮忙:
"多亏厨师手艺巧,
喜酒席上饭菜香。
奉劝厨师多喝一杯酒,
愿你们油盐满缸!"

阿支笑得坐不稳,
阿奈笑得热泪淌。
夸赞媳妇情意深,
魔虎越逼越刚强;
又夸儿子最勇敢,

第十一章 悲去喜来 Chapter Eleven New Beginning

and Zha Dong Pi Ran held a jug of wine.
They toasted to all the guests from one to the next,
and they were filled with joy.
With each bowl of wine,
they sang louder and clearer than before.

The groom sang the *Thank the Matchmakers* song,
every word expressing his deep gratitude:
"Many thanks to the matchmakers to preside over the ceremony,
where we can become a couple.
Please have an extra cup of wine
and accept our wish for you to enjoy both happiness and longevity!"

The bride sang to *Thank the Chefs* song
for their work for the wedding:
"It is due to the skill of the chefs
that the dishes for the wedding are so sumptuous.
Please drink an extra cup of wine
and accept our good wish that you will always have plenty of food!"

A Zhi was too happy to remain in her seat.
and A Nai laughed with tears running down.
They praised the daughter-in-law's loyalty:
the more ferocious the demon tigers, the stronger her will;
they praised their son for his bravery:

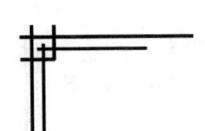

金笛 Jin Di

将那魔虎全杀光。
堂屋里面更欢乐,
姑娘小伙心花放。
男女各分两边坐,
饮酒对歌庆吉祥。
酒歌情歌尽情唱,
罚酒罚歌闹洋洋。

蜜蜂蝴蝶齐飞来,
祝贺新郎和新娘:

"祝你俩白头共到老,
贺你俩夫妻和睦日子旺!"

通宵达旦来祝贺,
一直闹到太阳出东方……

第十一章 悲去喜来 Chapter Eleven New Beginning

he killed all the demon tigers.
Inside the main hall it was even merrier,
young women and men bursting with happiness.
Men and women were sitting on each side of the hall,
drinking and singing responsorially to observe this auspicious occasion.
They were singing all kinds of wine songs and love songs,
merrily using the wine and singing as punishment.

The bees and the butterflies came together
to congratulate the groom and the bride:

"May you two grow old together,
with prosperous days as husband and wife!"

All night long the congratulations arrived,
until the sun rose up in the east…